Pendragon Rises

ONCE AND FUTURE HEARTS BOOK 3.0

TRACY COOPER-POSEY

STORIES RULE

EDMONTON • ALBERTA

Praise for the Once And Future Hearts series

It takes me back to the magic I felt when reading Mary Stewart's stories of Merlin. Tracy Cooper-Posey has written another winner!

As a long time, self proclaimed Arthurian Legend junkie I couldn't wait to dive into Tracy Cooper Posey's new series. Tracy once again proves to be a master story teller as she weaves the delicate threads of this beloved legend into her own.

Oh my goodness. Of course I was not sure what to expect with this but what I got was a wonderful story set in the time just before King Arthur. Invading Saxons, Romans, Kings, princesses, mysteries, Merlin, and romance? Wonderful beginning to a new series and I cannot wait to read more.

I also love the fact that her female characters are definitely not boring, whiny or TSTL.

Tracy Cooper Posey is brilliant at weaving stories with individuals that are completely believable in their thoughts and dialogue.

MAPS

Hadrian's Wall

GREAT
BRITAIN

• Segontium
• Yr Wyddfa

• Stonehenge
• Amesbury
  • Calleva

• Venta Belgarum

• Tintagel
• Dimiliōc

Locations in *Pendragon Rises*

Other locations in Britain

Great
Britain

• Maridunum

• Clausentium

• Lorient
• Carnac Lesser Britain
(Brittany)

Greater and Lesser Britain

PART ONE

Chapter One

Dimilioc Fortress, Duchy of Cornwall, 464 C.E.

Both Daveth and Cador were absent for the evening, which should have been warning enough, except Steffan couldn't see the empty places at the head table.

He found the small table at the back of the room, ran his staff along the bench and learned it was unoccupied. He rested the staff against the edge of the table, then slid onto the end of the bench, as was his custom.

The chatter in the stone room was louder than usual, disguising the sound of the evening meal being served by the slaves and servants. Perhaps that was why he missed the other signs.

From the odors, he judged that mutton was tonight's meal. And…something with warmed honey. Parsnips, possibly. Through the high open windows, he could smell the sea. It was a fresh scent, pleasant among the aged and sour smells in the hall. Dimilioc was five miles from Tintagel and three miles from the ocean. Everyone called Steffan a liar when he said he could detect the salt and the weeds which clung to the rocks and dried in the sun. Yet the scents were undeniable.

Someone thumped a mug in front of Steffan. He heard the wine slosh and felt the splatter on his hand. He reached out to locate the mug and raised it to his face and sniffed. It smelled like the sour wine Cornwall produced. He sipped cautiously.

He had discovered all sorts of additions in his mug on previous evenings. Soil was common. Food, too. Gobs of spit were frequent. On one memorable occasion, there had been urine.

It was just wine, tonight. He took a deeper mouthful and put the mug where he could find it again.

Another clatter told him a plate had been put in front of him. He waited and heard the wet slap of meat. "Thank you," he said, his voice dry.

No answer. That was also customary.

Steffan pulled out his knife and thumbed the edge. The blade was satisfyingly sharp. He put his left hand on the table, then brushed it sideways, looking for the edge of the plate.

Nothing. His hand swept all the way to the right. His fingertips touched the wine mug.

Someone had removed the plate.

A snigger from nearby told him what had happened. It was Maurgh's soft laugh. The high note was unmistakable. He or one of his faction had pulled the plate away while Steffan had been checking his knife.

"Awww…the priest can't find his dinner." That was one of the others. Steffan wondered how many of Maurgh's men were watching the by-play, enjoying what they thought was Steffan's humiliation.

Steffan brought the knife point down upon the table and rested his hand on the hilt. "Tutor," he corrected them. "Give me the plate."

"All tutors are priests," Maurgh said. He paused. "Or eunuchs. You're *sure* you're not a eunuch? You just said you are not a priest."

More laughter.

Steffan squashed the anger which wanted to rise. He was hungry. The more he argued with Maurgh over his lack of reasoning abilities, the longer it would take to get the plate back. He gritted his teeth and waited, instead.

Everyone nearby was chomping their food and drinking. Steffan's belly cramped.

"Let the sod have his meat," Maurgh said. "He's too good to sit with us Cornish men. He was in the High King's favor, remember."

Someone clapped Steffan on the shoulder. He hid his twitch of surprise. He had not seen the slap coming.

A metallic scrape sounded as the plate was returned to him.

"Enjoy your meal, eunuch," the breathy, low voice murmured in his ear.

Steffan traced the edges of the plate, then ran his fingers over the meal itself. The meat was still warm and felt as it should. He found the lumps of parsnip, sitting in a honey sauce to offset the peppery flavor. There was nothing inedible among them as far as he could tell.

He sawed off a lump of the mutton and chewed, wishing as he often did that he had a room of his own where he could take his meals. It would halt the pranks which Maurgh and other soldiers of the same quality found to be a worthy night's entertainment. It would also allow Steffan to eat without everyone watching him play with his food like a child.

The men at Maurgh's table also ate. He could hear them grind their food between their teeth as they spoke.

If all he must put up with tonight was the stealing of his plate, then it would be a normal, almost pleasant evening. It just didn't *feel* normal. For a moment, while gripping his knife and waiting for the return of the plate, Steffan wanted to lash out. Slice arms open and finger tips off.

Maurgh was being no more belligerent than usual. Steffan

forced himself to consider the real cause for the knot of tension in his chest.

At the end of their lessons today, Cador had touched Steffan's arm to gain his attention. "My father has spoken of me joining him at the High King's side."

Steffan hid the jolt Cador's confession delivered. Once, it had been Steffan by the High King's side, one of Duke Gorlois' most favored captains. Steffan made himself nod. "You are seventeen. It is reasonable that you finish your education now and take up your responsibilities as your father's heir."

"I *like* my education," Cador said. Steffan could hear the smile in his voice. "You make Latin make sense."

"You don't need Latin on the battlefield," Steffan replied. "You are a good warrior, Cador. You will grace yourself on the field and make your father proud."

"How would you know I am a good warrior?" Cador asked, with a soft laugh.

Steffan did not mind Cador's teasing. It was never cruel. "I listen to the other men. They watch you closely."

"They measure," Cador said, his tone dry. He sounded like a much older man. "Every day I am examined."

It was true, so Steffan said, instead, "When does he want you to join him?"

"He said 'soon'. I don't know what that means." Cador sounded pensive.

Steffan considered. "Ambrosius is still camped outside El-lisbury—"

"Amesbury," Cador corrected. "Remember?"

"Amesbury," Steffan amended. The town had changed its name to celebrate its status as the birth place of the High King. The massive stonework being rebuilt on the plains a few miles from the town had elevated it to one of the busiest places in Britain. "Amesbury is only three days' ride from here and these are times of peace. The work on the monument is likely to take many days yet. Months, even. There is time."

"They have been at it for nearly a year," Cador pointed out. "If Merlin is the all-powerful magician they say he is, then why does he not cast a spell and have the stones just raise themselves into position?"

"They say he *is* using magic," Steffan said. "The magic of music and mathematics…which are not your strengths at all."

"Then I will never be a magician," Cador said lightly. "What will you do when I go to my father, Steffan? Dimilioc is a military fort. There is no one else here to teach."

"No one worthy, at least," Steffan told him, the tension in his chest tightening just a little more. "I don't know what I will do," he admitted. "The Duke was kind enough to find me a place here. I cannot demand he find another."

"I don't think kindness had much to do with it," Cador said. "*Your* magic is with languages, Steffan. Also, I have learned to appreciate logic and reasoning because of you."

"You are kind to say so, Master Cador," Steffan replied. "Shall we meet again tomorrow? There is still time to acquaint you with Scipio."

"Another Greek?"

"A Roman general who knew much more about military strategy than you."

"I suppose, yes, we should, then. Tomorrow at noon. Thank you, Steffan."

Steffan listened to Cador bounce to his feet and hurry from the room, eager to stretch his body with riding and hunting, now that Steffan had thoroughly stretched his mind.

The conversation lingered in Steffan's mind through the rest of the afternoon, as he made his way to the stables and brushed and fed Avalloc. He took three times longer to complete the simple tasks these days. The pitchfork to shovel hay and the brush to tend to Avalloc's hide, and the sack of oats were never where they were the day before. Each day he was forced to hunt for them throughout the large stable.

As Steffan finished the last bites of his supper, the memory of the conversation returned to him, accompanied by the frustration which had been growing all afternoon. *Uncertainty breeds fear...* Who had said that?

He wasn't fearful. Yet the uncertainty gnawed.

"Watch out, Steffan!" came the cry.

Steffan turned his head, searching for the direction of the warning.

The tankard which hit him in the shoulder was still half-full of wine, which splashed onto Steffan's face and spilled down his front and back. The tankard itself was a heavy thing which sent a flare of pain through his shoulder.

Steffan hissed and grabbed at his shoulder. The tankard clattered on the flagstones beneath him. Wine dripped from his hand and thigh.

The laughter which broke out around him was from more than just Maurgh's table. It was a raucous sound. Fists and mugs thumped upon the table tops, signifying their great amusement.

For the first time Steffan wondered why Daveth did not shout for order. Daveth liked an orderly meal, even if it was loud with chatter. He sent men from the room if he didn't like their behavior, whether or not they had finished their meal. The custom contained the inclinations of men like Maurgh and his brethren.

"Look at the eunuch. He's wet himself!"

That earned even more laughter, as if it was the height of wit.

Steffan clenched his hand, weighing up whether it was worth responding. He was already frustrated. Reacting as he wanted to would not be fair.

He shook off the wine from his hand and the worst of it from his jerkin and trousers. The jerkin was leather and would not be harmed. He would have to coax one of the kitchen servants into washing the trousers for him, which meant finding something else to wear in the meantime.

That would take up most of his spare time tomorrow and he already faced the challenge of finding another position in another household somewhere…

No, he would not lash out at these men. They were just the last of a day's worth of irritations.

He turned back to his plate and felt the edge carefully. Then he cautiously ran his fingertips over the contents. It was as he had left it. The mug had not been a distraction for further mischief.

His shoulder throbbing where the mug impacted the heaviest, Steffan finished his meal. The parsnips tasted of wine, now.

He was close enough to done that he could have abandoned his meal and left the hall. Only, the temper stirring in his gut and chest made him stay where he was and eat, even though the parsnips did not go well with wine.

When he was completely finished, he cautiously sipped his wine once more, then drained the mug. He got to his feet and reached for the staff. It had been moved an extra foot along the table, too.

He gripped the staff and headed for the door. He always sat at the back of the hall. From here, he knew the way to the door and that there was nothing between the last of the tables and the wall which might trip him. If a man stood in his way, the tip of the staff would warn Steffan of it.

It had taken many weeks to learn to constantly sweep the staff from side to side to check for obstructions. After he had struck his shins and knees and his nose and elbows enough times, the lesson sunk in.

Steffan moved forward, the staff painting in his mind a picture of clear floor. When something snagged his ankle and pulled it out from under him, he was taken by surprise.

The yank was powerful enough to take him off his feet. Steffan landed on his back on the stones, the wind driving out of him. His head rapped sharply against the floor, creating sparks in his mind.

The laughter, this time, seemed to sweep through the whole room. All background conversation stopped.

Fury swept through Steffan. He gripped his staff and jumped back to his feet. He pushed his left hand farther down the staff and gripped it, listening, while his temper throbbed in his head, driving out wise thought.

There. There was the closest laughing man.

Steffan rammed the end of the staff into the laughing man's chest, hard enough to steal the air from *his* lungs. A coughing sound confirmed he had hit squarely.

"Hey!" someone protested, from behind him. Steffan reversed the staff and shoved it backward, aiming for the protestor. Another square strike.

The laughter halted as the man wheezed and groaned.

"Get the bastard!" someone shouted.

Steffan shifted his grip on the staff, waiting. Every man in this room was a warrior and not one of them had read a book. None of them knew—or they had forgotten, if they had known—that one of the most effective weapons in the world was the quarter staff.

Idiots. Fools.

As they surged toward Steffan, he raised the staff. Their sour breath and heavy steps told him exactly where they were. He didn't need his sight to deal with them.

Chapter Two

Tintagel, Duchy of Cornwall, 464 C.E.—the next morning.

ador's arrival at the gates shortly after prayers sent a ripple of whispers through the stone corridors. Everyone hurried to the Duchess' rooms to attend Igraine while she received Cador, driven more by curiosity than because their attendance was expected. Cador had not set foot inside the high stone walls of Tintagel for years.

A woman passing the door of Anwen's room hissed, "Hurry! The Duchess has called for us!"

Morguase and Morgan looked up from their slates. Morguase, who was twelve and just showing the first signs of adulthood in her small frame, frowned. "Why would Mother call for us?"

Morgan pursed her perfectly bowed, full lips. "I heard our brother comes to speak to her." Morgan was six, yet often spoke like a much older child. The doting and favors her perfect beauty engendered had not spoiled her at all. Instead, they had imparted a cynical maturity.

"How did you hear that, Morgan?" Anwen asked curiously, for both girls had been sitting at the table since prayers had ended. She moved over to the small chest by her bed and took out her brush and pulled it quickly through her hair. She had left her hair loose this morning, although that would not do for a formal reception in the Duchess' quarters. Not that anyone would notice, even if she did leave her hair out.

Morgan shrugged in answer to Anwen's question. "I just know."

It was possible she did know. Perhaps she had heard Cador's voice in the keep, below. Perhaps someone had spoken his name in the rooms beyond Anwen's. Or perhaps she had learned the truth a different way. Anwen was still deciding if Morgan's astonishing insights were the product of other-world gifts, or merely the fruits of an inquisitive and swiftly reasoning mind.

For sure, she was smarter than Morguase, who still struggled over her reading, while Morgan had barely needed to be taught her letters. Anwen would never speak of Morgan's cleverness to Morguase, who tried hard to please.

Morgan, alas, did not have to try hard to please anyone. A pout, a dimple, a sunny smile, and the toughest heart melted.

"Stand up, both of you," Anwen told them. "Let me see what you are wearing."

The girls got to their feet. Anwen inspected their gowns for stains and tears. Miraculously, both gowns were whole and clean. "Morguase, come here. Let me tie your hair back." She bent and retrieved the ribbon from her chest and bound Morguase's hair at the back of her neck and patted her shoulder.

There was no mirror for Anwen to check her own appearance, for which she was grateful. Her reflection in the wash basin was plain enough.

"Hurry, we must be in the room before Cador arrives," Anwen said. "If it *is* Cador," she added.

"It is," Morgan said, with a confident tone.

They moved along the narrow corridor. Anwen's room was in the depths of the main tower, while Igraine's rooms were, naturally, at the top. Anwen was lucky to have a room to herself. The other lady companions to Igraine all shared a single drafty chamber with windows which faced north. Anwen, though, needed a place to teach the girls their lessons. There was just enough space in the room assigned for those lessons to install a bed in the corner, too.

The circular stairs were full of women hurrying to the same place as Anwen and the girls. They climbed a step at a time up the narrow stairs to the Duchess' chambers and filed into the big anteroom.

This was one of the finest rooms in the fort. When the Duke, Gorlois, was home, the room was his reception chamber. When he was away, the chamber was for Igraine's use, as she acted on Gorlois' behalf in matters of domestic justice and dispute resolution. The chamber reflected that function.

It was not a square room. The circular walls of the tower shaped the east and west sides of the room, giving them a gentle outward curve. As the room was close to the top of the unscalable tower, which sat upon the impregnable rock of Tintagel, windows too small to allow the body of a man to pass through were not necessary. There were three windows in each curved wall. The two center windows were huge. Their sills were only as high as a man's knee, and they soared up at least as high as two men. It took three long paces to traverse the width of them. When the leather was lifted and folded to one side, as it was now, the view from the west window was breath-taking.

The west side of the tower dropped for the height of ten men to the curtain wall of the fort. The wall had been built upon the very edge of the cliffs which made the Tintagel headland. The cliffs dropped into the sea, far below. The sea churned and sucked at the rocks with ceaseless motions of deep green water. On stormy days it was possible to feel the spray of the waves, standing at the window.

Yet if one lifted their head to look directly out from the window, they saw nothing but clouds and birds and the endless green sea, clear to the horizon. Nothing of man was visible, unless a ship risked the dangerous navigation to the stony, tiny beach between the Tintagel headland and the mainland. The beach was at the foot of the narrow, natural rock bridge which was the only access to the fort.

It was said Tintagel could not be taken by any force known to man. For that reason, Gorlois kept his wife in this fortress, while his army resided in Dimilioc.

The two other windows on the curved walls were smaller and higher. Their view was only of the sky.

The east window looked out upon the fortress courtyard. Beyond the fortress walls and on the other side of the narrow channel between Tintagel and the shore laid the lands of Cornwall. Today, those lands were mist covered, the mist rolling over the jagged edges of the cliffs and down to the restless sea. Gulls and cormorants cawed as they fished for their breakfast.

The air passing through the chamber was redolent of sea and weed and green growing things. It was not unpleasant, even if it was a little chilly. Soon, the sun would touch the west wall and warm the stones and this room along with it.

It was another day in Tintagel, made novel by a most unusual visitor.

Anwen took the girls over to their mother. Igraine was just settling into the big chair where she would receive Cador. She smiled at them and held out her hand. Morgan slid her smaller one into her mother's hand, while Igraine studied Morguase. "You must stand quietly and listen," she told them. She glanced at Anwen and moved her head, with a glance to the side of the big chair.

Anwen shepherded the girls to stand to one side and behind their mother's chair. Anwen stood well behind the girls, her back almost against the rug hanging against the wall. She watched Igraine as the Duchess arranged herself and her gown to her satisfaction.

Igraine had such great beauty it was possible to admire the woman without a shred of resentment or envy. Her flawless features raised her above mere mortal womanhood. Even though she was no longer considered young, Igraine's skin was smooth. No scars or wrinkles marred her face. Her flesh was pale and her cheeks touched with the blush of an apricot. Her hair was thick, black and untouched by gray. It hung to her hips. Today, pearls had been woven through the curls and waves.

Her brows were firm, arching over her black eyes, which were large and expressive. Igraine's chin was small and pointed and her lips full and the color of strawberries.

Her perfection did not end at her chin. Igraine was a tall

woman and her figure, despite the carrying of multiple babies, was still slender. Her hips were perhaps a little wider than they had been as a maiden and her breasts fuller, although men liked such curves. Yet her waist was still small and she made the most of her advantages. She favored gowns which outlined her figure, and transparent veils—when she wore veils at all.

The necklace and earrings she chose drew one's attention to her slender throat and the line of her gown beneath.

Yes, Igraine knew how to portray her charms. She adjusted the folds of her blue gown now with particular attention upon getting it exactly right. As she put her foot upon the cushioned stool in front of her, she cleared her throat.

Anwen suspected she was the only person in the room who detected Igraine was nervous about the coming meeting. As Gorlois' second wife, her relationship with Cador, whose mother had been replaced by Igraine for failure to provide more children, had always been strained.

Cador climbed the last of the stairs and stepped into the chamber and everyone fell silent.

Anwen was startled. It had been several years since she had seen Cador even from a window of the tower. He had grown, in the meantime. He would be seventeen this autumn and he was already a man. He had dark blond hair which must surely come from his mother, the unfortunate Mari. He was taller than the steward, Daveth, who followed him into the chamber, and his shoulders and neck had filled out with strong fighters' muscles. Living amongst the soldiers at Dimilioc, Cador would have little choice but to become a fighter. He wore a well-used and burnished sword, and metal armguards which were the minimum armor for days when battle was not expected. He was tanned and fit and his gaze was direct…just like his father's.

He moved to stand in front of the big chair and bowed. "Lady Igraine."

"Cador, it is good to see you," Igraine told him and her tone was sincere. "This is a great surprise."

"I'm sure," Cador said, his tone dry. "Unfortunately, I have an issue I must deal with that puts me in a quandary. I thought you might have insight into the way my father would resolve the issue, if he were here."

Igraine blinked. "You seek my council?"

Anwen understood her surprise. When Gorlois was away serving the High King, as he had been for several years now, Cador was the nominal commander of Dimilioc, just as Igraine directed the affairs at Tintagel. However, for most of those years, the real manager at Dimilioc had been the steward, Daveth.

Anwen glanced at Daveth. He looked old, she realized with a start. He had gray in his hair which had not been there when she last saw him. His chin was unshaved, and the stubble was silver. His brown eyes were faded and the lines on his forehead deeper than she remembered.

Cador's smile in response to Igraine's startled question was small. "As strange as it seems, I believe you may be able to offer insight. The matter is not straight forward."

Igraine hesitated. "Perhaps you should tell me, then." She waved to a woman. "Bring Cador a chair and some wine."

"Thank you," Cador said.

"Daveth, how are you?" Igraine asked the steward, as people flurried about, finding a chair and calling for wine.

"I am well enough, my lady," Daveth said. His voice wavered. "This is a troublesome business, though."

A stool was brought for Cador and a second stool settled beside him. A cup was placed upon it and a platter with one of the last of the summer's apples sliced upon it.

Another servant handed Igraine her jeweled cup. Igraine murmured her thanks and raised her cup toward Cador.

Cador lifted his and with a nod of thanks, sipped.

So did Igraine. Then she thrust her cup to one side for someone to take it. Her gaze remained on Cador.

Cador skewered a slice of the apple with his knife and lifted it. "Last night I did not take my supper in the hall as I usually do. Unbeknown to me, neither did Daveth. We have learned the coincidence was...unfortunate."

"The men acted up, my lady," Daveth said.

Igraine's smile was not forced. "Men do, when not properly supervised. Especially military men."

"Yes, well…" Cador bit into the apple and chewed. "There is always someone who becomes the focus of their attention. Last night and I suppose for a great many nights before that, it has been Steffan."

Anwen's attention was caught.

Igraine spoke the question which rose in Anwen's mind. "Steffan? Are you referring to Steffan of Durnovaria?"

"Is that where he is from?" Cador asked, sounding surprised.

Daveth nodded vigorously. "That be the man, my lady."

A murmur ran around the room as everyone recognized the name.

Igraine sat back. "I thought he was dead," she said flatly.

So had Anwen believed. She knew of Steffan of Durnovaria only by reputation. Rumor of his exploits as a warrior and Gorlois' most favored captain had reached them even here in Tintagel.

In the years before Ambrosius had taken back Britain, when the Saxon raids had been at their worst, the young warrior from Durnovaria had burst upon the fields of war like a star blazing across the sky. A fierce warrior, a gifted fighter and a natural leader of men, he had risen through the ranks and become one of Gorlois' strongest captains. He was also the Duke's most favored officer, winning battles and skirmishes with novel strategies, rousing the men to fight with a fierceness and passion which dismayed the enemy before them.

When Ambrosius landed on the southern shores and swept up all of loyal Britain in his wake, Gorlois had been among the leaders and kings who followed the new High King into battle against first Vortigern and then the Saxons. Steffan had ridden with them and it was said Ambrosius called him "another Uther"—not for his prowess in bed, but in battle.

Only, Anwen could not remember hearing anything more of Steffan of Durnovaria since Doward had been taken. Like Igraine, she had presumed the man had been killed in a battle and no one evoked his memory after, just as they rarely spoke of others who had fallen. It was the price of war. Men died, women were widowed.

"Oh, he's not dead," Cador said. "Although I've heard some say he might as well be. In the year of Doward, the first year of Ambrosius' reign, Steffan met the Saxons in battle and received such a wound to the back of his head—"

"The back?" Igraine said. "You mean, the Saxons struck him from behind?"

"With one of their great war hammers," Cador said.

Anwen winced.

"The wound healed well enough," Cador said, "only Steffan

has been blind since."

Daveth rubbed his bristling chin, making a scratchy sound. He looked as uneasy as Anwen felt.

Igraine pressed her hands together. "How…unfortunate," she said. "Are you saying that in all the years since—how many is it?"

"Seven, my lady," Daveth said.

"You mean, for the last seven years, Steffan has been living at Dimilioc? My husband let him remain there?"

Cador put his cup down with a sharp tap of metal upon the stool. "It may appear to be charity to you, madam. I assure you it is not. For those seven years, Steffan has been my tutor. It is thanks to him I can speak the Saxon tongue when I must, plus Latin and Breton." He paused. "I would advise against arguing with him over matters of war strategy, history or reason, too."

Anwen was startled. A knowledge of languages was not unusual, yet the study of history and reason and war theory… that was the purview of scholars and priests.

"You have been taught by a military man?" Igraine asked, sounding as shocked as Anwen.

Cador smiled. "I am a better man for the education, I assure you. However, I am to join my father at the High King's court and Steffan's services would no longer be needed, even without last night's business."

"What happened last night?"

"The damned men pushed him," Daveth growled. Then he bowed quickly. "Forgive my curse, my lady."

Igraine gave him a small, stiff smile and turned her gaze back to Cador.

Cador sighed. "I've been up half the night interviewing everyone involved, which was too many, for my liking. I learned that during the evening meal, one of the men, Maurgh, decided to have some fun. There were pranks—"

"What, exactly, do you mean by pranks?" Igraine interrupted. A fine line marked her brow.

"He's blind, my lady," Daveth said, as if that was all the answer needed.

"Explain it to me," Igraine said. A whiplash of command edged her voice which widened Daveth's eyes.

Daveth rubbed the back of his neck. "About what you'd expect when men look for distraction. Taking away his plate. Throwing things at him he can't see coming. Moving his staff out of reach."

Anwen drew in a slow breath, reminding herself that the world of men was a harsher world than her own.

"And this is…usual?" Igraine asked, her voice low.

"I've seen it happen before," Cador said. "It's meant as a jest. I've seen the same men shove each other off their benches and laugh uproariously. Soldiers work hard. They play hard, too."

"I see," Igraine said, her tone tight. "So they played these jests upon Steffan last night?"

"And a bit more," Daveth said. "We weren't there to shut it down, you see."

"Yes, I gathered that," Igraine said dryly. "What happened?"

Daveth shrugged.

Cador reached for his cup. "As far as I can establish from the reluctant mumblings of the men, one of them tripped Steffan as he was leaving the hall. He fell heavily. Then he got back up again and fought them."

"*All* of them?" Igraine asked, her tone appalled. "With what? He surely does not still wear a sword?"

"Hasn't the need for one," Daveth said. "He used his staff."

Cador smiled. "I wish I had seen it. He put a dozen men in the infirmary, my lady. Broken arms, sore heads, bruises you would not believe. There are more limping around the yard this morning looking sorry for themselves."

A blind man had done this? Anwen didn't believe it.

Igraine looked as though she believed it even less than Anwen. There were other soft sounds of incredulity around the chamber.

"I am still not certain why you bring this matter to me, Cador," Igraine said. "It appears to be one of simple discipline. Punish the men involved, including Steffan, for brawling." She shrugged.

"It's not that simple, my lady," Daveth said. "Steffan is... well, he's not liked."

Cador frowned. "They hate him," he added, with a candid air. "I'm not sure why."

"Steffan always puts a good face on things for Master Cador," Daveth said. "Fact is, he's an angry man. No one at Dimilioc meets his expectations. He's too good for them. Unfortunately, he doesn't stint himself letting them know that."

Cador glanced at Daveth, startled. "*That* might be true enough," he told Igraine. "I've heard Steffan lecture many times about the discipline and morals and superior quality of the men my father keeps beside him at the High King's court, while the men who are left behind are lacking in all matter of skills and qualities."

"Naturally, my husband would take the best with him. They are needed."

"Indeed, my lady," Daveth replied. "Fact is, we can't keep Steffan at Dimilioc and we don't know what to do with him."

"Turn him out," Igraine said. "You would be better off without the disruptions."

"That is why I seek your wisdom," Cador said. "By rights, he should be tossed from the fort. Steffan wounded his fellow soldiers. Only, he served my father with the greatest loyalty and effectiveness and my father favors him still. He appointed him tutor and gave him a place at Dimilioc, teaching his own son. I cannot simply turn the man out. Father would be upset."

Anwen curled her hands into fists. Did no one care that Steffan had been provoked into fighting?

Igraine looked thoughtful. "I understand the shape of your problem now," she said, her tone one of agreement. "The Duke spoke to me about Steffan many times in the past, before Doward. He always spoke with admiration and respect. He would be disappointed indeed if we discard the man without careful thought."

She reached out her hand. One of the women pushed Igraine's cup into her waiting hand and Igraine sipped thoughtfully.

"We could find the man a monastery somewhere. The monks would care for him," Daveth said.

Cador shook his head. "As angry as the quality of the men and the life at Dimilioc makes him, how much angrier would Steffan be with the cloistered life at a monastery?"

"Should we mind what he thinks?" Daveth asked bluntly.

"In this case, I believe we must at least consider his thoughts," Igraine said. "At least, insofar as my husband would expect us to." She paused again. "He really taught you three languages, Cador? Including Saxon?"

Cador grimaced. "I can make myself understood in all the tongues, only Steffan says my accent is horrible."

"I understand Saxon is a difficult language to master."

Cador grimaced again. "It is horrible to learn. It made my jaw ache. And the sound of it is an affront to the ears. Only, to know the language of the enemy is a huge advantage in war. It will make my service to my father and the High King more valuable and for that, I am glad Steffan insisted I persevere with the lessons."

Igraine nodded. "Then, perhaps we should not waste this man's abilities." She thrust the cup out once more and it was plucked from her hand. "Bring Steffan here to Tintagel. He can teach my children."

Anwen drew in a sharp breath, cold fingers running down her back. She could not protest aloud, not here, yet fear touched her.

Morguase looked similarly horrified. "I don't want to learn Saxon, mama!" She at least could get away with a public protest.

"Latin, dear, will serve you well."

Morgan, Anwen saw, was smiling with delight.

Daveth looked doubtful as he ran his gaze over the two girls. "Well now, the man is blind. He'd be useless teaching the little ladies to read and write, begging your pardon, my lady."

"That part of their education is already well in hand. My lady, Anwen, will continue their reading lessons. Steffan can expand their education in ways Anwen cannot. It is a suitable solution."

"And this anger Daveth says the man carries?" Cador asked Igraine.

Igraine dismissed it with a wave of her hand. "Anwen will be there to offset his brutish ways. If he is fit enough to teach Gorlois' first born and heir, then he is more than qualified to teach the Duke's other children. It is done. Have the man brought here."

Even as relief trickled through her at the reprieve, Anwen could feel fresh horror building in her chest.

She must deal with this man? She had never been alone with a man in her life. How could she possibly protect the girls against a blind man who still had the strength and ability to bring a dozen men to their knees?

Chapter Three

nce Cador left, the rest of the fort returned to their normal affairs, as if the interruption had not happened. It was not their lives which were about to change, Anwen thought with some resentment.

She took Morguase and Morgan back to the room and put them at the table to complete the lessons she had set for them. Only, they were too full of questions to settle to the work.

"Is Steffan a really fierce warrior?" Morguase asked. "Will he shout at me if I get things wrong?"

"I've never met Steffan," Anwen admitted. "I won't let him shout at you," she added, for her short answer did not make Morguase look any happier.

Morguase's mouth turned down. Her nose wrinkled. "If he's such a great warrior, how will you stop him? You're old."

Anwen held in her reaction. Morguase sometimes unintentionally said things which were cruel. It merely meant Anwen had more to teach her. "Even if I am old, Morguase, do you think it is something you must point out?"

Morguase shrugged.

"You will coax no one into doing your bidding if you point out their failings," Anwen continued, ignoring the thudding of her heart. "Now, please, finish the line I asked you to write."

Morgan jumped down from the bench and went over to the stand where Anwen's harp sat. She picked up the harp. It was a knee harp, which was an awkward and heavy load for a six-year-old. Morgan carried it with small steps over to where Anwen sat on the edge of her bed. "Please play for us," she said, with an angelic smile.

Anwen breathed out the last of her hurt and smiled at Morgan. "Only if you finish your lessons while I play."

Morguase turned back to her slate and Morgan went back to the table, as Anwen set the harp upon her knee and ran her hand over the strings, listening for jarring notes. It was still tuned properly, so she let it make a rippling arpeggio.

"Something happy!" Morguase demanded.

Anwen nodded and plucked out one of the simple, gay tunes which everyone always liked, while she contemplated the future with growing unease.

LONG AFTER THE GIRLS LEFT to attend to their afternoon tasks—sewing and spinning and weaving lessons could be taught by any competent woman—Anwen remained in her room and read. She possessed few books, for they were difficult to find and expensive to acquire. The few she did have, she cherished. She read them often, only in the privacy of her room where no one would see her doing it. It was another reason she was grateful for the room and the door which kept out the rest of the world when she needed it to.

She knew she was reading to stop herself from thinking. She didn't want to deal with the wounded soldier, even in her thoughts. She had no experience dealing with men, especially not angry men. All her life had been spent among women.

The alert of the sentry on the tower over the gate forced Anwen to put aside the book. She rose and moved to the window. It was a narrow aperture, yet low enough for her to see into the yard, to learn who was about to arrive.

Three guards pulled open the heavy wood and iron gates, just in time to allow entry to five men on horses. They thundered into the yard, their cloaks flying and pennants flapping. More of the Duke's men from Dimilioc, Anwen guessed. They were all large and strong.

The horses halted, breathing hard. Slaves ran to gather their bridles and contain them as the men jumped to the ground.

As the horses were led away, the men removed riding

42

gauntlets, talking among themselves. One gave a soft call, halting the slaves. He moved over to the horses and lifted a long wooden shaft strapped to the horse's side.

A staff.

He carried the staff over to the group of soldiers and held it out.

The man who took it was the tallest of the group. His hand thrust out, then moved sideways until his palm smacked against the staff and he gripped it. This, then, was Steffan.

Anwen pressed her hand to her chest as her heart jumped. She had expected a blind man to look…well, blind. The only other blind person she had ever met was an old woman, whose eyes were milky and skinned with growth which blocked her vision. She was a wretched creature, shuffling about with her hands out, when she dared move off her stool at all.

Steffan, though, was identical to the other men in dress and manner. He rode the horse as if he could see. Had he allowed the horse to find its own way, then? He had thick dark hair, as most Britons did. It was unruly, though, with waves and locks which did not lie against his head. His fair skin was tanned as men generally were. His nose was straight, his brows thick and his jaw square. The chin was strong, too. His neck was thick and strong.

There was nothing wrong with his eyes as far as Anwen

could tell. They looked perfectly normal, although she was too far away to determine their color. He was even turning his head as if he was looking about the yard. Was he listening, instead?

He turned so his gaze—if he could see—was upon the tower itself. For a moment it seemed he was looking directly at Anwen where she stood behind the window.

She stepped back, her heart leaping and her breath shortening. Fright tore through her.

How was she to contain a powerful man like that, when a whole fort of soldiers could not?

Anwen reached for her harp. It was an instinctive movement. Her harp brought her comfort and no one was here to demand a song or tune from her which she did not wish to play. She sank to the bench and put the harp upon her knee and without pausing to consider, she let her fingers move over the strings. The notes were random and jarred against each other. Then a run of notes sounded among them which reminded her of music she had created, long ago.

Anwen recalled the older notes and the sounds they created and played the lilting, soaring melody.

Her heart and her mind lifted with the music. She remembered the first time she had played the notes—they had come to her while she watched the sea rise and fall, and the sun sink into it. That had been when she was younger and had not fully accepted her place yet. She had stood at the big window in Igraine's chamber—Mari's chamber, it had been then—and watched the birds hover and soar, completely free to glide upon the wind, as the sun set behind them. How she had longed to be out there, a part of them, as free as them!

Anwen yearned for that freedom now, too. She wanted to escape the coming days. She wanted to be rid of the fear which coiled in her.

As she played the music, bit by bit the fear did ease and her heart with it.

IT WAS COOL INSIDE. STEFFAN felt the touch of the milder air on his face and the whisper of echoes against the stone surrounding them.

"The Duchess will see you," the steward told Bryce and his men. "Go up to the top of the tower, where she waits."

Steffan hid his surprise. Bryce had not explained where they were going. His men hauled Steffan from the cellar where they had tossed him the previous evening, thrust his cloak at him and told him to put it on.

Then they shoved him at his horse and ordered him to mount it, before slapping its haunches to get it to move with them.

The sun on Steffan's face and the growing scent of the sea

told him they were riding west. The clatter of hooves inside a contained yard said they had arrived. Now, they were in a stone building and the steward spoke of the Duchess.

This, then, must be Tintagel. Why were they here? It could only be because of last night. Had they brought him to face the Duchess for the dispensing of a higher justice?

Surely, their feelings were not so injured?

Glyn, the youngest of Bryce's men and the most considerate, touched Steffan's elbow. "Stairs just ahead," he murmured. "Round and steep."

Steffan swept the end of the staff in an arc until he found the first and stepped onto it. Then the second. Two more, then he had the pattern in his mind and climbed as swiftly as the others.

As they climbed, music sounded. The notes seemed to ooze from the stone walls themselves—a trick of the air and the corridors, most likely. The notes were soft and clear. They climbed and fell and lifted into the air like birds on the wing.

Poignant feeling throbbed between the notes, weeping in loss.

Steffan's chest constricted. How could anyone listen to those notes and not want to beat their chest in anguish?

"Who plays such beautiful music?" he demanded, his voice rough, betraying his response to it.

"What music? Bryce growled.

"Can't you hear it?" Steffan said.

"I can hear it," Glyn said.

The notes climbed and climbed, making Steffan's throat ache. "The soul who shares such beauty must be just as fine."

Someone ahead of him snorted. "The lady Igraine is a beauty, although she doesn't play the harp." That would be the steward.

"Then who is it?" Steffan asked.

"Who cares? Shut up and climb," Bryce snarled.

"Who?" Steffan demanded. "Steward, you must know."

The steward didn't answer at once. He needed his breath to climb, Steffan presumed. Then the steward said, "One of the Duchess' women maybe, only I don't know of any who plays."

Abruptly, the music stopped.

Steffan drew in a deep breath, regret touching him. Now, all he could hear was the sea against the rocks and the unmusical caw of gulls.

From behind Steffan, someone said, "I think the older woman plays."

"Older…?" the steward said. "Oh, that one!"

"Ann," the man at the rear supplied.

"No, Anwen," the steward corrected. He snorted. "She is no beauty, or she wouldn't be companion to the Duchess all these years. No man wants her, or the Duchess would have lost her long ago."

Bryce's laugh was just as derisive. His hand slapped against Steffan's shoulder, startling him. "You lost more than your sight with that blow to your head, eunuch."

Steffan held his tongue. Let them laugh. To not hear the music properly was their loss.

THE SUMMONS TO IGRAINE'S CHAMBER was urgent, forcing Anwen to thrust the harp aside and not linger in her room. She slipped into the antechamber just as the visitors arrived at the top of the stairs.

Her heart back to jumping around like a moth caught in a downturned glass, Anwen moved to the dark corner where the wall hangings kept her back warm, behind the women already gathered there.

She threaded her fingers together, her gaze drawn to the taller of the men clustered in front of Igraine's chair. All the other men were staring at Igraine, as men usually did. Steffan did not. He stood facing the high chair, while his sightless gaze was to one side. He gripped the staff up by the top end, his elbow raised, which made the cloak fall back and reveal his bare arm, rounded with muscles. He wore a leather jerkin, buckled across the front, and no shirt.

Now he was closer, Anwen could pick out details she had not seen before. His skin was smooth with the fairness of youth, yet the contained way he held himself made him seem older. Wisdom and experience imparted the stoic patience he wore. He looked to be ten years younger than Anwen. When had he the time to build such experience?

This was the man who tutored Cador? It did not seem possible. He looked every inch the warrior he had been. He turned his head as a normal person did. It really did seem as though he was observing everything.

One of the other soldiers with Steffan bowed toward Igraine. "My lady, this is the tutor, Steffan. We was told to bring him to you."

"Thank you…Bryce, is it not?"

"Captain Bryce, yes, my lady."

"I requested Maurgh bring him to me," Igraine said. "I wished to speak to Maurgh, too."

Bryce hesitated, his eyes narrowing. "Maurgh was beaten enough to keep him abed this day, my lady."

"I see." Igraine studied Steffan. "Your name and reputation are known to me, Steffan of Durnovaria."

Steffan turned toward her and bowed. "Your husband has been generous and kind, my lady."

"Not without reason," Igraine said. "Although, you have tested that generosity of late."

Steffan's jaw rippled. "The Duke appreciates what others discard through their ignorance. I am a sharp tool, my lady, yet even my edges can be dulled if rubbed against stone long enough."

Anwen smiled. The soldiers around Steffan merely looked puzzled by his response. They had no idea Steffan had just called them stupid.

"Dull blades, rubbed hard enough, create sparks," Steffan added.

Igraine nodded. "Such was my suspicion. We would be wise not to waste your talents, Steffan. My husband would wish it so. There will be no further consequences for your actions last night if you agree to remain here at Tintagel and teach my children the languages you know—but not Saxon," she added, as Morguase sucked in a loud breath and opened her mouth to protest.

Steffan's face grew still. His throat worked. "Your children, my lady?" His voice was strained.

"My daughters," Igraine said. She tilted her head, which he would not see. "Do you object to tutoring women?" Her voice was soft. Dangerously soft. Igraine was comfortable with the power at her command as wife to the Duke of Cornwall. When it came to her children, she used that power without hesitation. Anwen had seen her order men flogged for failing to properly protect her daughters, and women ejected from Tintagel for neglecting an aspect of their care.

Igraine's voice warned him. Steffan shook his head. "No,

my lady. I would be honored." Only, his voice was stiff and his knuckles about the staff paler than the rest of his hand. He was hiding his true feelings.

It made him smarter than most men. Men usually tried to protest or bluster their way out of the lady's request, fooled by her loveliness into thinking she was incapable of independent thought.

Although, of course, Steffan could not see Igraine. He had only her voice to guide him and the dangerous tone had been warning enough.

Igraine relaxed. "Then it is settled. Welcome to Tintagel, Steffan of Durnovaria. You are welcome here."

Not by all, Anwen breathed to herself, her resentment building.

"Anwen?" Igraine called.

Anwen sighed and stepped forward a little. "My lady?"

"Come here," Igraine told her.

Reluctantly, Anwen moved through the phalanx of ladies to the clear space between the assembled ladies and the cluster of men in the middle of the room.

"This is Anwen," Igraine said. "She teaches my children to read and write, which will supplement your own lessons, Steffan. You will begin tomorrow."

Steffan turned to where Anwen was standing and his eyes settled on her unerringly, as if he really could see her.

Anwen pressed her hands to her chest, panic building there. *He sees me!* The thought was colored with the fear which had been building all day, and also with an emotion she did not recognize. A fizzing of her blood, which made her shudder.

As soon as Igraine rose to her feet, signaling the audience was at an end, Anwen escaped the chamber.

The man could find his own way to the room where he was to disrupt her life.

Chapter Four

Ilsa heard the argument from all the way across the open square. Ambrosius and Uther's raised voices were distinct, issuing through the tent opening and the walls themselves. She put down the sword she was polishing to listen.

Maela lifted her chin, her pale eyes narrowing. "Again?" she murmured, with a sigh. She lowered the armored jerkin she was working upon.

"It sounds as though it is about more than the lack of amenities, this time," Nimue said in her clear voice. She was on the other side of the tent, reading letters from Brocéliande. "Perhaps you should slip inside and listen, Ilsa. No one but Arawn will notice you."

Ilsa did not bother being offended. Nimue, with her power and her youth and her white golden looks, drew the eye of everyone. Ilsa wore dull green and brown as usual, which she found useful for slipping unnoticed between trees and across valleys.

She put the sword aside and moved out of the tent. It had rained this morning and now a fine mist was rising from the ground as the sun burned off the last of the puddles. Four rows of tents outlined an open square. The High King's big pavilion made up one entire side. The ladies' pavilion was on the other side, while the nobles and kings' tents ranged on either side, making up the rest of the square.

The ground squelched under her boots as Ilsa hurried across the square. There were few people outside, yet. The rain had driven everyone indoors.

Surrounding the inner square of tents were more tents and shelters and camps, housing the senior officers. Beyond them were the shelters for the lesser ranks of soldiers. At the edge of the camp, the roughest lean-tos and makeshift shelters protected the lowliest foot soldiers.

Just beyond the perimeter laid the town of Amesbury itself. It was too small to offer housing for anyone but the High King. Ambrosius wisely refused the hostel they put aside for him. "I will camp with everyone else," he told them. "Mine is a court which travels, although we will remain until the work of building the monument is done—another reason not to turn someone from their home."

That had been eight months ago and tensions had risen over the summer as the limitations of the impermanent accommodations wore upon the men. Fighting broke out among the troops. Arguments were rife among the leaders.

Ambrosius and Uther, who had seen eye-to-eye through years of fighting and campaigning against the Saxons, were just as quick to come to shouts.

Ilsa turned sideways and moved through the gap between the nearly closed flaps of the High King's tent. If she avoided touching the flaps, she would not change the light shining through them and signal her arrival.

The carpets and furs spread upon the ground inside. Dozens of men stood upon them and Ilsa knew them all. These were Ambrosius' leaders. Most were kings in their own right, who had faithfully supported Ambrosius for the last seven years, working together to oust the Saxons from Britain forever.

Only in the last year had Ambrosius succeeded in driving the Saxons back to the original shoreline territory ceded to them by Vortigern. There, the Saxons remained…for now.

Ilsa moved around the backs of the men, passing Mabon and Ban, Gorlois and the thin, tall Pellinore and Ector, who always stood together. Those two were perhaps the youngest of the captains Ambrosius kept near to hand.

Arawn saw her. He stepped back, which let Ilsa move to his side. His hand touched hers. He didn't look at her. He was watching Ambrosius and Uther.

Uther stood in the center of the circle of men. It never bothered him when forced to stand alone, which he often did—Uther's opinions ran counter to everyone else's. It didn't help that he was usually right, especially in matters of battle and war.

He was staring at his brother, his anger showing in his eyes and the way his jaw worked and the stiffness of his shoulders.

"If we do not secure the north, it will be Vortigern's flood years all over again," Uther ground out.

Ilsa looked at Arawn. He leaned toward her. "Word from the north," he murmured. "Catigern is raiding again. Lot and Urien do nothing."

His quick explanation outlined the entire argument for Ilsa, for it was not the first time she had heard it. The north had always been and still was a wild land which resisted the control of the High King—*any* High King. Vortigern never tamed it despite a decade spent there, fighting for domination against the Picts, the Saxons who fled there, the hill tribes and the Celts who hated him.

Ambrosius did not try to dominate. Instead, he met with the heads of the northern kingdoms, one by one, and forged alliances. He would let the kings fight for their own lands, which would act as a bulwark for the southern lands.

Two of those petty leaders were Lot, king of the Orkney Islands and sprawling lands to the south, and his younger cousin Urien, Duke of Rheged, to the southwest of Lot's borders. Between them, they covered most of the north, along with a handful of smaller kingdoms and duchies and tribal lands—all of which looked to those two for direction.

Lot and Urien had sworn allegiance, yet they were as wild as their lands. Their idea of allegiance held only so long as personal gain could be made.

Catigern, Vortigern's rebel son, ran with the Saxons who remained in Britain. While Ambrosius pursued the Saxons, Catigern had been contained, too.

Now peace was declared, Ambrosius turned to peace-time pursuits. That included the rebuilding of the standing stones. Ambrosius wanted the stone circle as a monument to the three hundred kings and leaders whom Vortigern and the Saxons had slaughtered in Aquae Sullis, the year Ambrosius returned to Britain.

Catigern was testing Ambrosius' tolerance. He and his Saxon cohorts had raided into the west three times in the last year. Uther had driven them north onto Lot's lands, where the terms of the agreement insisted Uther break off and leave them to Lot and his men.

Now, Lot and Urien were doing nothing to control the raiding parties.

It did not sit well with Uther, who preferred direct action to solve a problem. From Uther's expression, Ilsa judged Lot's and Urien's insolence had pushed Uther too far.

"A large party. A show of force," he told his brother. "A month or two and I could have the entire north cleared out."

Ambrosius shook his head. "No. It would violate our treaty with the northern kings."

"They have already violated the treaty!" Uther shouted back. "They do nothing! Let me demonstrate the effectiveness of our men! It will stiffen their loyalty."

"Until they have broken the agreement, we will do nothing, do you hear?" Ambrosius said. "Inaction is not enough to call them traitors."

Uther steamed, his jaw working.

When Ilsa first met Uther, he had been a chaffing lieutenant under Ambrosius' direction, longing for freedom to fight the war for which he had trained his entire life.

The return to Britain gave him that freedom and he reveled in it. Uther and war were made for each other. He blazed as brightly as the star which gave his family the name of Pendragon.

War seasoned him, Ilsa reflected. It seasoned them all. Every man standing in this tent had faced overwhelming odds and learned the extent of his courage and strength. They were all quiet men, assured and confident in their abilities to lead and fight. They did not boast or revel in their accomplishments. They grimly bent to the next task their High King demanded of them.

Uther, too. He was close to forty years of age, now. He wore a full beard the same deep russet as his hair. The beard and the high forehead made his blue eyes blaze and glitter. So did his will. He grew more powerful with each passing year, with more than just physical strength.

It was little wonder he found peace a burden.

Mabon cleared his throat. "The men *are* bored, my lord," he told Ambrosius, his tone apologetic. "Infractions and punishments are increasing daily."

Ambrosius, who could blaze as brightly as his brother when his passion was roused, blew out a breath, his shoulders relaxing. "Yes," he said heavily. "They are."

"Do not send me on another courier errand, brother," Uther warned. "I have fetched my last stone for you."

Ilsa glimpsed Arawn's smile as he lifted a hand to cover it.

The errand Uther referred to had been one of Uther's most successful campaigns. Ambrosius directed him to deal with the Irish tribes, who threatened Britain's western lands with their ferocious raids and weakened Ambrosius' ability to attack the east and the north, for he must constantly guard his back.

Ambrosius told Uther to "take the heart out of Ireland." Uther did exactly that.

Merlin unexpectedly attached himself to Uther's expedition. Uther had no time for Merlin's ways and no respect for a man who refused to pick up a sword. In the matter of Ambrosius' plans for Britain, though, they were in full accord. Uther grudgingly took Merlin with him.

After battling the tribes to a standstill with his small force, Uther captured their leader. The Irish considered a hill in the center of the island to be sacred. It was crowned by a ring of giant stones they called *Chora Gigantum*. It was within the ring where Uther beheaded their leader.

Then Merlin directed Uther's men to tear down the ring and bring the key stones back to Britain, including the black altar stone. The five giant stones and the altar stone were rolled and floated back to Britain. Using waterways and rivers, they were brought within five miles of the stone dance on the plains.

Then, inch by inch, the stones were transported to the old ring, which Merlin planned to raise once more.

The engineering and calculations needed to transport the stones and raise the ring taxed the brightest minds of the land. The project also strained Uther's leadership skills, for the work was physically demanding. Every man who looked to Uther was conscripted—and Uther was not spared, either.

Yet the stones were delivered and even now Merlin was working to finish the project.

Uther called the mission an errand, yet it had routed the

Irish, who had not stepped foot in Britain since.

Ambrosius considered Uther for a long moment. He had let go of his own anger, although Uther still fumed.

"It is not yet time to loose you upon the north," Ambrosius said at last. "We must give Lot and Urien time to prove their fealty, or the work I have done to build the northern ramparts will be for naught."

Uther opened his mouth.

"No, Uther," Ambrosius said. "Ector…?"

Ector was a short young man with sandy hair and a round face. He was the new Count of Galleva, whose lands were to the south of Rheged. Ector drew himself up straighter. "My lord?"

"I think it is time you went home to see your new wife," Ambrosius said. "Hunt boar in that Perilous Forest of yours." As he spoke, he kept his gaze upon Uther.

Uther's anger checked. His eyes narrowed as he looked from Ector to Ambrosius.

Ector bent his head. "I can do that, my lord. Should I take my men with me?"

"That would be appropriate," Ambrosius said in agreement. "Take your time, Ector. Visit your neighbors. Share wine and gossip."

Ector smiled. "Perhaps boast about how Ambrosius sees and hears everything which happens—or doesn't happen—in

Britain?"

Uther scowled. "Talk does not move men of action."

"The power of stories would surprise you," Nimue said from the tent opening, making everyone turn to look at her. She smiled. "There are so many fine stories. Consider the story of how Uther defeated Claudas and turned his lands to waste. Uther's success in Ireland, when he plucked the heart of that land and brought it back to Britain. Ambrosius' victory over Vortigern at Doward, where he did not lift a single weapon."

Uther's smile was small. His eyes danced.

"Fear, brother," Ambrosius said. "Fear can bring a man to his knees well before a sword need be raised."

Chapter Five

She constantly checked the closed door, as if staring at it might tell her when the odious man was to arrive.

Her skittishness communicated itself to the girls. Morguase could barely focus upon her slate, while Morgan frowned as she wrote, marring her smooth little brow.

Morgan, unlike her older sister, did not need a reason to learn. She absorbed her lessons with ease, her genuine curiosity leading her.

Anwen slid onto the bench beside Morguase and coaxed her to read back her letters and words, correcting the formation of the letters with forced patience. Morguase was a less than ideal scholar. She saw no use in learning how to read. Her future as the daughter of the Duke of Cornwall was predetermined. She would be married to a leader, perhaps even a king, to cement an alliance. Then she would bear children and run his household. Morguase, like most people, did not understand how reading would enhance such a future, despite Anwen's assurances that being able to read provided unexpected benefits.

The lift of the latch on the door alerted them.

"In here," came a gruff voice, as the door swung wide.

"Thank you," came another, deeper one.

Anwen swung her legs over the bench and got to her feet, her heart thudding hard. "If you're coming in, come in," she snapped. "All the warm air escapes while the door is held so."

He stepped into the room, moving as a sighted person would, except that the tip of the staff swung out in front of him, sweeping from side to side. He halted two paces inside the door, which put him in the middle of the room. He turned his head, as if he examined it.

"You are Steffan, then," Anwen said. She closed the door behind him, which just missed his back. He was taller than she had guessed from watching him among the other men. She was tall for a woman— an unladylike feature, she had been assured more than once— yet her head only just passed his shoulder.

He seemed to glance over his shoulder as she latched the door. "You are Anwen."

Morgan giggled and slapped her hand over her mouth.

Steffan looked at the girls. At least, he seemed to. He

turned in their direction. "And you would be Morgan and Morguase," he added.

Morguase pushed her slate to one side. "Why do you swing your staff about like that?" she demanded.

"Because I don't know the room yet." The foot of the staff knocked up against the foot of the stool and he scraped it over the legs of the stool.

Morgan, disturbed by his unusual actions and gruff speech, slithered off her bench. She skirted him with a tiny gasp and gripped Anwen's hand, her shoulder against Anwen's hip.

"This is a bench?" Steffan said.

Morguase, who sat upon the bench, narrowed her eyes. "You can't see!"

"Clearly," he replied, reaching past her with his other hand and laying it against the table. "Table. There is a bench behind it, against the wall?"

"Yes," Anwen said. This is what he meant by knowing the room. "A higher table is against the connecting wall and— "

He held up his hand. "I will find them," he said shortly.

Morguase looked at Anwen, offended by his peremptory tone. Anwen shook her head and put her finger to her lips.

Morguase instead watched the man skirt around her, stepping to the corner of the table. He ran the side of the staff along the edge of the table, then tapped it against Morgan's bench. He touched the wall behind it, then ran the tip of the staff along it until he reached the corner.

He found the high table where Anwen's few books were stacked, and her meager collection of garments, folded neatly. His staff slid along the front of the table, while his hand ran lightly over the objects on top of it.

When he touched the harp, he paused. His fingers brushed the strings softly, and they sighed.

Morgan gave a gasp. Her grip on Anwen's gown tightened.

Anwen bent to murmur in Morgan's ear, so the man would not hear her. "He won't hurt it."

"I would be a fool if I did damage an instrument which makes such sweet sounds," Steffan said, making Morgan gasp once more.

Steffan had already moved on. He reached the end of the table. His staff found the wall between the table and the bed. He lifted his chin, as if he was peering through the high window above. "This is the eastern wall. I can detect wet straw in the stables. Brine, too."

"One can smell brine anywhere one stands in Tintagel," Anwen observed, her tone dry. "We *are* perched upon a cliff which drops directly into the sea."

"The straw scent is stronger and fresher. This window faces the courtyard."

The staff ran along the wall, then tapped up against Anwen's bed. Anwen moved out of the way, bringing Morgan with her, as Steffan moved down the length of the bed and found the wall it hugged, then the other corner. The tall lamp stayed in that corner until it was needed to light the work upon the table.

He found and measured the width of the door with both hands, then swept the staff along the wall to touch the other end of Morguase's bench, nodding as he reached it.

Then he rested the staff on the floor and gripped it at the top, as he had in the Duchess' chamber. "You will move nothing in this room. It should remain as it is."

Hot fingers clutched at Anwen's chest. "Who are you to tell us what we can and cannot do in this room? It is *my* room."

He shifted his chin so it appeared he was looking at her. "It is a room with a purpose common among four of us at least," he replied. "If I am to teach effectively, I cannot waste my time searching for objects which are not where they should be."

"And what must we do when the lamp is required to see? Stand in the corner beneath it?" she snapped.

He frowned. "At least have the courtesy to inform me when the lamp is shifted." His tone was mild.

"How are you supposed to teach us, if you can't see?" Morguase demanded. "You can't read anything if you can't see."

"Knowledge doesn't always come from what is written," he shot back.

Morgan tugged on Anwen's dress. "He isn't like other priests," she murmured. "He's rude."

Steffan drew in a sharp breath. He had heard that, too, then. He dropped his chin and addressed Morgan as if he could see her. "I am not a priest, little one."

"What are you, then?" Morgan asked.

"I was a warrior once. I served your father." His mouth shifted into a hard grimace. "Now I serve him again by teaching you Latin and Greek and Breton, among other things."

"Anwen teaches us," Morgan said. "I can read." She considered Steffan. "You cannot," she added, her tone superior.

Anwan shook Morgan's hand. "Now *you* are being rude."

Steffan lifted a brow. "Do you know what *barba* means, little one?"

"My name is Morgan," Morgan said, with the full haughtiness of a child raised in a royal household.

"And do you know what *barba* means, little Morgan?"

Morgan scowled. "No."

"It means beard," Anwen said. "It is Latin."

"Indeed," Steffan said. He spoke to Morguase. "Have you heard anyone say *barba tenus sapientes*?"

Morguase frowned. "My father *says* it sometimes, after

meeting people."

"And what does *sapientes* mean?" Steffan replied.

Morguase shrugged.

Steffan frowned. "Do you know?" he insisted.

"He cannot see you shrug, Morguase," Anwen said.

Steffan's frown smoothed out. "*Sapientes* is the present tense of *sapiens*, of which you are one."

"I am?" Morguase looked offended again.

"*Homo sapiens*," Anwen murmured. "Humans. People."

"Creatures with the ability to think," Steffan added. "So what does *bara tenus sapientes* mean?"

"What does *tenus* mean?" Morgan asked, her tone curious.

"As far as, up to, down to…" Steffan replied.

"Beard, as far as, thinking," Morgan murmured. Her hand loosened and fell away from Anwen's. "Thinking as far as a beard?" she guessed.

"Very good," Steffan replied. "Put another way, a man who is said to be *barba tenus sapientes* is said to be as wise as far as his beard."

Both girls frowned.

Anwen held her tongue. She understood what Steffan was doing.

"What if a man has no beard?" Morguase demanded. "Does that mean he isn't wise?"

"The Romans think a man with a long beard is wiser than

others," Steffan said. "Or perhaps he is just older and has had time to grow his beard. An old man is often a wise man, or he would not have grown so old."

"That's silly," Morguase said. "My father shaves, and he is the wisest man in the world."

"He is a wise man indeed," Steffan said, his tone sincere. "What the Romans mean when they say a man is *barba tenus sapientes* is actually the opposite. They mean a man might *look* intelligent yet be far from it."

"Then they're being sarcastic when they say it?" Morguase asked.

"It is called irony," Steffan said. "You are in the middle of an irony right now. Both of you."

"We are?" Morguase asked, astonished.

"You say a blind man cannot teach, yet I have just taught you some Latin and the meaning of irony," Steffan pointed out. "There is also the secondary irony...do you understand it? About measuring a man's beard?"

Morguase frowned, looking inward. "Women don't grow beards," she murmured. "Romans don't think women can be measured for wisdom?" She frowned. "They don't think women can be taught," she finished, her scowl deepening.

Steffan spread his hand. "Yet here I stand, teaching young women." His voice was dry.

Morguase looked indignant and offended. Morgan

frowned, her small mouth puckering. "You don't want to teach us," she said.

The staff scraped on the stone floor as Steffan shifted his feet. "I want you to understand the gift of knowledge, no matter where it comes from, even if it comes from a man who cannot read. You presumed, both of you, that because I cannot see to read, I am incapable of teaching. You measured me by my beard."

Anwen squashed the flare of appreciation she felt for the multi-faceted lesson he had imparted. She didn't want to admire the man.

Morgan's mouth opened. Morguase had the grace to look ashamed. She glanced at her sister, then at Steffan. "We did," she said softly. "I am sorry, Steffan. I didn't understand."

"I'm sorry, too," Morgan said in her lilting high voice.

Steffan nodded. "And now you have a complete understanding of what *barba tenus sapientes* means. That is enough for today. Both of you may leave. I must discuss future lessons with Anwen. Be here tomorrow at the usual time."

Irritation flared in Anwen at his high-handed directions. She remained silent, though. She could not dispute him in front of the girls, for it would damage the fragile rapport he had just built with them. For their sake, she would not jeopardize his ability to teach them well.

"That would be after prayers and breakfast," Morgan said.

"That is when I will be here," Steffan confirmed.

"Go now," Anwen told them. "Enjoy the rest of the morning as you wish."

"Thank you, Anwen," Morguase said as the two girls left.

Startled, Anwen stared at the door that closed behind them. Morguase had never thanked Anwen before.

Steffan stepped over to the bench and table. Instead of sitting on the bench as Anwen had expected, he swept his hand over the table, then sat on the edge. He propped the staff in the crook of his arm and rested his hand on it.

He appeared to gaze at her.

"Why does it look as though you can see me?" Anwen demanded, her insides jumping uneasily.

"In a well-lit room, I can see shadows and shapes," he said, his tone dismissive. "When you move, I see the shape move." He tapped the staff. "It occurs to me that I may have measured by beard length, too."

Anwen threaded her hands together. "A woman teaching?" she guessed.

"Very good," he said with a small smile. The smile changed his face, made the harsh strength grow warmer. "How is it you were taught to read? I've never met a woman who could, not outside a nunnery."

"Nor within one, I would hope," she replied.

His smile grew a little more. "Tell me. Are you the daughter of a privileged king?"

Anwen flexed and twined her fingers. "My father was a simple war chief. I don't believe he saw a single coin in his whole life. My mother died when I was small, so he gave me to the nuns to care for me while he waged Cornwall's campaigns. There *was* a nun who could read. She taught me."

"That was kind of her."

"Kindness had nothing to do with it," Anwen said. "I was an impossible child. Opinionated and inclined to more mischief than the nuns could tolerate. They needed to distract me."

"Capture the mind and the heart follows," he murmured. "And were you tamed by words?"

Anwen cleared her throat. Such a personal question! She had never spoken about her childhood before. No one had ever asked. "It wasn't words which tamed me," she said, shifting on her feet.

"Ah. Then something else did the deed. What was it?"

Anwen moved over to the high table and rearranged the books he had scattered in his exploration. "Did they tell you anything about me?"

"Should they have?"

"I know what they say," she said bitterly. "The old woman in the corner. The ugly one."

"You are not ugly."

Anwen whirled. "As if you would know."

He shook his head. "There are people whose voices beckon attention."

Anwen snorted. "I cannot sing. My voice is not light and pretty like Igraine's. Did you ever see her, before your sight was taken?"

"She is a great beauty, to be sure," Steffan said. "That was not my meaning."

"I speak too harshly at times," Anwen admitted.

"When you speak at all," he added.

Anwen pressed her lips together. "It is not my place to speak, except to Morgan and Morguase, when I teach them."

"That is the world's loss," Steffan said.

Anwen shook her head, irritation building. "If you seek my cooperation by complimenting me, you will fail. I know my place too well, Steffan of Durnovaria."

"You are fortunate in your certainty."

"Am I?" Her voice emerged sour and dry. "My father died in battle when I was fourteen. Gorlois brought me to Tintagel, in return for my father's life of service. I was made a companion to Gorlois' new wife, Mari. Mari ignored me— as she should. I was young and naïve, despite my education. An ignorant child. I spent years in the corner, where no one noticed me. No man wanted me— I have no dowry and what man would want a wife with more education than him?"

Steffan raised a brow. "One who is not a fool?" he asked.

Anwen dismissed the notion. "When Mari was put aside, I was twenty-three. Two years later, Gorlois married Igraine, who insisted I remain in her household out of charity, I am sure, for I have nowhere else to go. I have been here ever since. I do not delude myself with notions that anything might change in the future. I will live out my days alone, the unnoticed companion of a great lady. Tell me, would you truly find it a comfort if you knew your place with such certainty?"

"I might," Steffan replied, his tone still soft. "You, at least, *have* a place."

"So do you. You are the Duchess' appointed tutor."

"Ah. That." His mouth turned down.

"Is it really such a burden to teach women?" she snapped.

He did not answer straight away. Even if he were not blind, Anwen suspected that at that moment, he would not see her. His thoughts were far away. "'Tutor' is a title given to me. It is not the one I would take for myself."

"As if any of us has a choice in the matter," Anwen said dryly.

He got to his feet with a flex of muscles and sinew and the room seemed to shrink around him. Anwen resisted the need to move out of his way. She was not in his way, even though he seemed to take up all the spare space in the room.

"I was born the son of a soldier and was expected to be a soldier, too. And so I was. *That* is my true place. It remains my place in here." He touched his chest.

"How is it you came to read, then?" she demanded. If he could ask impertinent questions, so could she. "I mean, you can read, yes? You must have learned, to acquire your knowledge of languages, before you lost your sight."

He shook his head. "No. I could not read and I still cannot, even if I could see the letters. I learned, Anwen of Tintagel, from *listening*. I sought those who could read, those who spoke the languages I wanted to learn. I spoke to anyone who might provide insight."

"Insight into what?"

"Into the workings of fate and the meaning behind it," he said bitterly. He lifted a finger toward his eyes. "I wanted to know why."

Anwen could find no response which did not sound callous. To remind him that God did not explain himself would bring Steffan no comfort. None of the platitudes about patience and humility fit with the physical man before her. "Did you learn why?" she asked, instead.

"I am still searching," he replied. "You are I both chaff at our places. Yet, there could be use in the place where we find ourselves."

"How so?" she demanded.

"Your books. I felt them. Do you read them to Morgan and Morguase?"

"They are too young for Plato," Anwen said quickly.

"Greek…" He gripped the staff. "You know Greek."

"And Latin," Anwen replied stiffly.

"But…" He frowned. "Why, then, does Igraine want me to teach them, if you can?"

"I suppose, because she does not know I speak either language," Anwen said.

"You didn't tell her?"

"She did not ask."

His knuckles whitened. "The woman in the corner…" he murmured.

Anwen straightened her back and raised her chin. Then she remembered he would see neither of those actions. "It is the Lady's will which forces me to endure your presence. You might make it tolerable for both of us if you confine your thoughts to the education of the girls."

"An impossible task," he returned and reached out with his spare hand, searching for the door. "My thoughts roam too far to be contained to such a simple chore. However, while I am in your presence, I will channel them to the task at hand."

"That would please me greatly."

He opened the door. "As I am to channel my thoughts, I cannot care one way or the other about your pleasure." He nodded in her direction. "Tomorrow, we will begin."

He shut the door behind him with a soft click of the latch.

The room was no longer warm. Anwen shivered.

Chapter Six

I tell you, this sort of stupidity will increase, the longer we sit upon these wind-blasted plains," Uther said, his tone one of warning. He strode beside Arawn and Gorlois as the three headed for the edge of the war camp, threading through the tents and shelters.

Ilsa could only keep up with them by skipping along and breaking into a jog every few paces. All three of them failed to notice she was trailing them. Their expressions were tight with concern.

Soldiers stepped out of the way, snapping off salutes as they passed by.

"There is always stupidity when soldiers grow idle," Gorlois said in his gravelly voice. His hair, which was a lighter red than Uther's thick dark russet and even Ilsa's own auburn, lifted in the wind made by his passage.

"Let us learn the facts, before we condemn the conditions," Arawn added.

Uther scowled. "Good luck with that," he murmured.

Ilsa suspected Uther would be right once more. The report of a brawl ending in murder, which had them sprinting for the edge of the camp to investigate, would end with the same puzzling lack of explanations as so many minor infractions had, lately.

The location of the brawl was easy to find. A large circle of men gathered around the body. Uther pushed through the men, then shoved enough of them aside so Ilsa, Gorlois and Arawn could step into the space in the middle. A man laid on the damp ground, face down. It was not clear what had killed him, although he rested in a pool of blood which was sinking into the weed-tufted mud.

Another soldier stood on the far side of the circle, his head down and his breath billowing in steamy clouds, for the morning was chilly. He had the powerful arms of a sword-fighter, with bronze arm guards and a good cloak over his shoulders. His nose was crooked from being badly set.

This was no simple, untrained recruit. He was a disciplined soldier. Yet a bloody knife laid at his feet and two men held his arms. An officer wearing Cornwall's white cloak, which was a dirty gray and tattered at the hem, whirled to face them as Uther and the others pushed into the circle. The officer had close-set eyes and a crease over the bridge of his nose, which gave him a mean, squinty expression. His jaw flexed

80

when he saw them.

"My lords, there's no need to concern yourselves with this matter. I have it in hand."

"It's a matter of murder, isn't it, Madog?" Gorlois said.

Madog rubbed his jaw. "It depends on how you look at it, my lord."

"A man lies dead," Arawn pointed out, his tone mild.

Madog shook his head. "It isn't that simple—"

A whisper and a shuffling of the surrounding men alerted everyone. The edge of the circle separated, as Ambrosius and Merlin walked into the center. Merlin glanced around the circle, his gaze missing nothing. Men cowered when his gaze touched them.

Ambrosius moved up to where Uther confronted Madog and the captive soldier. "What happened here?" he demanded.

Merlin didn't join the tight knot of men standing by the body. Instead, he prowled the circle. Ilsa, who was not included in the center, either, monitored the tall man's restless steps.

Merlin's gaze fell upon Ilsa's face and she shivered, for his deep black eyes seemed both lifeless and depthless. It was like looking into a night sky bereft of stars. Merlin was strange at the best of times, yet he was friendly when he spoke to Ilsa and warmth of a sort showed in his eyes. Now, he was a stranger.

No wonder the men flinched from his gaze.

Ilsa's heart pattered uneasily.

She pulled her gaze from Merlin for the officer, Madog, was speaking nervously.

"It's nothing, my lord," Madog assured Ambrosius. "A thing which happens when an army is camped for too long."

"Murder is nothing?' Ambrosius asked, his voice dangerously soft.

"'twasn't murder," Madog replied. He pointed at the dead man. "He took a camp girl away from another."

"By the gods, man, I don't condone the killing of *any* man over a woman!" Gorlois burst out. "Especially not an officer of mine!" He turned to Ambrosius. "My lord, I apologize. This is not a behavior I tolerate—"

Ambrosius held up his hand. "I want to hear this," he said softly. "The officer who slew the man…what does he have to say about this?"

The man being held lifted his head. He was also wearing one of the white cloaks of Cornwall. "Braises was beating the girl because she wouldn't cooperate."

Gorlois' face turned as red as his hair. "So you *killed* him?"

The man shrugged, an abbreviated movement because his arms were held. "I didn't mean to. It just happened."

"Where is the girl?" Ilsa asked.

The one called Madog glanced at her. His eyes rolled.

"Who gives a damn? Gone for the surgeon, I suppose. He split her eye open."

"Speak civilly, man," Gorlois growled. "You're addressing a queen."

Madog glanced at Ilsa again, startled.

Ambrosius waved everything aside, his gaze still on the captive officer. "What do you mean, it just happened?"

"I don't know," the man said heavily. "I wanted to stop him beating the woman. Then…it was like a cloud came over my thoughts. Then he was lying there, where he is now." He seemed stoical, even indifferent about-facing execution, which was the sentence for cold-blooded murder.

"For the sake of Mithras, Merlin, will you stop that incessant pacing?" Uther bellowed.

Everyone looked at Uther, startled.

Uther threw out his hand. "He's a wolf among sheep. Stirring up the men with that blank gaze of his."

Ambrosius jerked his head at Merlin, who crossed the space in the middle of the circle, heading for them. He stepped over the dead man's legs with his own long ones, then whirled to look down at the body.

Ilsa's heart lurched once more. No one but she could see Merlin's face, for she was far from Ambrosius' group.

Merlin's gaze ran over the body, as if he was seeing it for the first time. Then his eyes widened and grew blank and still.

He straightened with a snap, as if someone had pulled him up by his hair.

"For the king shall fall and rise again!" he cried, in a voice which was deep and booming and not his own.

Ilsa drew in a shaky breath.

Everyone spun on their heels to look at the tall figure in the center of the ring.

"What did he say?" someone muttered.

Merlin threw out his arms, in a gesture which encompassed the entire camp. "The white dragon has fallen! The red dragon has risen! And so it will again! The path of the once and future king lays before all of you, for his time has come. The winter shall witness his fall and his most glorious rise, for he comes! He comes!"

The muttering of the men grew louder. They drew away, the tight circle fragmenting.

Merlin gave a groan which sounded as though he was in mortal pain and fell to his knees. He thrust out a hand, propping himself upright and spoke. He used no language Ilsa knew or recognized. She clenched her hand against her chest, which ached with tension, her breath held.

No one around Ambrosius moved, either.

Merlin's guttural voice ground on, rising and falling, making the hair on the back of Ilsa's neck prickle hard and send shivers down her spine. She did not understand what he was saying, yet the tone implied dark deeds and misery.

She edged around the circle toward Arawn and the men and saw Merlin's face. Her fear fled.

Agony contorted his features. The strange eyes were not his. Did something or someone speak through him the way they spoke through the Lady of the Lake, as Merlin had once explained to her, many years ago?

He fell silent, his chest heaving. His eyes rolled up and his arm bent.

Ilsa threw herself forward, with barely a thought except that Merlin was not himself and in pain. She caught his shoulders as they sagged toward the mud. He was shuddering, his eyes closed.

Ilsa rested his head on her knees. This, she remembered, too. *All one can do is ensure they do not come to harm while they writhe so*, he had said, while protecting Nimue's head.

"Everyone, return to your billets!" Gorlois bellowed. "Break it up! There's nothing to see here. Go on. Go!"

"You heard your sire!" Madog shouted. "Get out of here, you mangy curs!"

"Madog, take Garnet to my tent. I'll deal with him there," Gorlois said.

Merlin shifted and twitched, his eyes closed. It was as if someone moved his limbs about for amusement. Ilsa pressed her lips together and held onto his shoulders, so he would not roll fully into the mud, as the sound of men muttering and squelching across the mud faded.

"Here," came a gruff voice.

Ambrosius' thick red cloak settled over Merlin, the edges trailing in the dirt.

Ilsa looked up. Ambrosius stood over them, his gaze dark as he studied his son.

"Once he is himself again, I can arrange for him to be taken back to his tent," Ilsa said.

"You have practice dealing with what ails him?" Ambrosius asked, surprised.

"I have a little experience," she admitted. "He is not ill, my lord. He would tell you he is suffering from the raw power of having gods speak through him."

Ambrosius grunted. "I've heard him say such things before, yes. He's stopped moving now."

Ilsa looked down. Merlin's eyes were tight slits, as if the low dawn light was too bright for him. Awareness gleamed in them.

"Here. I will help him back to his tent," Ambrosius said. He bent and slid his arm under Merlin's back and hoisted him to his feet. "Can you walk?" he asked him.

"A little," Merlin croaked.

Ilsa caught Ambrosius' cloak as it fluttered toward the ground and bundled it up in her arms. She followed the pair as Ambrosius walked his son through the maze of campfires and billets. Everyone who saw them turned their gazes away, as if they were giving them privacy which was rare here.

The interior of Merlin's small tent was spartan spare, with only a single mat to protect feet, a small chest and a pallet in one corner. The pallet had thick furs upon it.

Ambrosius grunted with effort as he laid Merlin upon the furs, then crouched beside him and studied him. His brows were tightly furrowed.

"This will not harm him," Ilsa assured him. "Merlin will sleep and when he wakes, he will be as normal."

For a long moment, Ambrosius did not move. His gaze shifted to her as she settled on her knees on the ground beside him and pulled a fur up over Merlin. "Your sons must be near grown now, yes?"

Ilsa gave a soft laugh. "Not quite, my lord. Alun is seven. Elen is five. Arawn Uther has just turned two."

"You have watched over them while they are sick, yes?"

"Oh, yes."

"Then you know a little of what I feel right now."

Ilsa glanced at Ambrosius, startled, for deep feeling shaded his voice. "He is your son," she murmured. "Of course you feel helpless. It is quite natural."

"Is it? This power he wields…it frightens normal men. It makes me afraid for Merlin. What price will he pay for the use of it?"

"I think you are looking at a part of that price right now."

Ambrosius settled on the ground, one knee bent in front of him, his gaze on Merlin's peaceful face. "Merlin found me when he was nearly a man. For all the years before that meeting I thought myself childless. I assumed Uther would take my place, when the time came."

"Merlin has assumed that, too. He has no interest in ruling," Ilsa assured him.

"I know." Ambrosius' jaw worked, as if he struggled with a thought. "Merlin told me that between him and Uther, they would make another king. The greatest king of my line."

"My lord?" Ilsa asked, puzzled.

"The once and future king," Ambrosius said softly. "I suppose I am the 'once' part of it." He glanced at Ilsa and grimaced. "In all these years, Merlin has never prophesied my personal future, until today." He got to his feet. "I'll have food sent for you to break your fast and for Merlin, when he wakes."

Ilsa watched the High King leave, his shoulders square, as the meaning of what he had said coupled up with Merlin's shouted prophesy. She shuddered as she put it together.

Merlin had seen Ambrosius' death, which would happen before mid-winter.

Chapter Seven

The air was still and few sea birds called. The older folk muttered about summer storms being the worst as the household shuffled into the chapel for morning prayers and devotions.

As a companion of the Duchess, Anwen was permitted to sit on a bench behind Igraine, while most of the household stood or knelt as was required. Over their heads, Anwen could see Steffan standing at the back of the chapel, his staff in his hand, his gaze on the ground.

Just a glimpse of him made her heart squeeze and thrash like the waves against the cliffs.

She had supposed that being alone with and talking to a man would require constant fortitude and guarding of her honor. She had heard lurid tales from Igraine's other women. From their stories, Anwen gained the impression that at the first possible moment a man would push his physical attentions upon a solitary woman, using his strength and weight to convince her to fall in with his wishes.

The little exposure she'd had to men who lived in Tintagel convinced her the women were not exaggerating, for Anwen was aware of male gazes following her as she crossed the yard, making her heart leap as it was now.

Or else, the women said, a man would pay no attention to the woman at all. He would barely notice her, only to demand she serve him food and drink and look as pretty as possible while she did it.

Steffan had done neither. He spoke to her as if she were a man, as if the ideas in her head and the words she spoke were worthy of his attention. He did leer at her…well, he could not leer. Only, she did not think he would even if he could see her. Not that any man had ever leered at her. She was not a beauty like Igraine. Even when Anwen was younger, plain was as charitable a description as could be spared for her.

Her hair was plain brown and lighter rather than darker. It was neither a pretty gold nor a pleasing Celtic black. It was thick and abundant and when she let it loose, it brushed the back of her hips. Yet it hung in straight hanks, with no interesting curls or waves. Her face was not objectionable, although it was not pretty, either. Her eyes were also brown, as were her brows. Her nose was straight and perhaps a little long, her lips were neither thin nor full and they did not beckon as Igraine's full lips did. Anwen's skin was Celtic pale, without scars or blemishes, yet it was not brushed with a delicate blush of color or dewy with youth.

She did not have curves the way Igraine did. Her breasts were full yet not large enough to draw a man's eye. Her waist was small, but so were her hips. Her legs were longer than most women's. Her feet were long, too. Not as long as a man's yet they were not pretty and delicate the way a woman's ought to be.

Anwen had spent many nights when she was younger, totting up the sins of her appearance, wondering if they were the sole reason she did not draw men's gazes the way any silly young thing new to the court tended to do. It had been many years since she agonized over her shortcomings, though.

Last night, she had not lingered upon the long list of grievances. She considered them for only a short while, in light of the startling realization that Steffan could see none of her flaws.

Was that why he treated her as he did? For a while, when he spoke of their places in the world and the work ahead of them, she forgot this was the angry man she was expected to control and direct.

His anger had been there—it bubbled silently at the bottom of his words and thoughts, driving what he said. Yet he did not vent his anger upon her the way they said he had done to the soldiers at Dimilioc.

In fact, talking to him was interesting. When she had shuddered in anticipation of having to speak to a man alone, "interesting" was not a possibility she had entertained.

When prayers were done, Anwen passed through the kitchen and scooped into a bowl a spoonful of the oatmeal and dried fruit stewing on the fire. She took the bowl back to her room. It was not required of her to sit with the other women to eat, for which she was grateful. She sat at the teaching table instead. While she ate, she turned her thoughts upon the coming day.

Before she finished her bowl, the latch clicked up and the door opened. Steffan moved into the room with the same confidence a sighted man would. The staff stayed tucked under his bulging arm.

He knew the room now, she realized.

He shut the door. "Anwen?"

"At the table," she said. "Have you eaten? I did not think to bring more food with me."

He lifted his spare hand. There were three of the cook's flat oatmeal cakes wrapped in a cloth. "I thought you would be with the other women."

"You planned to eat alone?"

"I will not eat with the other men." He moved over to the table, only pausing at the last second to bend and touch the edge of it. "May I?"

"The bench in front of you is empty," Anwen told him.

"That is not what I asked. This is your room. Do you mind if I eat here?"

"And if I say no?" she asked curiously.

"The horses in the stables are undemanding company," he said dryly. "They do not snore, either."

"You sleep there as well?" she asked, appalled.

"Is there somewhere I am expected to sleep of which no one has informed me?"

Anwen stared at him. "Surely a bed can be found for you."

He shrugged. "Straw is very comfortable. I have slept upon it for many years."

Anwen struggled to encompass that. "They gave you no bed at Dimilioc, either?"

"I considered it a blessing," he said. "Eating with the men was trial enough."

Anwen's gaze dropped to the cakes in his hand. He had come here, expecting to eat alone. He made no move to sit, though.

"Oh, for goodness sake, sit down!" she said, abruptly irritated.

He moved toward the table until his knee touched the bench, then stepped over it and sat. Another sweep of his hand across the table told him it was clear. He put the cloth on the table and spread it beneath the cakes.

Then he lifted the first and bit into it hungrily.

Anwen made her attention return to the bowl before her. She ate slowly, enjoying the tart taste of the fruit. She risked staring at the man on the other side of the table, for he could not see her do so. Women had warned her many times that boldly staring at a man would embolden him to take liberties. That could not happen with this man, though.

Her gaze fell to his bare arms and the muscles which moved beneath the flesh as he shifted them. Tendons in his neck flexed as he ate. Even sitting upon a bench, he was full of movement. Vitality emanated from him which conflicted with his blindness.

Her gaze shifted to his sightless eyes. He had oddly colored eyes. They appeared to be green right now, yet when she saw them yesterday, she could have sworn they were brown. They were perfectly normal eyes. If she had not seen him quarter the room yesterday, and feeling the shape and placement of the furniture, she would have supposed he could see just like any other man, now.

Then she processed how swiftly he was eating. "You are hungry?"

"Yes," he said, around a mouthful of cake.

"Did you not eat your fill at supper last night?"

"That would require sitting with the other men." He shrugged.

"You had no supper at all?" Anwen asked, appalled.

"Hunger was the more attractive choice," he assured her.

Anwen remembered Cador and his man, Daveth, talking about the "entertainment" the men at Dimilioc found through taking Steffan's bowl from him, and throwing things at him. She glanced at Steffan's spare hand, which was curled protectively around the last cake sitting on the cloth. Likely, the entertainment had not stopped with simply stealing his food.

She shuddered. "You would be best to eat all your meals here," she said shortly, before she could reconsider the wisdom of asking a man to return to her chamber so frequently throughout the day.

Steffan lifted his head. He swallowed the mouthful of cake and frowned. "Do you eat your supper here?"

"Often," she admitted.

"I prefer to eat alone."

"Then I am sure the wet straw in the stable will be a sufficient table for you." She returned her attention to her bowl, to finish the last morsels.

Neither of them spoke again, until Morgan and Morguase pushed into the room and settled at the table for their morning lessons.

"Must we write more today?" Morguase complained as Anwen retrieved the wax slates from the high table in the corner. "I want to learn more Latin."

Anwen hesitated.

"Do both together," Steffan told Morguase. "Write the phrase you learned yesterday. Do you remember it?"

"A man is as wise as his beard is long," Morguase said.

"And in Latin?" Steffan challenged her.

She frowned.

"*Barba*," Morgan said, taking her slate from Anwen.

"*Sapientes*," Morguase added, as Anwen slid the other slate in front of her.

They both picked up their styluses and bent to write the words, spelling them out together.

Anwen leaned over to look at their slates. "That should be an 'i' and an 'e' in *Sapientes*," she told Morguase. "Not two 'e's."

Morguase looked at Steffan. "Is that right, Steffan?" she asked him.

He hesitated. "If Anwen says that is how you write the words, then it is right."

Morguase looked at Anwen, startled. Then she turned back to her slate once more.

She did not challenge Anwen after that. The lesson continued, with Steffan introducing simple Latin words for objects in the room. Anwen helped them write the words.

The time passed quickly. When Anwen heard the women coming down from the Duchess' chamber to head for the kitchen for their noon meal, she took the girls' slates from them.

"You have done well this morning," she told them, as she sent the girls from the room.

Then she put the slates away. "I am going to find food for myself," she told Steffan, collecting the bowl she'd used for her breakfast. "I will see you tomorrow morning."

She had her hand on the door latch when he spoke. He did not turn to face her, but spoke to the tabletop. "I suppose…I could eat here, after all."

Anwen struggled with the hot mix of feelings which sprouted at his observation. "You do not need to make it sound as though you are conferring a favor upon me. I like being alone and I withdraw the offer."

He turned about, lifting his legs over the bench and facing her. His eyes looked gray now. Storm clouds. "I do *not* like being alone," he said. "It is not a condition I experienced until…"

Until he was blinded and suddenly, no one sought his company.

Anwen shifted on her feet. "You seek to make me feel pity for your plight and give up my solitude."

He shook his head. "I prefer to eat alone, for more reasons than to avoid the bad manners of other men."

Anwen rolled her eyes. "You cannot have it both ways. Either you want company or you want none. Pick one and hurry, for I am hungry and there is lamb stew."

"Mutton, actually. The smell is unmistakable," Steffan said. "Someone should explain to the cook about the power of rosemary as an aromatic."

"You try my patience!" she said and stalked from the room.

She found one of the staff in the kitchen and asked them for two bowls of the stew simmering in the big cooking pot on the fire. There were loaves left over from breakfast and she took one of the smaller ones. Juggling the hot bowls and the loaf, she carried them back to her room.

The room was empty.

Anwen ignored her disappointment. That left more for her to eat.

She settled at the table, the wall at her back, and broke off a hunk of the loaf, dipped it in her stew and ate.

The door unlatched and swung open. Steffan entered, carrying a stoppered flask and two cups in one big hand.

Anwen lowered the bread, her heart pattering.

He sniffed. "Bread, too. A feast." He put the flask on the table and settled the mugs, then sat. He leaned the staff against the wall, then sat and swiveled to face the table and put his hands upon the surface.

His sightless eyes moved to where she was sitting. There was an expression on his face which Anwen did not understand.

"You must forgive the impertinence," he said.

"What impertinence?"

He moved his hands across the table, feeling his way with his fingertips. They brushed over the bread and the bowls, including hers, the handle of her spoon and the back of her hand. Then he moved them back over to the other bowl. He picked it up and put it in front of him.

Then, with the same waving of his fingers, he found the flask and the cups. He unstopped the flask and put his finger into the cup and poured the watered wine. When the liquid touched his finger, he stopped pouring. He took his finger out and shook it off, then pushed the cup toward her.

"*That* impertinence," he said, his voice strained.

Anwen stared at him, her heart thudding with more than unease. This was why he preferred to eat alone. He didn't like being alone. Yet he did not like people seeing his fumbling uncertainty, as he explored his food with his fingers and dipped them into his drink so he knew when to stop pouring.

He was embarrassed.

How mercilessly the other men must have tormented him for his awkward groping, to bring him to such a quandary!

Anwen picked up her spoon once more. "I do not care one way or another about your manners," she said, keeping her voice neutral. "So long as you do not need me to entertain you with gossip and conversation while you eat, you may remain."

He sat motionless for more of her heartbeats. Then he drew a breath and let it out. Silently, he poured the second cup of wine, then licked the end of his finger.

"Tonight, I will bring napkins, too," Anwen added and ate.

Chapter Eight

rawn should be out drilling his men, seeing to their duty rosters, and training the youngest recruits. Her children should be in the big tent where all the other small children who traveled with the High King's court remained during the day. There, they learned lessons or played, while supervised and guarded by wives and soldiers. Sometimes they were permitted to walk upon the plains, with a suitable guard to escort them. That would not happen today, for the cold, overcast morning had turned into a chilly, rainy afternoon.

Ilsa longed to be warm. The idea of mulled wine and warm furs had sustained her while she watched over Merlin until his sleep had become natural and relaxed.

Only, Arawn was moving about the tent in impatient circles, while Ban and Bors, both red in the face with frustrated anger, tried to talk over the top of each other.

Arawn spotted Ilsa as she ducked under the flap and relief

showed on his face. "These domestic crises are endless," he told her.

"What has happened?" she asked, glancing at Bors and Ban. They were both handsome men, with clear eyes and skin, tall and well built. They favored closely cropped beards which outlined their jaws and strong chins.

Neither looked handsome nor happy right now.

Bors scowled at his brother. "The stupid git got Lady de Maris with child, that is what has happened."

"Oh…" Ilsa said, her heart sinking.

It was an open secret that Ban had been sharing Suzanna de Maris' pallet while her husband was patrolling the Saxon Shore borders at Ambrosius' direction. Ilsa could even understand why Ban was drawn to the woman. She was fair, with dark hair and eyes which reminded Ilsa of Elaine, Ban's wife.

Ban shoved his hand through his curly hair. "It might not be mine," he said. "There are other possibilities."

Ilsa winced. It was true Suzanna was free with her favors, although not of late. She had devoted herself to Ban's company for some months, a fact which had not escaped most of the encamped army yet had apparently eluded Ban.

Or perhaps, Ilsa thought, studying Ban's unhappy features, he preferred to believe Suzanna had no attachment to him.

Ilsa glanced at Arawn, who had returned to pacing. "This is not good. What message does it give the army, if their leaders cannot contain themselves?"

"Exactly!" Arawn said, throwing out his hand, looking at Ban and Bors.

Ban shook his head. "You think setting a good example will cure the illness which strikes this place?"

Ilsa glanced at Arawn, startled. They had spoken about the declining morale in the camp more than once and wracked their minds for solutions. "Idle men make for mischief of the worst kind," Arawn had growled. "It's not just a matter of keeping them occupied and happy—they stop caring about everything when the rot sets in. Sentries stop patrolling diligently. Guards don't bother challenging everyone who passes. Men become slower to respond to emergencies and alerts. It's dangerous, Ilsa."

Ilsa had never thought peace might be dangerous. Now she understood why it might be so, among this company of highly trained and dangerous men who had spent their lives fighting wars and now had none left to fight.

"It has been nearly a year since Ambrosius pushed the Saxons behind their own lines," she murmured. "It is too long to hold an army together in this way." She glanced around the temporary shelter. It was warm and comfortable, but only constant vigilance made it that way. Tents sprang leaks when least desired. Mud always tracked inside. The flaps and the hems of the tent let in drafts and chills.

Ban looked at her. "A year we've been held here, waiting for Merlin to finish the damned monument to the fallen. A year too long. We fought for seven years. Seven!" He pushed his hand into his hair and clenched his head. "I left my new bride the day after the wedding and I haven't seen Elaine since and that was *eight years ago!*" He spun to plead his case with Arawn. "You must understand, Arawn—I do not regret a single year of the time we have spent fighting for Ambrosius and Britain. I would do it all again. This waiting, though…I am so sick and tired of this place!"

Arawn came over to Ban and pressed his hand upon his shoulder. "I know, friend. I know. I will speak to Ambrosius on your behalf and see if a dispensation can be made. I think it is time you went home."

Ban shuddered. "Just to behold the forest again would ease the sickness in my chest. To see Elaine…"

Arawn shepherded the pair to the tent opening, assuring them he would speak to Ambrosius at the earliest moment. Then he came back to Ilsa and took her in his arms.

He was warm against her and Ilsa sighed.

"I thank the gods you are here, every single day," Arawn murmured. "I would look as Ban does, if you were not. Every deprivation and discomfort my selfish need has put you through, I will spend the rest of my life redressing and I will do it happily."

"I'm glad I'm here, too," Ilsa said against his chest. "Although I must admit, sometimes I yearn for the softness of our bed in Lorient."

"We can't go home," Arawn said heavily. "Not until the High King gives us leave and even then, I would not. We must stay to witness the final resting place of the fallen ones, Ilsa. We must honor them."

"I agree," she said, her voice muffled.

"Although, perhaps this endless waiting has an end coming into view. I was talking to the engineers this morning." He took her shoulders and moved her away from him so he could see her face. "They say the work on the standing stones is nearly done and will certainly be done in time for the ceremony."

"In time?" she asked, confused. "Won't the ceremony be scheduled after the work is done?"

Arawn shook his head. "There is some special alignment of the stones and... Merlin and the other mages would give a better explanation. Even the engineers are convinced there is only one day of the year when the ceremony can be held."

Invisible fingers walked up Ilsa's spine. "When?" she asked, her throat tight.

"Dawn, at mid-winter," Arawn told her. "By years' end, we could be on our way home, Ilsa."

Mid-winter.

Ilsa tried hard to show enthusiasm for Arawn's news but could not.

Mid-winter and the fall of the red dragon…and the coming of the once and future king.

GORLOIS RETURNED TO TINTAGEL UNEXPECTEDLY, in the late autumn. He rode with a small, fast retinue of men. Ambrosius had given him only twelve days leave. Eight of them were taken up with travel from and the return to Amesbury.

The entire fortress fell into hysteria when they realized he had returned. Women giddily donned their best and prettiest gowns. Men bathed in the rivers and the sea. Everyone scrambled to look their best.

Morgan and Morguase were even more distracted by their father's return, crowding up against the window which looked upon the square for a glimpse of Gorlois among the men. Even before the horses had been led away, Anwen declared no more lessons would be given until Gorlois left once more. Morgan did not protest, and Morguase's hasty departure left the door swinging.

Anwen smiled as she shut the door once more and came back to the table to stack the slates.

Steffan had already placed them in a neat pile and held them out to her.

"You should change, too," Anwen told him, taking the slates.

"Why?" he asked, sounding startled.

"When Gorlois learns that you are teaching his daughters, he will expect you to present yourself to him."

Steffan's eyes narrowed. "I had not thought of that," he admitted and got to his feet.

"There is no rush, though," Anwen said.

"He will not expect everyone to attend him in the upper chamber immediately?" Steffan asked, raising a brow. He reached for the staff.

"I thought you fought by Gorlois' side?" Anwen replied.

"I did," Steffan said, with the flex of his jaw which Anwen had learned was a sign the conversation had strayed into painful territory for him.

"Then how is it you do not know that the very first thing Gorlois will do upon his return is shut himself in Igraine's bedchamber?"

Steffan's unseeing gaze settled on her face. His smile was small and for a moment, heat flickered in his eyes.

Anwen's breath evaporated between one heart beat and the next. It was simply not there. Her heart knocked heavily. Her limbs shook, while the core of her grew warmer.

What was happening? It felt as though the room had suddenly grown far too hot.

Steffan cleared his throat. "How would I know that?" he asked, his tone reasonable. "Gorlois has never brought his wife with him on campaigns."

Anwen tried twice to speak. She tore her gaze away from his face and closed her eyes. With a deep inhalation, she could speak evenly. "You should go."

He did not move.

"Go!" she said, her voice tight.

Steffan moved to the door.

"A moment!" She hurried to the narrow table against the wall and grabbed the white, folded garment on the top of the pile. "Here. Take it."

Steffan held out his hand. She laid the garment on his palm. He curled his fingers over it. "What is it?" he asked.

"A shirt. I suggest you wear it when you present yourself."

He felt the cloth in his hands. "You made this? For me?"

"Do not flatter yourself. It was found in the storeroom among a great many others. I had it washed, that is all. It should fit. The man it belonged to was a giant."

He nodded and gripped the shirt in his fist. "Thank you."

"Now go," she said irritably.

He left without another word.

IT WAS NOT REQUIRED THAT Igraine's women attend Gorlois,

yet Anwen found herself climbing the circular stairs anyway, drawn by the bubbling good humor drifting through the corridors. Gorlois' return had energized everyone.

She found her customary spot between the big window and the wall tapestry. The tapestry showed the final bloody battle of Macsen Wledig, with his great sword picked out in yarns of extraordinary fineness. They were gray threads, although in the right light, the sword glowed silver and white.

Gorlois emerged from the inner sanctum with Morgan's small hand in his. Morgan's face was shining with happiness. Morguase trailed behind them.

Gorlois did not let go of Morgan's hand when he reached the big chair. He lifted her up and settled her on his knee. Morgan giggled and stroked his chin and the thick red beard which grew there.

Anwen smiled. Morgan approved of this change in Gorlois' appearance.

Igraine emerged from the chamber as the last of the household assembled in the antechamber, facing the big chair. She took up her place beside the chair. Her hair hung freely about her shoulders and tumbled down her back, making her look younger than she was. The loose gown she wore looked hastily donned, too.

Gorlois looked about the almost-circular room, scanning the faces. He wore a pleased expression. Igraine had often spoken of how much Gorlois enjoyed the comforts of home and the simple life to be found here.

Then his smile checked. He frowned, peering. "Steffan...?" he said. He lifted his hand and beckoned. "Is that really you?"

The attendees in the room stepped aside, clearing a path for Steffan, who was easily taller than all of them.

He moved along the path they had made, the staff swinging in low arcs. "It is I, my lord." He stopped before the chair. He had donned the shirt she gave him, then put the jerkin back on, too, to hold in the excess of material. The shirt was over-large even on him. He had left off his cloak. "Does the High King still camp beside the standing stones, my lord?"

"He does," Gorlois said. "You look extraordinarily well, Steffan. Why are you here and not in Dimilioc where I left you? Have you abandoned Cador?"

"Cador was no longer in need of my services," Steffan said. "He awaits your summons with a rare eagerness."

Gorlois smiled. "I will take him back with me," he said, his tone warm. "It is time. More than time. Still, I am puzzled. Explain why you are here."

"Steffan teaches Morguase and me, father," Morgan said. "Mother told him he must."

Igraine stood with her gaze upon the room and did not move. Gorlois considered her, his smile fading. "Is this true, Igraine? What extraordinary circumstances would bring you to such a decision?"

Anwen watched Steffan, not Igraine. His knuckles whitened upon the staff, yet he wisely remained silent. Gorlois did not like to be interrupted.

Igraine turned to face Gorlois, her smile stiff with tension. "It is a decision which Cador and I arrived at jointly, my lord."

Anwen nodded to herself. Bringing Cador into the matter would rebuff some of Gorlois' anger, although Anwen wasn't certain why Gorlois *should* be angry about the decision. Clearly, he did not like the idea of Steffan tutoring his daughters.

Gorlois opened his mouth to speak, then glanced around the room at the entire household, who stood watching the drama with avid interest.

"Everyone leave," Gorlois said abruptly. "Now. Steffan, you stay. Igraine, you too. Someone send for my son! I would speak to him as soon as he gets here."

There was a shout—Anwen thought it was Parry, the steward, shouting for a messenger to saddle and go with all haste to Dimilioc to summon Cador.

Silently and with clear reluctance, everyone filed out of the room, including Igraine's women. Anwen moved up behind the last of them.

"Anwen, stay," Igraine said quietly. She glanced at Gorlois. "Anwen continues with their lessons, too."

Gorlois considered Anwen, his eyes narrowed.

Her middle shifting uneasily, Anwen went back to the place where she had been standing.

The room emptied and echoed.

Gorlois kissed Morgan's cheek and put her on her feet. "I must speak to Steffan alone," he told her. "You and your sister run along."

"I want to stay," Morgan said. "Steffan is *my* tutor."

Gorlois blinked. "Very well," he said. "You must remain silent, hmm?"

She nodded and sat on the footstool in front of the chair, her chin on her fists.

Gorlois lifted his hand and beckoned Steffan closer. Then he shook his head, as if he had only just remembered the man was blind. "Come closer, Steffan."

Steffan moved the staff out in front of him and cautiously stepped closer. Then Morgan jumped up and ran over to him. She gripped the bottom of the staff and drew him forward until he stood beside the stool. "There," she said, and sat once more. She kept a grip on the staff, too.

Gorlois tilted his head, studying his daughter. Then he raised his gaze to Steffan. "Do you still miss war, Steffan?"

"Always, my lord," Steffan said softly. "These times are grand beyond ken. The great deeds we hear about..." He shook his head. "Yes, I miss war," he finished.

"Your sight has not improved?"

Improved? Startled, Anwen straightened, her attention pricked.

Steffan did not seem to find the direct question offensive. "Sometimes, I glimpse things—I see them as you might, from the very corner of your eye. Distorted and hard to understand. Once, I saw snow falling…or perhaps it was merely light playing in my mind, making me think I saw what everyone else could. When I am relaxed, I sometimes see…" He swallowed. "The merest hint of vision," he finished, his voice hoarse. "Then it is gone."

Gorlois tapped his fingers on the arm of the chair. "So there has been no change," he concluded.

"It is as the surgeons suggested," Steffan said, his tone one of agreement. "I do not hope. They gave me none."

Gorlois nodded. "Igraine, please explain why you brought Steffan here."

Igraine touched her hair in a nervous flutter. With short sentences, her voice strained, she told the story of how Steffan had arrived at Tintagel and why. Wisely, she made it seem that Cador was as complicit in the decision as she. Gorlois had no patience for feminine sensibilities such as empathy and pity, while he could understand a strategic decision.

Gorlois listened without interruption until she fell silent. He brooded, his gaze on Steffan. Then he swiveled on his chair and looked at Anwen. "You...what is your name?"

Anwen jumped. "Anwen, my lord."

He pointed to the stone floor in front of his chair and she moved over to the spot and faced him, her heart thudding.

"You were teaching my daughters before Steffan?"

"I still do, my lord."

"How so?" he demanded.

"Steffan provides the language, and I teach Morgan and Morguase how to write it down and read it back."

"Barba tenus sapientes," Morgan intoned.

Gorlois looked at his daughter with a startled expression. "That is Latin, isn't it?"

Morgan nodded. She bounced off the footstool and reached up on her toes to touched Gorlois' chin. "It means you are a wise man because you let your beard grow back."

Gorlois gave a soft, short laugh, yet puzzlement lingered in his eyes.

Morgan put her hands behind her back, her sweet face sunny. "Actually, it doesn't mean exactly that, although it *is* ironic you came home with a beard, Father."

Anwen hid her smile. Steffan didn't bother. He grinned.

Gorlois tapped the arm of the chair, and it seemed to Anwen that his irritation was building. "You are a soldier, Steffan. You were born and raised a soldier, and have lived a soldier's life, always. I cannot ignore the...roughness such a life imparts. While you taught my son, it was not an issue. Now, though…do you understand my concern?"

Anwen did. Her heart sank. Gorlois would presume that Steffan shared the barbaric values of the soldiers in Dimilioc and his standing army. Why would he think otherwise? Even the story of how the men at Dimilioc had treated Steffan he considered to be proof all soldiers were beyond redemption.

Morgan tugged on her father's hand. "But Father, Anwen tells him what to do and he does it."

Steffan turned his head, his gaze settling on Anwen, as if he had known she was there all along.

Gorlois looked from Steffan to Anwen and back. "Is this true?" he asked.

Anwen dropped her gaze to the floor, confused. She did not think it was true that Steffan obeyed her. She had been charged with controlling him, although she knew in her heart that Steffan behaved civilly for reasons she did not under-stand. Only, if she said so aloud, she would reveal her own uselessness.

"My lord," Steffan said, his tone even. "I speak Breton, Lat-in, Greek, Saxon and a little of the dialects the hill people use. I do not know how to write any of it or read it back. An-wen does. She also knows and can play the most beautiful music a man can ever hear. Between us, we can ensure your daughters are accomplished and educated, a prize for any king."

The appeal to his political aspirations did not stir Gorlois. He frowned. "You would settle for such an ambition, Steffan? You rode and fought with Uther and drank with him. You were celebrated the length of Britain. Ambrosius praised you. All that, and you expect me to believe you would be happy teaching girls Latin conjugates?"

Steffan gripped the staff until his fingers turned white. "Happy, my lord? No, I will not pretend it is an ambition to which I aspire. It *is* a worthy next task after preparing your son for the rigors of war." He swallowed. "I would rather ride with you, my lord, but as I cannot, I am grateful to have the chance to serve you in this way."

Gorlois drummed the arm of the chair.

"Father, Steffan says knowledge comes from more places than books," Morgan said. "I *like* knowledge. I like understanding things. Let him stay. Please."

Gorlois sighed. His gaze shifted to Anwen. "I will allow this only as long as you are part of it. A soldier never stops being a soldier. You will offset his ways. You understand?"

Anwen swallowed. "Yes, my lord."

Gorlois nodded. "It is settled, then. Have everyone return. I would hear what has happened since I left."

Anwen slipped around the influx of people as they returned to the antechamber, her heart thundering. She felt as though she had narrowly escaped dire consequences she hadn't been aware she was at risk of suffering.

Was a soldier always a soldier?

She didn't think it was true. Only who was she to dispute the Duke of Cornwall? She was nobody, a middle-aged spinster whose name everyone forgot. How could she possibly know more than he did?

Only a few minutes after she reached the sanctuary of her room, Steffan arrived, too.

Anwen wrung her hands together. "I do not think Gorlois fully understands you," she said. "Those things he said about you being a soldier, his worry you might revert to barbarism and harm his daughters…it's ridiculous!"

Steffan did not sit, either. "Oh, he knows me well enough," he said mildly.

"I've heard the stories about what soldiers are like," Anwen said. "The…the raping, the pilfering…the spoils of war. I have heard it all, many times. You are not like that."

"I was a *good* soldier," Steffan said, his voice calm. "I was a leader of soldiers. Soldiers only obey men they trust, men like them."

"I do *not* believe it," she said, her voice trembling. "Even if you once were like that, you are not, anymore."

Steffan grimaced. "Yet I would give up everything I have to get that life back."

Anwen stared at him. "No," she whispered. "How could you?"

He shook his head. "Not for the women and the riches, although they were a nice reward. I mean, to *serve*, Anwen. To properly serve, to fully use every skill I have to help Cornwall and the High King find peace for Britain. To be a part of such great doings…" He paused. "That privilege has been taken from me forever." His voice was bitter.

Chapter Nine

 rawn shook Ilsa awake. She blinked in the deep
darkness of the tent. "What is it? What time is it?"
"Very late. Very early," he whispered. He tugged on
her arm. "Nimue asked for you. She is in the High
King's tent."

Ilsa sat up and glanced at the silhouettes of her sleeping
children on the other side of the tent. "Why? What has happened?" Someone stood outside the tent with a flaming torch,
sending leaping shadows over the fabric.

Arawn got her to her feet and dropped her gown over her
chemise and tugged it into place, as she slid her arms into the
sleeves. He handed her the warmer cloak and bent and
pushed her shoes into place.

Ilsa pulled the cloak around her shoulders and shivered.
Arawn drew her from of the tent. He took the torch from the
soldier standing just outside. "Stay here," he told the man.
"No one goes into the tent. Hear?"

The man nodded.

Arawn picked up Ilsa's hand and pulled her across the dark, empty square. The stars overhead gave little light.

There was more light in the King's big pavilion. Ilsa could see men moving about inside, including in the inner room where Ambrosius slept.

"Arawn…" She pulled on his hand, slowing her steps.

Arawn turned back to her, the flames from the torch jumping and hissing at the abrupt change of direction. "The King is ill," he said, his voice low.

Ilsa pressed her hand to her heart as it creaked. She was too afraid to speak another word. Instead, she moved forward again, hurrying for the big tent.

She ducked under the arm the guard thrust out to stop them and left Arawn to deal with him. There were too many men standing about the outer section with their hands on their swords, as if gripping them hard enough might change the news.

Ilsa stepped around them and into the inner section of the tent. Ambrosius had a real bed, which the people of Amesbury had pressed upon him while he stayed outside their town, as thanks for the invaluable protection his army provided them. He was lying in that bed now and appeared to be unmoving. His face was pale and sweat dotted his temples and throat.

Nimue was bent over him, her hand on his forehead.

Uther paced the carpet between the bed and the canvas wall of the tent.

Merlin stood in the darkest corner, farthest from the lamp, his black eyes glittering as he watched his father.

Ilsa touched Nimue's arm. "I am here. How can I help?"

Nimue glanced at her. "The time you made your son ill, after he swallowed those berries…?"

Ilsa glanced at Ambrosius. "He ate something noxious?"

"He was *poisoned!*" Uther hissed, rounding on her.

Nimue glanced at Uther. "We do not know that for certain. He says his stomach burns. We must remove what is there."

"He says…?" Ilsa asked delicately, for Ambrosius was clearly beyond the ability to speak.

Nimue rolled her eyes. "I can hear him," she said. "We have little time. Help me."

Ilsa pushed up her sleeves. "We need a bundle of the reeds growing by the pond. Enough to make the thickness of my thumb, tied together."

Nimue glanced at Uther.

"I'll arrange it," he growled and strode to the opening into the other side of the tent.

Ilsa listened to him give low, strident orders. Booted feet ran from the tent. Everyone moved swiftly but almost silently. No one would risk rousing the camp with such bad news. Not yet.

The reeds were brought to them. Ilsa and Nimue sent everyone from the tent, even from the outer side. "There is no need for anyone to see what happens next," Ilsa told Nimue, as they struggled to bring Ambrosius into a sitting position.

Merlin, though, would not move. He didn't speak. He remained a silent statue in the corner.

The work of expelling the contents of the King's stomach was messy and difficult. While Nimue held his jaw open, Ilsa inserted the reeds deeply enough to cause his gorge to rise and make him vomit.

At least Ambrosius was aware of none of it, she thought, until Nimue sighed. "He says the burning is diminishing."

Ilsa had the bowl of offensive matter taken away. "Burn it and bury the remains," she told the slave.

They bathed Ambrosius' flesh with cool water, and Nimue listened, a furrow on her pale brow. "We must wait and see."

A little while later, Uther returned, to resume his pacing.

Ilsa sat on the corner of the thick rug which Uther paced upon, her back against the foot of the bed. She was tired beyond belief, yet sleep was far away. From the light falling against the sides of the pavilion, she judged that sunrise was not far away. As they waited, the light grew.

Nimue stood by the side of the bed, staring down at Ambrosius, as unmoving as Merlin.

The sounds of the camp stirring for the day rose about the tent. Fires were stirred and cooking pots settled onto coals. As the guards changed outside the tent, with a rattle of armor and exchange of words, Uther hissed and turned to Nimue. "Surely enough time has passed? Well?"

Nimue didn't move.

Uther grabbed her arm and hauled her about to face him.

Ilsa jumped to her feet. "Uther, no!"

He gripped Nimue's arms and shook her. "*Look* at me! Tell me!"

Nimue's gaze shifted from the inner focus Ilsa recognized, to settle on Uther's face. "There was too much of it. It has gone too far. We have only slowed the pace of it."

Uther grew still. "What are you *saying?*" His blue eyes blazed with emotion. He knew already.

Ilsa put her hand on his arm. "Uther..."

He shook Nimue again. "Tell me." He ground the words out.

A solitary tear rolled down Nimue's cheek. "I cannot save him."

Uther roared, his arm lifting high, ready to strike her. Nimue did not move. She watched him calmly.

Ilsa shoved him. He was so much larger than her that all she could do was disturb his balance. It was enough. Uther dropped his arm.

"Get out," he told Nimue. "Go far from here. I do not want to see your face again."

Nimue's throat worked. "This is the last time you will see me, Uther Pendragon. I vouch for that."

She moved out of the tent. Even in the bright sunlight shining through the thin fabric walls, she gleamed and shimmered with power.

Uther dropped to his knees beside the bed and gripped his brother's hand. He bowed his head.

MORGAN'S SCREAMING PULLED ANWEN FROM her bed before she was aware she was even awake. She threw her cloak around her chemise and ran barefoot through the cold stone corridors to the big chamber the two girls shared, brushing her hand along the wall so she did not cannon into it.

People were stirring, coming sleepily to the doors of the dormitories and chambers, asking what was happening. No one had the sense or was awake enough to coordinate the movements needed to light a torch and the guards had extinguished those which lit the corridors.

Anwen slipped past them all and pushed the heavy door open. It was dark in the chamber, too, but Morgan's screaming told her exactly where the girl was. From the other side of the room came an echoing whimper.

"It's all right, Morguase," she said. "Morgan is having a bad dream, that is all."

She groped for the bed and found the edge of it, then moved up to the head and felt for Morgan. The little girl thrashed and moaned. As Anwen laid her hands on her, Morgan screamed once more, making Anwen jump. It was a panic-filled sound.

Anwen gathered her into her arms and rocked her. "Shh....shh, Morgan. It's just a dream. Wake up, little one. Wake up!"

As she rocked Morgan, Anwen heard people calling for light and muttered conversations in the corridor outside. The orange glow of lamplight showed where the door was, then moved closer. Before the lamp could be brought into the room, though, a big silhouette filled the doorway.

"Anwen?" Steffan asked.

"I'm here," Anwen confirmed. "Five paces, and you'll find the bed."

He took the paces, and whoever held the lamp behind him also came into the room.

Morgan shivered in Anwen's arms, although she no longer moaned. Anwen kept up her rocking.

Steffan crouched down by the side of the bed, his head tilted, listening.

"You heard her screaming all the way from the stables?"

Anwen breathed, keeping her voice down.

Steffan let out a breath. "The horses, too," he said in agreement. "They'd have bolted if not for the doors."

Anwen's gaze dropped to his bare shoulders and chest. He wore only his trousers.

Morgan gave another little shudder, pulling Anwen's attention back to her. "Steffan, see that Morguase is comforted. Across the room, another five paces."

Steffan rose to his feet.

More fuss sounded at the door and more light built. Gorlois moved into the room. He wore a belted robe and his hair stood at angles. Thrust into the belt was a long knife. "What happened?" he demanded.

"A dream," Anwen murmured.

Morgan heard her father's voice and stirred. She lifted her tear-stained face toward him. "The High King is dying!" she cried.

Gorlois came to a halt, three paces from the bed. His eyes widened.

The roused household standing in the corridor behind Gorlois muttered nervously, passing the news along.

Gorlois looked from Anwen to Steffan, who sat on the other bed, soothing Morguase with soft pats. Then he seemed to shake himself. "A bad dream indeed," he said gravely. "But only a dream."

Morgan wound her arms about Anwen's neck. "He must go back," she murmured to Anwen. "Before it is too late." Her voice was still that of a six-year-old girl, yet the certainty in her tone belonged to a much older woman.

Anwen shivered.

"What did she say?" Gorlois demanded.

"That you must return to the High King, my lord," Anwen said.

Gorlois stared at his youngest daughter. Then he shook his head. "The nervous mutterings of a child," he said. Doubt colored his tone. His gaze moved to Anwen. "Or is it?" He took a step closer and his hand curled around the hilt of the knife. "Does my daughter have the Sight?" he asked.

Anwen patted Morgan's back as the child shivered. "I know nothing about such matters," she said truthfully. Yet all the times Morgan had ever spoken of events in the future, the times she had been aware of news which was yet to reach Tintagel—and all the occasions when Anwen had dismissed the unsettling hints as the parroting of a small child who overheard far more than adults realized—all those moments rippled through her mind, a cascade of memories. "It is… possible," she admitted to Gorlois.

He swallowed. She could see his throat working in the dim light. "The King was in perfect health when we left, or I would not have come away."

Morgan turned her head to look at Gorlois. "The poison wasn't in him, then."

Even Anwen shuddered and the mutter in the corridor rippled down the length of it.

"Poison…" Gorlois breathed. "The gods save us." He was no longer a concerned father investigating a troubled daughter, but a leader considering the greater implications of an ailing king. "If the Saxons learn of this…"

Then he bent to speak to Morgan, who clung to Anwen still. "Are you certain he is dying, Morgan? Or was this just a dream? I must know before I order the men to give up their time here and return. It is a four-day journey."

Morgan looked at her father. Her chin lifted. "He is dying." Her voice was still that of an older woman. "If you leave now, you will return barely in time."

Gorlois stood. His grip on the knife tightened. He looked at the lightening sky through the window. "Dawn comes. We will ride as soon as it is light enough to see the way."

He whirled and left.

Anwen settled Morgan back on the bed and wiped her wet cheeks with the corner of her cloak. "You must try to sleep now. Tomorrow, if you still remember this, we can speak of it."

"I will remember this always," Morgan whispered. She curled up on her side and closed her eyes. The dark lashes settled against her soft cheeks and she breathed softly and slowly.

Anwen marveled. The child was already asleep.

She stood and rearranged the furs over the top of her.

Parry, the steward, stood at the door, holding a lantern, the flame burning orange. His eyes were wide. "The King is dying?" he breathed. Fear distorted his face

Anwen hesitated, doubt gnawing at her.

Steffan moved closer and said in a low voice, "We will know nothing until the Duke sends word back."

"Yet he rides for Amesbury, because his daughter said he should," Parry said, his tone awed.

"It is a practical thing," Steffan said. "If the King is in good health, then no harm is done if Gorlois returns early. If he is not, then—"

"Then the child is proved a witch," Parry breathed.

Anwen gripped the sleeve of his robe and shook it. "Hush!" she said harshly. "Have you no sense, man? You cannot speak of witches so casually."

"She *knew*!" Parry breathed, fear making his voice tremble.

"If she did, then it is simply the first emanations of the Sight," Steffan said, startling Anwen. Most fighting men were wary of the unseen power of people with the Sight. They found comfort in what they could see and touch, what they could control. Yet Steffan spoke as if he was experienced in such matters. He put his hand on Parry's shoulder with unerring precision and squeezed. "There is no need to panic the household with talk of magic. You have a position to uphold. Set an example, Parry."

Parry swallowed and nodded. "You are right," he said, his voice still shaking.

"In the light of day this will seem far more prosaic," Anwen added. "Perhaps an early rising may benefit us all. Listen. The Duke's men are stirring already."

Echoing through the corridors came the sound of men shouting. Out in the yard, too, there were more calls. Torches lit the yard. Horses snorted and whinnied as the men prepared them to ride.

Parry raised a brow. "They will need food for the road. Drink to see them on their way. I must rouse the cooks…" He turned and left, taking the lamp with him.

The room plunged back into pre-dawn darkness, making Anwen gasp and blink.

"He took the lamp, yes?" Steffan said. Anwen felt his hand on her arm. "Here. The door is this way." He drew her across the floor.

Anwen took small steps, her hand raised in front of her. She had been staring directly at the flame of Parry's lamp and now she could see nothing at all. Her heart pumped hard, dispensing fear.

"It's all right," Steffan assured her. "The door is right here. Wait, the air is too still…it must have swung closed."

She halted and he brushed past her. The door swung open. Air shifted against her face. Anwen lifted her hand, reaching for the door itself, so she would not run into it.

Her hand brushed up against warm flesh. For a heartbeat which seemed to last for a year, her fingertips rested against the warmth and the solid muscle beneath.

Her heart slammed into her chest, hurting.

She snatched her hand back, breathing hard.

The darkness in front of her shifted. Steffan stepped out of the way. He had been blocking the tiny amount of light in the corridor, shed by lamps and torches far away. It was enough light to show her the outline of the doorway and the seamed stone of the corridor walls beyond.

Anwen blinked. "I can see the way, now." Her voice shook. Her whole body rippled with a wave of sensation which made her weak.

"So can I," Steffan breathed, his voice low and hoarse with something which made her weakness increase.

Anwen stumbled from the room and fled to her chamber.

Chapter Ten

ou must make him drink the potion at least three times during the day," Nimue told Ilsa, as she pushed garments and possessions into the saddle-bags sitting on the ground. Nimue was already wearing dark, sturdy travel clothes.

Ilsa hefted the heavy flask of liquid Nimue had pushed in-to her hand. "I am not a healer," she said. "Wouldn't a sur-geon serve Ambrosius better?"

Nimue straightened. "No one can heal the King now." She touched the flask. "This poppy concoction will make him comfortable, at least. He will need more of it each time, to-ward the end."

Ilsa blinked away the hot ache in her eyes. "I cannot do this…"

Nimue cupped her cheek. "Have courage," she said. "While the men tear themselves apart adjusting to the news, you will help Ambrosius." Her small smile faded. "It will be very bad for a while, Ilsa. Uther is not ready. He thought he was. Now he stands upon the brink he knows he is not…and his grief will distort his judgment, too."

"I am just a woman," Ilsa breathed. "I cannot help him."

Nimue merely smiled once more. "Watch to the north and the west," she said, and closed the saddlebags.

"Saxons?" Ilsa breathed, her fear expanding in her chest.

"When they learn about Ambrosius, they will try to take advantage of the chaos he leaves behind." Nimue wound a dark cloak about her shoulders and pinned it. Ilsa realized it was the first time she had seen Nimue wearing anything but white. The glow of her features had not faded, though.

"Do you have messages I can pass on for you?" Nimue asked.

Ilsa shook her head. "With the ships running all summer, we have been sending letters constantly, and Ban took many back with him."

Nimue hugged Ilsa. "I return to Brocéliande as the gods demand, yet my thoughts will remain with you and yours here, where the future shapes itself."

Ilsa gave in to the worry which had been nagging her for months. "Will I ever see Lorient again, Nimue?"

Nimue squeezed her hand. "Yes, Ilsa. You will return to Lorient. Your children will know their heritage, too."

Ilsa shuddered. "Thank you," she breathed.

Nimue did not smile.

FOR TWO DAYS, THE SUDDENLY empty Tintagel seemed to ring with echoes and whispers. Gorlois took not only the small contingent of men he had arrived with, but nearly every able-bodied man in Tintagel and Dimilioc.

"If the King really is dying, then my husband will need every man to hold back the Saxons, who will try to take advantage of his fall," Igraine had explained to her women, the next morning. Anwen had been summoned to attend, leaving Steffan to deal with the girls. The reason for the summons became clear after Igraine dismissed the women and beckoned Anwen to her side.

They were in Igraine's private chamber, with the large bed and thick wall hangings, the cushions and drapes and silver trays. Igraine sat in the chair by the window, watching the sea. "Is it true what Gorlois told me, about Morgan?" Igraine asked her. "Have you known all along?"

Anwen clenched her hands. "I have known nothing for certain, my lady, and I still do not. The duke places greater faith in Morgan's nightmare than would I. She sometimes shows remarkable knowledge, although she likes learning and absorbs facts the way moss draws up water."

"The duke gambles," Igraine said. "When he reaches the

King, he will send a message. We will know then if Morgan is merely a good student or something more."

Anwen returned to her room and the task of teaching, her thoughts troubled. The daily routine swiftly settled the household, so it felt as though Gorlois had never arrived and left so precipitously.

Only, the visit had left its mark, which Anwen learned two days later.

It began with a simple question from Morgan. The girl had been unaffected by her night time terror and Anwen forbore from asking her about the dream. It would be cruel to remind her of the upset if she did not remember it.

Others in the household did not have the same consideration, though, Anwen discovered.

Morgan tapped Steffan's wrist, which both girls had learned was an acceptable way of drawing his attention to them. "When you fought beside my father, Steffan, did you get to meet Merlin the Magician?"

Anwen raised her head from Morguase's slate, which she had been correcting. "Why do you ask that, Morgan?"

"Canna, the goat herd, asked me if I was like Merlin," Morgan said. "I didn't know who Merlin was, so he told me how Merlin was the most powerful magician in Britain. He cast a spell that drew the standing stones in Ireland all the way to Britain, floating on the air. He made dragons fight and he said a magic word and Vortigern dropped dead, miles away."

Anwen's lips parted. She had not heard such tales before. All she knew for certain was that Merlin was Ambrosius' son, and had the Sight, which made him unsuitable in some way to be the High King's heir. Everyone had always known that the High King's brother, Uther, would be the next king.

She cast about, wondering what she might say to Morgan in the face of such fantasies.

Steffan laughed, a long, low belly-shaking sound which seemed genuine. He leaned back on the bench and gripped the edge of the table, balancing himself, as his mirth rocked him.

Morguase hitched farther along the bench, away from him. She had been silent for the last two days and Anwen wondered if she resented the sudden interest and concern over her little sister.

Morgan put her chin on her fist, watching Steffan laugh, a frown marring her smooth forehead.

Steffan got himself under control once more. He wiped his eyes. "Is *that* what they say of the man?" he asked Morgan. "The tales have grown in the telling to the point where I no longer recognize them."

"They're not true, then?" Morguase asked, with an eager note in her voice.

"There is a kernel of truth in them," Steffan said. "That is all."

"What is the kernel, then?" Morgan asked, also eager.

"I can assure you, no dragons fought each other," Steffan said. "No *real* dragons."

"Dragons aren't real, anyway," Morguase said to her sister, with a chiding tone.

"Two dragons *did* do battle, though," Steffan added.

Morgan smiled, pleased.

"The white dragon was Vortigern's emblem," Steffan said. "Ambrosius and Uther Pendragon use the red dragon. When Ambrosius defeated Vortigern at Doward eight years ago, you could say that dragons fought each other, although there was little fighting in it, for Merlin did most of the work."

"With a magic spell?" Morgan said hopefully.

"Merlin told Vortigern what was in his future," Steffan said. "He prophesied death and ignoble defeat, and that all history would forget Vortigern. Vortigern so feared that future, he sought to change it. He abandoned the fort he was holding and rushed to Doward, which they say is impregnable. It was there Ambrosius defeated him."

Anwen drew her breath to warn Steffan that he should say little more about the style of Ambrosius' defeat. Talk of burning out a keep while people were in it was not something a child who already suffered nightmares needed to hear.

Even Morguase seemed interested in the tale. "Then there

was no magic at all?" she asked.

Steffan shook his head. "Not in the way the goat herd thinks."

"But Merlin does have the Sight?" Morgan asked.

"Do you understand what that means, Morgan?" Anwen asked.

"Mary the cook told me. It means someone who can see the coming weather and tell whether a baby will be a boy or a girl, before it is born."

"Shepherds and fishermen can do that," Steffan said. "Merlin does have the Sight, Morgan. It lets him see the future, sometimes, or things which are happening right now, yet far away."

"Then he *is* a magician," Morgan breathed, delighted.

"He's just a man," Steffan said. "And the Sight *hurts.*"

Both Morgan and Morguase stared at him, startled.

Anwen could feel the same astonishment curling through her. "It hurts?" she asked.

Steffan nodded. "When the gods speak through him, Merlin is ill afterwards. Sometimes for days. He writhes upon the ground while they speak and he often doesn't know what he has said until someone tells him. I have seen him in the midst of it. His whole body contorts, as if invisible hands prodded him with sharp knives."

Morguase smiled, while Morgan looked thoughtful.

Anwen approved of this sobering telling of facts. She coaxed Steffan further by saying, "What of the standing stones he lifted and flew to Britain?"

Steffan nodded. "He *did* bring the heart of Ireland to Britain. I heard Cador speak of it, for his father wrote to him about the feat. Merlin didn't use magic, Morgan. He used knowledge." He tapped his temple. "Merlin is a master of mathematics and engineering. He floated the stones to Britain not on the air, but by barges sailed across the sea. He used block-and-tackle to tear them down. He uses the same engineering tools to raise them again, on Salisbury Plain. They will be the monument marking the death of five hundred kings and leaders, murdered by Vortigern's betrayal of them to the Saxons, the year Ambrosius returned to Britain."

Morgan's and Morguase's eyes shone.

"Then Merlin is truly clever," Morgan said.

"Very clever indeed," Steffan said. "He doesn't just acquire knowledge. He uses it."

Morgan nodded and sat up, her hand dropping. "I will be very clever, too," she said firmly.

"Only if you learn your lessons well," Anwen said.

"Can you teach me mathematics and engineering?" Morgan asked.

Steffan's sightless gaze met Anwen's. His brow lifted. "I cannot, for I am not a master," he told Morgan. "Although, if you show promise, I am sure a suitable tutor could be found for you."

Morgan's smile was incandescent.

Morguase shifted on the bench once more. "Why do you use your staff sometimes and at other times you do not?" she demanded.

"Morguase, you cannot ask such—" Anwen began.

Steffan lifted his hand. "When did I not use the staff, Morguase?" he asked, his tone gentle.

"The night Morgan dreamed about the King. You came into the room as you come into any other room and you didn't have your staff. You've never been in that room before. How did you know the way?"

Steffan shifted on the bench so he was facing her. "I was directed by Morgan's screaming. When I was inside, there were many more people running and talking and it told me where to go, too."

"You told my father you can see, sometimes," Morguase said. Her tone was accusing. "Blind people can't see. Are you really blind?"

Steffan's smile was tight. "I cannot see you right now, Morguase, although I have grown good at guessing about appearances from the sound of people's voice and the way they talk and what they do."

Morguase's shoulders straightened. "What do I look like?"

Steffan considered. He held his hand out and raised it. "You are this high."

"You can tell that from my voice."

"Black hair," he added. "Black eyes like your mother, and her chin. Your father's white skin, but none of the freckles. And you are wearing…" He paused. "Blue," he finished.

Morguase smoothed the blue gown over her knee. "You cheated," she said. "You can see more than you admit."

Steffan's smile was wry. "It is cheating to be given the smallest glimpse of light, which everyone around me takes for granted?"

Morguase's gaze shifted away from him. Her cheeks tinged pink.

Morgan tapped his wrist. "You sometimes look as though you can see."

Anwen nodded, for this was true.

"I have learned to compensate," Steffan said. "We have other senses which are blunted because our sight tells us nearly everything we need to know about the world around us. Take sight away, and the other senses grow stronger. Much stronger."

"What are senses?" Morguase said.

Steffan reached out and tapped on Morgan's wrist. "Touch is one."

"Hearing things," Morgan said.

"Yes. And taste," Steffan said. "Although taste is not as useful as touch and hearing...and smell."

Morgan giggled.

Steffan smiled, too.

"Then you really can't see anything at all?" Morguase pressed.

Steffan hesitated. Anwen knew he was weighing, deciding. Then he said, "Sometimes, I get the faintest glimpse of things, then they are gone again. It doesn't last."

"Everything goes black?" Morgan asked.

He shook his head. "It isn't blackness I see. It is light and color."

"Color?" Morgan said, her interested rising yet again. "Is that why you know Morguase is wearing blue?"

"She is?" Steffan smiled, pleased. "The colors I see are not related to the colors you see. They are representations, I think. Emanations of feelings or movements."

Morgan wrinkled her nose. "That doesn't make any sense."

Steffan considered. "Very well. Look at Anwen and tell me what colors you see."

Both Morguase and Morgan looked at her. Anwen cleared her throat. She realized she was smoothing down her dark brown gown the same way Morguase had straightened hers and made her hand stay still.

"Brown," Morgan said flatly.

"Yes," Morguase added. "Dark brown, all over."

"What I see when I look in Anwen's direction is gold," Steffan said.

The girls stared at him in disbelief.

"She isn't wearing gold," Morguase pointed out.

"I'm not seeing what Anwen wears. I see something else. The essence of her. I see glowing golden brown."

Anwen's heart pattered. She made a fist of her hand, resting on her knee. "And what do you see of Morguase?" she asked, deliberately turning the conversation.

Steffan smiled. "That is easy. The color of strawberries."

Morguase laughed. She liked that.

"And me?" Morgan asked.

Steffan's smile faded. "I do not know for certain. Perhaps, a pretty lilac?"

Morgan's mouth pursed and her nose wrinkled.

Anwen watched Steffan's face. He could not see, yet his eyes could be expressive. She watched them shift and move away from Morgan and knew he had lied.

From the corridor outside the door came shouting. "A messenger! A messenger comes!"

With it came a buzz of conversation and calls, as everyone reacted to the arrival of news. Feet ran. Doors slammed.

A slave pushed open the door to Anwen's chamber. "The lady bids you attend her at once," he said breathlessly and slammed the door once more.

"Does that mean she wishes to speak to me or you?" Steffan wondered aloud.

"We should all go, just to be sure," Anwen said, as relief touched her. The conversation had become uncomfortable, although she was not certain why. She wanted everyone to think only of languages and letters or the arriving news. "Morgan, let me inspect your gown. Yes, that is clean enough. Tie your chemise strings properly. Morguase...yes, you are very neat today."

Morguase beamed and ran from the room. Morgan followed. They called to each other as they traversed the corridor to the big circular stairs.

Anwen stood and brushed down her own gown, smoothing out the folds and arranging it properly. Steffan remained upon the bench, his head down, as if he was deep in thought.

Anwen did not consider waiting for him. He was capable of finding his own way to Igraine's chamber.

Only, as she moved to the door, his hand shot out. He gripped her wrist. She gasped at the uncanny accuracy of his reach. "How did you know I was there?"

He swung his feet over the bench and stood. It put him far too close to her. There was barely a hand-span of space between them. "Scent, air movement, sound. The glow which marks you wherever you are." His voice was low. He drew her wrist up toward his shoulder.

"What are you doing?" she demanded, pulling at his grip.

"Confirming you are as I see you."

"See…?" Her breath caught as he brought his other hand to her face and touched it. Her flesh sizzled at his touch and she shuddered. "Steffan—"

"Shh." His fingers ran over her face, her hair and her throat. They came back to her face and rested there. "Beautiful," he breathed.

"Then you are truly blind."

He shook his head. "I suspect I am the only one who sees you properly." His fingers stroked.

"Stop that," she whispered, for his touch was sending hot waves through her.

"Why?" he breathed.

She could not speak of the throbbing which weakened her. Instead, she reached desperately for harsh facts. "I am old, Steffan."

His fingers shifted. "There are no wrinkles here. I would not care if there were."

"I am older than you."

His hand slid down her throat, leaving sizzling flesh in its wake. His fingers rested over her heart. "You are not older, in here. Here, we are the same."

Her entire body wanted to reach through the tiny space between them and surrender to him. Her eyes ached as sour knowledge prevented her. "You dally with me because I am to hand. If you really knew me, if you could see me—"

"I do see you," he breathed. His lips hovered only inches away.

She turned her head away. "If you really did, you would know my fear."

He turned her chin, so she looked at him once more. His gaze was steady. It truly seemed as though he studied her. She shivered.

"I know your fear," he said, his voice low. "I see your longing, too." He reached behind him, unlatched the door and opened it.

Relief touched her, as he held it open for her. She went to step through, but he caught her arm, making her heart leap again.

He leaned close to her, so the warmth of his big body enveloped her like a cloak. "One day, you will be mine," he breathed in her ear.

Then he released her. She was free to stumble into the corridor, her heart slamming and her body shrieking with competing tensions.

Chapter Eleven

The messenger was just emerging from Igraine's chamber when they reached the hall at the top of the stairs. He was dusty and travel stained, as messengers tended to be. He nodded at Steffan and Anwen as they passed.

Anwen knew the man's face. "One of Gorlois' riders," she breathed.

Steffan nodded. "Drusant," he added.

She looked at him, startled.

"He likes olives," Steffan said.

Anwen cleared her throat and moved toward the inner chamber. Steffan followed. He did not ask her to guide him. He never asked anyone for that service. He tapped his way across the floor and stepped through to the inner chamber.

Igraine was alone except for one lady and Morgan and Morguase. The Duchess sat in the big chair by the window. There was a letter on her knees. She picked it up and held it toward Anwen. "Drusant told me most of what is in here. Please read it to me."

Anwen took the letter and read.

Madam:

I write in haste. We came upon Drusant one day from Tintagel. He has messages from Uther, which he shared with me and I now bid him to give to you. We ride with even greater speed to Amesbury.

The High King is dying, just as we feared. You must gather and prepare the household for travel when the time comes.

Uther believes the Saxons will rise in response. He rides north as I write this, to counter the attack he anticipates.

Drusant will share more.

Cornwall.

The signature was a great flourish of unformed lines, for Gorlois did not read. His scribe's lettering was well formed and easy to read, though.

Anwen gave the letter back to Igraine.

Igraine looked at Steffan. "You rode with my husband, Steffan. You can explain this. What does it mean for Cornwall and Britain? For us?"

Steffan leaned on his staff. "What else did Drusant have to share, my lady? That may shed more light."

She pressed her full lips together. "Only gossip. The army, the kings, the senior leaders, are divided over Uther's orders to ride north. There are allies in the north, they say, who will stand for Britain."

"Uther seeks Catigern," Steffan said. "Those who oppose Uther's taking of the throne once Ambrosius is dead will draw around Catigern. If he removes him, then they will have no focus and no leader."

"He thinks of politics at a time like this?" Anwen said.

Igraine looked at her, startled.

Anwen shrank back toward the wall. She had spoken without thought. Her throat tightened.

Steffan, though, responded as if her speaking her thoughts was perfectly normal. "What I remember of Uther is that he is driven by emotions more than he should be. He would be a greater leader than Ambrosius if he could contain his violent passions. Everything I have heard about him since only confirms that impression. I do not believe he thinks of politics at this time, except it gives him an excuse to act in the face of a situation he can do nothing to change."

He grieves, Anwen interpreted.

Igraine frowned. "I do not follow, Steffan."

Steffan hesitated. "Uther is a man of action, my lady. He cannot act to save his brother, yet he can act to save his brother's kingdom, so he acts, no matter how rash the act may be."

"Is it rash?" Igraine asked.

"We approach the depths of winter. Travel in the north will be hard on the men and the horses. He also risks offending the northern kingdoms, who prefer to control their own territories. If he fails to find and kill Catigern, his hunt for the man will foment the very opposition he fears. Only, Uther is not one for sitting about the home hearth and staring at the flames." Steffan shrugged. "If he succeeds, he will win the breathing space he needs to take the crown and stabilize the kingdom."

"It is a risk worth taking, then," Igraine summarized.

"It is a very high risk, which is why the leaders are divided. Uther is perhaps the only man in Britain who might succeed at such a task, though."

Igraine lifted the parchment. "And why does my husband instruct me to prepare for travel? It is close to mid-winter, as you say."

Anwen sighed.

Steffan did, too. "Because the Duke wants all of Cornwall to attend the High King's funeral, my lady. No lesser honor will do."

WHEN THE THUNDER OF MANY approaching horses sounded from the north, Ilsa rose stiffly to her feet and moved to the outer room of the High King's tent. Arawn and Gorlois, who had returned only two days ago, and at least a week before anyone expected him, also watched the tent flap.

"Is that Uther?" she asked dully.

Arawn kissed her temple. "There was no challenge from the sentries. It is him."

Ilsa tracked the beat of the horses as someone rode them at high speed through the camp, to the center where they stood. Through the opening between the tent flaps she watched the horses burst into the square. Uther's great roan climbed the air with his front hooves, as Uther hauled on the reins. Uther rode the creature as he would a toothless mare, barely noticing the wild movements of the horse. He slid off the saddle as the creature blew heavily and tossed the reins to the boy who sprinted to catch them.

Uther strode across the square, pulling off his gauntlets. In the light of the torches which flared and jumped in their stands around the square, his hair gleamed redly, and his eyes glittered with harsh light.

He ducked under the flap and straightened, taking in the gathering of officers.

"Success, my lord?" Arawn asked, his voice tight.

"Catigern was beheaded at dawn yesterday morning and his

head put on a spear for the Saxons to find, just south of Galleva." Uther tossed the gauntlets aside. "My brother?"

Ilsa drew in an unsteady breath. "He is dead, my lord. Not two hours ago."

Uther's gaze skittered and shifted. Then he gathered himself together and looked toward the inner room. "Did he speak at all?"

"Only to Merlin," Ilsa said. "And not of affairs of state, Merlin says."

Uther nodded. "I will speak to Merlin, anyway. Find him for me." He pushed into the inner chamber.

Mabon stirred. "Does anyone know where Merlin went?"

"I'll find him," Ilsa said.

She moved out into the square, wrapping her cloak firmly around her, for the night was beyond cold. Merlin had left the King's tent the moment Ambrosius died. He would not be far away, even though he preferred solitude.

She checked his smaller tent and found it empty, then asked everyone she came across, no matter whom, if they had seen him.

Their answers lead her to the pond at the far southern edge of the camp. It was surrounded by rushes and the water was dank enough that no one but ducks used it, and even they had fled at the end of summer.

Merlin was there—not a tall figure gazing toward unseen

horizons, but a young man bent and shivering in the cold. He wore no cloak and his breath blew heavily in the frigid air.

He sat on his knees at the edge of the rushes, gripping the frozen grass as if it would keep him stable.

The black emptiness which had held Ilsa still and whole since Ambrosius had passed shattered between one hurtful breath and the next. Her heart ached.

She dropped to her knees beside him. "Merlin…"

He shook his head. "I didn't see it. I couldn't stop it." His voice broke and his shoulders shook.

Ilsa pulled him to her and rested his head on her shoulder. "The gods give and the gods take," she whispered. "All we can do is go on."

Merlin wept.

PART TWO

Chapter Twelve

Steffan waited alone in the freezing pre-dawn air. He was surrounded by thousands of people but was not aware of them. His agony was too great.

He did not need to see to know the funeral procession made its way through the throng. People had traveled in the depths of winter to this iron-hard plain to pay their respects to the first king to unite all of Britain in centuries. Steffan heard the crunch of the boots of the men who carried the pall, for despite there being so many people, the silence was absolute.

No torches lit the way. They moved in starlight only, for even the moon had set. Steffan's vision was a complete and rare, black nothingness. Not even the colors which normally danced and shifted showed themselves.

The boots moved past and Steffan turned to face them as they tromped away.

Then they halted.

Over the heads of the people standing around him, Steffan heard the Christian priest speak of an afterlife and eternal peace. Then a different holy man spoke of rewards and rest.

Words, all of them. Just words. Was nothing worthy of marking such a passing?

More movement. A hushed, muffled sigh from everyone around him. From attending too many funeral rites, Steffan knew Ambrosius' body was being lowered into the burial chamber. The shallow chamber had been hastily constructed beneath the massive black altar stone, which would stand in the center of the ring of stones Merlin had rebuilt.

Then, a silence which throbbed with waiting.

Steffan's heart beat hard. He'd heard the talk of the circle of standing stones. No one had been allowed near them in the five days mourners gathered in Amesbury, so it was all just rumors.

Then, light. Against his face, lifting the darkness from his eyes. Colors played. Warmth touched his skin.

Everyone gasped or drew in their breath.

The sun must have risen directly in front of where Steffan was facing. Light didn't just dance, it flared, like the flash of lightning. For one suspended heartbeat he saw the giant's dance in all its splendor. Black stones against the dawn in the east, turned silver with mid-winter frost. Gargantuan monoliths capped in a stupendous circle. Thousands of people stood among and outside the stones, tramping down the frozen earth, huddled in their cloaks and wraps and furs and blowing thick clouds with each awed breath. Their faces were all turned to the east, where the sun lifted over the horizon. The dazzling disk laid a beam of light from the horizon to the inner pair of great stones which marked the solstice. Blinding light speared the narrow aperture between them, to touch the place where the altar stone would be returned when this deed was done.

The bright flare didn't last. Overwhelmed, Steffan's eyes failed. He gripped his temples, covering them, as the light speared the back of his mind with pain. He bent, biting back his groan. He propped himself up with his staff as his head throbbed and his heart ached.

Merlin had said he would crown Ambrosius' resting place with nothing less than light itself. He had kept his promise.

So passed the greatest man Steffan had ever known.

A hand touched his wrist, light and uncertain. "Steffan? Are you ill?"

What was it about her voice which made him pause, every time he heard it? It was not the light tones of a young woman. The timbre and depth of her voice caught his ear and his mind. The unexpected dry notes, which spoke of weary wisdom, were fascinating.

At this moment, though, all her voice contained was simple

concern. As a minor duchess, among kings and queens and their courts, Igraine and her women would have stood at the back of the crowd. Had Anwen crossed the standing stones themselves to reach him? Had she been watching him?

Steffan made himself stand upright, wincing as his head throbbed and pulsed. "The light hurts. It is nothing. Once I am inside, the pain will pass."

Her fingers gripped his wrist properly. "Everyone is leaving now, anyway," she said. "Let me take you back to the Duchess' cart. You can at least ride back to Amesbury."

He let her lead him, this one time, for there were people all around him and he didn't know this place at all.

As the cart jolted and creaked over the rough track made by the passing of thousands of workers who had built the standing stones, Steffan reflected that, without the single blow of a Saxon hammer, his marking of the passing of such a great king would be far different. If he could still see, he would have stood among the officers surrounding Uther, able to watch every moment.

Instead he had only listened. The magnificence of the standing stones which marked Ambrosius' grave was lost upon him. How pathetic his tribute had been!

It wasn't until they reached Amesbury when another loss jarred him. Ambrosius' death was not a forfeiture, not when he had achieved so much for Britain and her people. This, though…this was a sacrifice. Why had he not looked for her, in that brief moment of vision? He might have seen Anwen as she was, not as his mind painted her.

AMESBURY WAS BUILT UPON AN open plain with little but grasses and stones. Building, here, did not require the heavy and difficult work of clearing forests to make room. As a result, the town sprawled east from the banks of the Avon and the solid stone bridge the Romans had built to cross the river.

The market square in the middle of Amesbury was an open space of cobbled stones far larger than the only other market place Anwen had ever seen in her life, at Isca Dumnoniorum.

She guided Steffan's fingers to the open gate at the back of the cart, while twisting her head to look around her, her eyes wide. The other women, including Igraine, had already alighted. They gathered about Igraine protectively and moved toward the tables.

There were braziers everywhere about the square, giving warmth and light to the day—although the sky was cloudless overhead. Around the edges of the square were many long tables. Some of them were merely boards resting on barrels, hastily put together by the townsfolk to host the royal company. A meal which was both the breaking of the overnight fast and a feast in celebration of Ambrosius was served upon the tables. Everyone was provided a platter or bowl, upon which the hot food was ladled.

There were porridges and stewed fruits, roast lamb aromatic with rosemary and pork with crackling rind. Winter vegetables cooked with more herbs and gravy and sweetmeats to satisfy any appetite. Bread, thick and crusty and still warm from the ovens, was heaped in baskets.

Pitchers filled with mulled wine and others with the rich white wine native to the region dotted the middle of the tables.

The steam from the hot food lifted into the air, as everyone gathered about the tables to eat.

The aroma of hot bread was overpowering, making Anwen's mouth water. Her heart sank, though, as she watched the mourners stand at the tables, talking as they ate. She turned to Steffan as he took his staff from the cart and tucked it against his shoulder.

"There is food to be had," she told him. "Although there are too many people here, all of them strangers, and everyone serves themselves. We can find an inn on the outskirts, instead."

Steffan tilted his head, listening to the clack of the wine pitchers and platters and the buzz of conversation. "It smells delicious. Why should you be deprived? Perhaps…" He frowned. "If you would gather two meals, we can find a place away from everyone. If that suits you?"

Relief touched her. "Yes, it suits me. Stay here. I will return shortly."

She hurried to fill two platters with meat and vegetables, selected hunks of bread and took it all back to the cart.

Steffan had not stood idle while she was gone. His staff was propped against the cart and his cloak hung from the top. Steffan rolled the second of two empty barrels up to the cart. A stack of similar barrels rested against the wall of the nearest building.

There were few people on this side of the marketplace, for the tables of food were on the other.

Steffan stood the barrel he was manipulating on its end beside the first.

"Here," Anwen said, holding out a platter. "Pork and vegetables and bread on the side."

He took the plate and sniffed.

"I want hot wine, too," Anwen said, putting her platter on the first barrel. She went back to the nearest table and poured two mugs of the wine. No one stopped her or tried to speak to her, which was normal. Igraine would be at her husband's side, she presumed. Even though Anwen was one of Igraine's companion ladies, the work of teaching Morgan and Morguase removed her from that company. She would not be missed.

Not that she minded. The ladies of Igraine's retinue and Mari's before her were spiteful when the great lady was not present.

Anwen took the wine back to the cart. Steffan had put on his cloak, for the morning was chilly, but furled it over his shoulders to eat. He sat on a barrel, his long legs letting him keep his feet upon the ground.

Anwen carefully placed the tankards on the floor of the cart behind them, where they could reach them through the slats on the side of the cart. Then she picked up her meal and tried to arrange herself on the barrel. It was too high to sit. Her platter jiggled, threatening to spill the meal upon her.

Steffan held out his hand. "Give it to me."

"How did you know?" she asked, handing him the plate.

"I know that irritated sigh of yours," he said.

She scowled and hoisted herself onto the barrel. Then, because her feet did not reach to the cobbles and she had no desire to swing them like a child, she lifted her feet, too. She and crossed her ankles and rearranged her gown around her knees and over her feet.

Then she took the plate back. "Thank you."

Steffan returned to eating. He had not waited for her and his plate was nearly empty.

Anwen ate quickly, using the bread to sop up the gravy. She was starving.

This was the first time in her life she had traveled beyond the borders of Cornwall. She did not like traveling. It was a dirty, uncomfortable experience. The cold was unrelenting. They were never in buildings with doors and windows which could be closed against the outdoors.

Yet the most surprising thing about traveling was that she was often hungry. Meals were chancy upon the road, unless one stopped and set up camp to prepare a proper meal or found an inn which could serve such a large company. As the message summoning Gorlois' household to Amesbury insisted they arrive before mid-winter, stopping on the way to eat properly had been impossible.

Most of the food Anwen had eaten in the last few days was cold—a snatched handful of dates or other fruit, cheese, or dried and salted meat. At first, there had been bread to gnaw upon, although the bread had soon run out and no chance arose to replenish their supplies. Most of Britain was on the road, summoned to Amesbury just as they were. Towns and their bakeries were stripped of supplies before they reached them.

After decades of Saxon raids and internal wars, most of Britain had little food to spare even for those who could pay for it. The lands they traveled through seemed barren. They passed no fallow fields or harvested crops. The herds and flocks she spotted were small, the creatures lean and sallow.

Few birds flew overhead. People hid away from the large company traveling the roads. Anwen was left with the impression that life clung by the fingernails. A year of near-peace had not been enough to reverse the shortfalls and deprivations of a generation.

This was the first hot meal she had tasted in five days.

"Is traveling always so rough?" she asked Steffan.

He smiled. "Try traveling upon horseback and carrying all your armor and shields and weapons, from earliest light to sunset."

"That is how an army travels?" she asked.

"When not in enemy territory, yes."

"And when you are in enemy territory?"

"Your armor is worn, your weapons held in your hands and you trust your horse to follow the others and find his own way, for you dare not put down your blades to pick up the reins. No matter the heat or the discomfort, you remain alert, while your sweat gathers beneath your armor and your brain cooks in your head, because you wear a war helmet and dare not put it aside, either."

Anwen shuddered. "This is the life you like so much?"

"There are ugly sides to any life," he said. After a pause he added softly to himself, "Yes, there is good and bad everywhere."

He twisted to put the empty plate on the boards of the

cart. With a sideways motion of his hand, he found the nearest cup of wine and picked it up. He sipped and nodded. "Good."

"What's this, then?" came a rough voice from the corner of the cart, making Anwen gasp. "The eunuch keeping company with a woman?" The man stepped around the cart, his arms crossed. He was a short man, yet solid with muscle. He wore the white cloak of Cornwall over his shoulders. His leathers were stained and his armguards slashed. His arms were thick with muscle. His muddy brown eyes shifted from Steffan to Anwen and back.

"Maurgh," Steffan said, lowering his mug. "I did not realize roaches like you were invited to attend. I'm glad you stayed with the Dimilioc end of the company. The road was foul enough without your presence."

Anwen recognized the name. This was the soldier from Dimilioc who had made Steffan's life so unpleasant, Steffan had beaten him with his staff.

Anwen slid her half-eaten meal onto the cart. She wanted her hands free.

A second man moved around the cart. This one was taller and also wore Cornwall white. His armor was of better quality. "There are fresh pitchers over…" His voice trailed off, as he looked from Maurgh to Steffan, to Anwen. His eyes narrowed. As he had deeply set eyes and a crease over the bridge of his nose, narrowing them made him looked both angry and puzzled. "Steffan of Durnovaria. How the mighty have fallen. Look at you."

Obeying her instincts, Anwen plucked Steffan's mug from his hands and put it back on the cart.

Steffan didn't seem to notice. His chin turned, making it appear he was looking at the second man. "Madog. You keep appropriate company."

"That would be Captain Madog, to you," Madog said.

"Nah, it wouldn't," Maurgh said, with a cruel quirk of his mouth. "He's a eunuch now. Not a drop of soldier left in him. He teaches children." He spat.

Steffan did not appear to react, although Anwen could see a pulse throbbing at the base of his neck. He didn't shift off the barrel. "Gorlois must be desperate to promote the likes of you, Madog."

Madog's scowl scrunched his creased eyes even more. "You always were too good for us men. Off drinking with princes and kings. Only, I'm a captain now...and you're no one."

Anwen sucked in a breath at the cruel words.

Steffan gripped her arm and squeezed gently. It was a warning to remain silent.

She swallowed.

"Look, he's reaching for help," Maurgh taunted. "Can't even feed himself without a nurse." As he spoke, he shifted his boots, moving in tiny increments. His gaze flickered toward the cart.

Anwen stifled another gasp. Maurgh was aiming to take Steffan's staff away from him, the one he had used to beat him at Dimilioc.

She untucked her feet and let them hang. The staff was on the other side of Steffan from where she sat. Maurgh was closer to it than she and she didn't know what she might do to prevent him from taking the staff.

Madog laughed. It was thick with derision. "Maybe it's a good thing you're blind, Steffan. You always found the only beauty worth bedding within a day's ride. Now you can't tell you're reaching for the plainest hag of a woman in Amesbury." He paused, considering. "Ugly is all you deserve," he added.

Anwen froze, her heart jolting.

Maurgh lunged for the staff. Anwen's throat locked tight. She couldn't draw breath to warn Steffan.

It didn't matter. Steffan heard or felt Maurgh's motion and guessed his intentions. He stood and snatched his hand out and sideways, to grip the staff just as Maurgh got his hand on it.

They grew still, both pulling at the staff. Steffan seemed to stare directly at Maurgh.

Maurgh snarled. "Eunuch."

"Fool," Steffan replied in a flat voice. He jerked the staff forward, toward Maurgh. The top of it rammed into the underside of Maurgh's jaw. The man staggered backward with a sharp click of his teeth, his breath escaping with a grunt.

Madog leapt, as if he had been waiting for this moment—and perhaps he had. He was a cruel man and he was a soldier. He had survived enough battles to be promoted to the higher ranks of Gorlois' army, so he knew how to fight with or without weapons.

His fist crashed into Steffan's jaw. Steffan didn't see it coming as a sighted man would. He didn't brace himself. The blow sent him staggering across the cobbles, his staff scraping across the stones.

He recovered quickly—more quickly than Anwen thought he might after such a hit. Steffan pulled the staff closer and gripped it with a hand at one end and the other nearly halfway down the length of the staff. He lunged at Madog, the staff lifting high, as if he could see exactly where the man was. Perhaps he could—he saw shapes and colors. What color would Madog be? A deep, dirty bruised gray, Anwen hoped.

The staff slammed across Madog's shoulder with a thud which seemed to echo. Madog cried out and his arm fell against his side, useless. Steffan rammed the staff into his stomach and Madog gave a sickly grunt and folded onto his knees, his hands at his stomach.

Maurgh leapt upon Steffan's back, his fingers hooked into

claws, as he reached around for Steffan's face. Steffan staggered up against the barrel upon which he had been sitting. He gripped Maurgh's wrist, to stop the fingers from digging into his flesh.

Anwen grabbed a mug of wine. It was still nearly full, which made it heavy. She jumped up on the barrel, gripped the cup in her hand and swung her fist at Maurgh's face.

Like Steffan had been, Maurgh was not braced for the unexpected blow. He grunted and fell from Steffan's back. He sprawled heavily. Hot wine sent up steam from his shoulder and back.

Madog surged to his feet with a growl.

"Behind you!" Anwen shouted.

Steffan whirled, bringing up the staff, blocking Madog's arm, which he had been bringing around for another blow at Steffan's face.

Madog didn't like that. His face twisted with fury. He stepped sideways and ducked under the lifted end of the staff. He rose in front of the barrel Anwen stood upon. His fist buried itself in her stomach.

The pain was immense—too much for Anwen to even gasp. Her knees folded. She fell onto the barrel, then tipped off the side onto the cobbles. The impact jarred her. Her bones creaked. The last of her breath pushed out of her.

"Anwen!" Steffan shouted.

She couldn't find the breath to reassure him. She moaned, her knees curling up around the hand she pressed to her stomach. The meal she had just eaten stirred uneasily.

Her lack of answer triggered Steffan. With a roar, he wielded the staff, swinging it in three sharp blows—into Maurgh's chest as he rose sluggishly to his feet, dropping him back onto his rear; against the side of Madog's flat face, making his jaw snap sideways and blood to spray; then a slam into Maurgh's temple, making his eyes roll backward and him to fall back upon on the cobbles.

Madog fell, too. He laid on his face, his hand making weak scrabbling motions at the stones.

"What in Mithras' name is going on here?" The roar came from behind Anwen and she could not straighten or move to see who it was, although she recognized the voice. It was Gorlois.

Steffan turned to the voice, lowering the staff. He was breathing hard. The staff rested upon the ground once more and he held it as he always did, as a guide, not a weapon.

Madog moaned.

More running steps sounded—Anwen could hear them through the ground beneath her ear. Gasps and wordless exclamations. More people gathered around Gorlois.

"Steffan, what have you done?" Gorlois demanded, anger thickening his voice.

"We…had a discussion," Steffan said.

Hands pressed against Anwen's arm. "Can you get up?" It was Igraine's voice. "Help me lift her to her feet," Igraine added.

More hands gripped Anwen's arms and tried to raise her. The movement hurt and she gave a soft cry and curled her knees back against her belly.

Gorlois glanced at her and frowned, then back at Steffan. "This is a day of peace, of reflection. Yet you fight like a drunken recruit after his first battle."

"There you are, Gorlois," came another voice, from the far corner of the cart, on the other side of where Steffan stood with two men sprawled at his feet. The man who strode around the cart was tall, with burnished dark red hair and a full beard and ferocious blue eyes which glittered with life and intelligence. He was a man at the prime of life, with youthful looks leavened with wisdom and experience.

He had broad shoulders beneath the thick, fine cloak. His clothing was richly embellished and his armguards were of finest gold, reinforced with polished copper, so they shone as red as his hair.

Red hair. Blue eyes. An air of command. It was the first time Anwen had ever seen him, yet she knew she was looking at Uther, the new High King of Britain.

Uther came to a halt, his eyes widening. He took in the

men on the ground, Steffan's position between them and Gorlois's angry face. Behind Gorlois a dozen other people strained and pressed to see what the fuss was about.

Gorlois swallowed. "My lord, this is just a minor matter. I would not spoil this day with domestic squabbles. Let me clear this up, then attend you."

Uther, though, swung his gaze back to Steffan. "Steffan! Gods above! It *is* you!" He stepped over Madog's still body and thrust out his hand, the other gripping Steffan's shoulder. "Look at you! You look *exactly* the same!"

Steffan couldn't see Uther's outstretched hand and didn't reach for it. "My lord Uther," he said, a small smile touching his mouth. "This is…unexpected."

Uther looked down at his hand, which hung empty. He frowned. "I forgot," he murmured. He picked up Steffan's wrist and pushed his hand into Uther's.

Steffan gripped his hand hard, the tendons in his arm working. "Uther," he said, his tone pleased and warm. Then his smile fled. He turned his head. "Anwen?"

Anwen took a slightly deeper breath. "I'm here." Her voice was weak and pathetic.

Uther frowned. His vital gaze ran over her. "So a woman is at the root of this. I should have guessed." He let go of Steffan's hand, then walked over to where Anwen sat on the cobbles.

The women who had been trying to help her drew back, perhaps worried what the High King might do. Everyone knew of his legendary temper.

"My lord, I do apologize," Igraine said quickly. "Anwen is one of my women, although she has an independent spirit…"

Uther bent and gripped Anwen's arms. He lifted her to her feet with little visible effort.

She gasped as he steadied her. His gaze was kindly. "Are you hurt?"

Anwen caught Gorlois' gaze upon her, just behind Uther. Gorlois shook his head. She understood. This should be contained within Cornwall. "No, my lord, but thank you for your help," she said, trying to make her voice sound as strong as his.

"Yes, thank you, my lord," Igraine added, from just behind Anwen.

Uther's gaze shifted from Anwen to Igraine. His smile faded. Anwen was close enough she saw his eyes widen slightly. His lips parted.

Anwen shifted so she was not standing in front of the High King. She glanced at Igraine.

Igraine stood as still as Uther, her gaze on the High King's face. Then Igraine remembered where she was and who she was. She dropped her chin and stared modestly at the ground, bringing her morning veil closer around her face.

Gorlois moved up beside her. "There has been no time for formal introductions, my lord," he told Uther. "May I present to you the Duchess of Cornwall?"

Uther stirred and glanced at Gorlois. Then his gaze slid back to Igraine. A tiny furrow appeared between his brows. "You are welcome here, Lady Igraine," he said. His tone was absent, as if he spoke the words automatically.

Igraine was forced to look at him once more, to acknowledge the welcome. Her eyes were wide as she dropped into a shallow curtsy. "King Uther," she acknowledged. Her voice trembled.

Anwen's heart thudded in response to the heat and tension swirling between the two. Neither of them moved, while they were surrounded by people who pushed and leaned, trying to see what was happening.

Gorlois's eyes narrowed as he took in the two still people. His face tightened. He could sense the tension, too. He gripped Igraine's arm, his fingers digging in. "Come, wife," he said. "Let us take this concern out of the King's sight and deal with it in private." He pulled on her arm.

For a moment, Anwen thought Igraine would resist her husband's tugging and her heart leapt with alarm.

Then Igraine drew in a tremulous breath, turned and let herself be pulled away.

A tall man with dark hair and a petite woman with red hair

the same color as Uther's swept up beside Uther. The man took the King's arm and spoke to him quietly, shepherding him as he spoke. Uther drew in a breath of his own, blinking. He frowned as he listened to the man.

The three of them moved in the opposite direction to Gorlois, huddled together as they conversed.

Anwen felt as though a disaster had been only narrowly diverted.

"Anwen?" Steffan called. There were too many people swirling about in the little space between the cart and the nearest building for him to risk moving.

Anwen moved to where he stood, his grip hard on the staff. Walking made her stomach ache, although she no longer felt as though she would be sick. She touched Steffan's arm. "I'm here."

He frowned. "What in Hades just happened?" he demanded, his voice even lower. "The air wasn't that thick when we faced armed Saxons."

"I think," Anwen said slowly, "a civil war may have just been averted."

Chapter Thirteen

Ilsa held the tent flap aside for Arawn to lead Uther inside. She dropped it behind them and pulled the edges together to discourage interruptions.

Arawn pushed Uther toward the big chair at the back of the outer room of the pavilion. "Sit and draw breath, Uther."

Uther turned to face him. "What is this? My captain telling me what to do?" A dangerous note colored his voice.

Arawn hesitated. He recognized Uther's tone, as did Ilsa. Eight years of campaigning with Uther and Ambrosius had taught them to take care when Uther's anger stirred.

This was no time for delicate side stepping, though. Ilse moved around the two so she was facing Uther. "Arawn is not your captain right now. He is your friend. And I am your cousin, Uther. We speak as friends now."

Arawn nodded. "You have never hidden your indiscretions, Uther. The gods know men have admired you for them and for your tirelessness. The Lady Igraine is no camp follower, though."

Uther's jaw worked. "What are you prattling about?" he demanded, with a patently false innocent air. "I was talking to another old friend and greeting his leaders."

Ilsa laughed. "Uther, *no one* who saw what just happened will believe that."

"I've seen you fall for women too many times to miss it," Arawn said. "You've risked baleful husbands before but this… this is an altogether different matter."

Uther swallowed, his eyes narrowing. "I am your king…" he growled.

"Not until Easter," Arawn said sharply. "We're just cousins and friends, trying to warn you to think this through."

Ilsa gripped Uther's sleeve. "Gorlois is your most loyal ally. He supported you and Ambrosius from the very beginning. He has not left the King's side since Ambrosius landed in Britain and his army has fought your wars valiantly."

"If you slight Gorlois," Arawn continued, "if you pursue Lady Igraine, then Gorlois will be forced to redress the insult. You would risk open war against your strongest ally, just to bed a woman?"

"And if you think that is a small price to pay," Ilsa continued, "remember what happened when Vortigern and Catigern fell out. The Saxons took advantage of the moment of weakness and flooded across Britain, slaughtering everything in their path. It took your brother seven years to wrest back control of the country, after that."

Uther flinched. His gaze slid from Ilsa to Arawn. Then he sighed and dropped into the chair and put his chin on his fist. "You speak truly," he said. "I am not that much of a fool—I would hope I am not, at least."

Ilsa drew in a breath, relief touching her.

Arawn let out his own breath in a gusty exhalation.

Uther dropped his hand. "By the gods, she is beautiful, though! No wonder Gorlois kept her locked up in that great fortress of his."

Arawn's gaze met Ilsa's.

Uther pushed his hand through his hair in a mannerism Ilsa remembered. She had not seen him do that in years. It was a habit from the days when he had been frustrated beyond belief, perched upon the very brink of war but not yet unloosed upon Britain.

"There is a day of feasting to get through," Arawn said sharply. "Then the camp can be struck and Amesbury can return to being a village. The sooner we reach permanent accommodations and a decent hearth for the winter, the better. We've tallied here too long."

"Are you cold, Arawn?" Uther asked, sounding surprised. His gaze ran over Arawn's layers of furs and wool.

"Are you not?" Arawn shot back, irritable. "It is midwinter—long past time for sane men to be tucked inside. It is eight years, now, since I last slept on a real bed."

Uther got to his feet and rested his hand on Arawn's shoulder. "After the coronation, you should go home, you and Ilsa. You well deserve it." His grip tightened. "A day of feasting, hey? One where I do not tear the country apart by insulting my ally."

"That would be nice," Ilsa murmured, her voice tight.

Uther patted her cheek. "You know me far too well, kinswoman," he said. "Let me surprise you, for once." He winked and left the tent. "Let's find some wine, Arawn!" he shouted from outside.

Ilsa dropped into the chair Uther had vacated, trembling.

Arawn let his head roll back and blew out his breath once more. "And now he will insist upon us keeping him company while he drinks himself to a standstill."

Ilsa gave him a shaky smile. "Tomorrow's headache will be a small price to pay if it helps us avert a disaster."

BEFORE ANWEN HAD FINISHED EXPLAINING what had happened between Uther and Igraine, and Gorlois' reaction, music began in the square beyond the cart. The space between the cart and the building where they stood emptied of everyone but them. Even the two men Steffan had beaten stirred from their positions on the ground and crept away.

The music was sprightly, with pipes and harp and a quick drum beat designed to make feet tap.

Steffan, though, frowned. "Uther has an eye for women—"

"Which everyone in the land knows about," Anwen assured him.

"He has never tarried with one so dangerous, though," Steffan added.

"He didn't tarry," Anwen said. "He hid his reaction and let himself be drawn away by his friends. There wasn't a wrong word spoken by either of them."

"He hid it?" Steffan sounded even more startled.

"He tried to. It was enough for everyone to pretend nothing was wrong, yet I *saw* his face, Steffan. It was as if he'd taken the end of your staff right against his heart."

Steffan considered. "In the short time I knew him, Uther never hid any lust he felt. He was open about it, which made the men admire him all the more. *And* stand back and cheer as he indulged himself." His frown deepened. "No one could cheer about this, though. It would force Gorlois to act, which would split the army...this is not good, Anwen."

She sighed. "That is why he let himself be led away, I think. He knows it, too." Her heart pattered unhappily. "What can we do about it? I am not Igraine's favorite companion. I never have been. She would not listen to me."

"And I am no longer a soldier with a channel to Uther," Steffan said bitterly.

Anwen gripped her hands together. "Those men…Maurgh and Madog…they are the people you miss, Steffan?"

His clear gaze shifted to where the men had been lying, as if he could see them there. "Maurgh and Madog and others of their ilk…they are the worst type of soldier. No, they are not the people I miss. The people I miss are like Uther, who has worked his entire life to fulfil his brother's dream of a peaceful Britain. I miss people like Gorlois, who are faithful and stalwart and ruthless in the protection of their leaders. There are dozens more. Arawn and Mabon and Bors and Ban, all of them good kings and leaders of men, dedicated to a greater vision than their own little kingdoms. I am not their equal yet because Uther liked me, I got to meet them and know them." He swept his hand out. "There were others. Ector and Pellinore and Cadfael's son, Bricius. Even Cador will be among them, now. They are the next generation of great men. They are the people who will change our world. And yes, I miss the company of such men."

Anwen pressed her hand to her chest. The light, happy music seemed such an odd note, compared to Steffan's ringing voice. "No wonder you chafe from the company you keep now."

Steffan shifted, as if she had startled him.

"Women and children and Latin," she added. "How mundane it must all seem. No wonder you are angry all the time."

Steffan jerked. "Angry?"

Wary, Anwen said, "You have much to be angry about."

Steffan's knuckles whitened on the staff. "That is what they say about me? That I am angry?" He seemed astonished. "You believe that, too?"

She swallowed. "When you first came to Tintagel, it seemed you were, yes."

"And now?" he asked, his tone tight with control.

"I don't know what others see—"

"I don't care what they see," he growled.

"You scare me," Anwen said, her heart jumping at his growl.

He grew still, as if he listened to something she could not hear.

"Sometimes," she amended.

"Sometimes…" he muttered heavily.

"You must understand," she said quickly. "I had never spoken directly to a man, before I met you."

He drew in a deep breath. "Not once? Not at all?"

His astonishment made her cheeks heat with shame. "I have lived in the women's quarters at Tintagel all my life," she said, unable to lift her voice above a murmur, for it seemed so pathetic.

"Then this is the first time you have traveled beyond Cornwall." He shook his head. "The first time I crossed the Severn, I could barely stay on my horse for terror. The mountains to the north are so much bigger, the trees taller, the enemy stronger and more ferocious—everything was new. How is it you have shown nothing but calm gracefulness since we left Tintagel?"

"I wasn't afraid," Anwen said. *Because you were there.* The words stayed in her mind, unspoken, yet shocking. The presence of a blind man had changed a journey which terrified Steffan to one of simple wonder for her? How could that be?

"Then you have courage far beyond mine," Steffan said. "I already suspected it was so. Now I know for sure." He moved over to where the cart sat and rested the staff against it. He held out his hand. "Come here."

Her heart jumped. She went over to him. With a great hesitation, she put her hand in his. "Why?" she asked suspiciously.

"There is music and there is dancing. Let me prove I am not as angry as you think." He pulled her gently around the cart. She could see in the greater square beyond that couples were stepping out dance formations in time to the simple tune.

Panic swamped her. "No," she said, her voice nearly bodiless. She pulled on Steffan's grip, trying to drag herself back behind the cart.

"No?" he asked, halting.

"No. No dancing," she said. "I beg you."

Steffan's smile was puzzled. "I've never before met a woman who does not like to dance." His smile faded. "Or is it the company you object to?"

"No. Neither," she said quickly, still pulling against the hold he had on her hand. "Please, Steffan, let me go."

He frowned, moving closer to her. He didn't release her hand. "What *is* your objection?" he asked.

Her terror built. She would die of shame if he forced her to speak it aloud. "Ugly old hags don't dance," she said desperately.

His eyes seemed to darken. "Neither do blind men. Tell me truly, Anwen. Why will you not dance with me?"

"I don't know how!" she cried and turned her back on him, her shame complete. Her arm twisted about her middle, for he did not let go of her hand even as she whirled away from him.

He came up behind her. She could feel the heat of his body against hers, warming the chill air of the day. "You've never traveled and you've never danced," he breathed. "Then there is something which terrifies you, after all." He laid his hand on her shoulder. "Come here."

She resisted and shook her head, forgetting for a moment he would not see the movement.

"Come, Anwen. Back behind the cart," he said gently.

She would be hidden behind the cart. That seemed safe. Anwen let him draw her back to where his staff rested against the end of the cart. He didn't pick it up. Instead, he pulled her into the middle of the open area between the cart and the building.

"Now, curtsey," he told her and bowed.

For a moment, fear blossomed once more. She stood frozen.

"Go on," Steffan told her.

"How did you know I had not?" she breathed.

"When you move, the air brushes my face. Curtsey, Anwen."

She gripped the folds of her gown with clammy fingers and curtsied, spreading the skirt out of the way.

"Now, do you hear the music?"

She nodded. Then she cleared her throat and added, "Yes."

"On every second beat, take a step toward me. Three steps. Ready?"

Her heart racing, she nodded again. "Yes."

"One, two," and he took a step. Anwen did, too.

"Three, four." Another step.

"Five, six." The last step.

His hand found hers and lifted it high and they swayed closer as the other dancers had been doing.

It was quite natural to take the step backward. She did it without instruction.

"Now around," he murmured.

She walked around in the tight circle, just as he did. He found her hand once more and this time they moved around in a single circle, their joined hands in the middle.

He released her hand. She turned and moved back three steps.

"On the beat this time," he said.

Three steps forward. Hands together, raise and sway…then to circle and circle again.

Her heart beat wildly. *I'm dancing!*

The tune ended. Another began immediately. This one was slower and far more sedate, to give the musicians a chance to catch their breath. Anwen recognized both the tune and the dance, for she had sat in the corner of the courtyard at Tintagel more than once on late summer evenings, watching dancers come together, their heads close.

Her heart pummeled at her chest as Steffan's arm came about her waist. He turned her just as she had seen other men do with the women in their arms. Steffan's gaze seemed to settle on her face.

"Can you see me?" she whispered.

"Almost," he breathed. "Perhaps, if I stop being angry and you stop being afraid, I might *really* see you."

"Like you saw the standing stones?" she breathed.

He shook his head. It was a small movement. "I suspect that seeing you won't hurt at all."

Her breath caught in her throat as he leaned down and pressed his lips to hers. They were no longer dancing. She was in his arms, held there by the touch of his mouth.

It was delightful. It surpassed any hint other women had given about the pleasure of kissing. Anwen sighed into his mouth.

His tongue touched her lips and pressed deeper.

Anwen recoiled backward. "You can't kiss me."

Steffan let his hands drop. "Why not?"

"I'm…" Old. Unworthy. "There must be someone else you want to kiss more," she said awkwardly.

Steffan considered it. "No, there isn't."

Her heart would not stop hurting. She pressed her hand to her chest. "You're playing with me. I'm Anwen, who everyone overlooks…"

Steffan shook his head. "What sort of man would I be, if I did that to you? I'd be no better than Madog and Maurgh."

She wrung her hands together. "You deserve a younger woman…a sweet maiden."

"Sweet maidens are still-green fruit plucked too early,"

Steffan said. "You are the ripest of apricots at the end of summer, when the flesh is still smooth, blushed pink by the sun and the juice bereft of any touch of tartness. You are ripe with potential, Anwen of Tintagel. Those who overlook you…they are the blind ones." He held out his hand. "Come here."

It was impossible to not take his hand, although her fear made her speak. "You should know…I've never…" Her voice strained to silence.

"Kissed a man? I do know." He touched her lips with his fingers. "That is my good fortune." His voice was low and thick with an emotion she did not recognize.

His lips pressed against hers once more.

It was easier this time to let the pleasure spread through her. Still she trembled with fear and inexperience. He lifted her arms and wrapped them about his neck, which made her strain on her toes and rock against him, her balance precarious. He pulled her against him with an iron-strong arm and held her there.

The kiss deepened. His tongue brushed hers and she made a sound she had never heard herself make before, a deep moan which seemed to pull from her middle.

Steffan's mouth released hers. He did not lift his head. He was breathing hard.

So was she.

The air on her back, where his arms were not covering her,

was cold compared to the heat between them. She shivered.

Steffan let her go—all but her hand. "I know where it is warm," he said. "Will you come with me?"

Maid, she might be. Old and overlooked, too. Yet she had heard enough talk among the women to understand what he was asking her. Anwen realized her hand was shaking in his. Her whole body trembled.

She reasoned it out, as she had reasoned all decisions in her life—the few she had ever had the power to make for herself. There would be no husband in her future. She accepted that now. She had known it for some years. There was no chance she would ever fall in love. No man would dream of falling in love with her, either.

If the gossip of the women was true and the acts of men and women were as pleasurable as they said, then why should she not take a little of that pleasure for herself? She had learned she liked kissing—kissing Steffan, at least. She had learned the woes of travel and how to dance. Why not this, too?

Anwen cleared her throat twice before she could speak. "I will go with you," she told him.

Steffan drew in a deep breath. He took her over to the cart and picked up his staff, then led her away.

Chapter Fourteen

The stable he led her to was large and filled with horses and straw, which made it warmer than the room in which Igraine's women had slept the previous night. The horses barely looked up from their slack-hipped nibbling as Steffan pulled Anwen through the stalls to the gear room at the end. A workbench against one wall was covered in bits of bridles and saddles being repaired. On the other side was a pile of hay, taller than a man at the back and sloping to the floor at a gentle angle.

Steffan laid his cloak upon the hay, put his staff against the wall and drew her against him. As she trembled, he kissed her. "Do not fear me."

"I do not. Not now," she whispered. She didn't finish the rest of the thought. There was a comfort in knowing he could not see her. He did not see her plain looks and her undistinguished hair.

Or she thought he did not.

He eased her clothes from her in slow, gentle stages, which broke with her understanding that a man would find the fastest route to access a woman's body—a flip of a skirt, a torn bodice... Steffan did neither and she marveled at the difference, even as she shivered in the warm, still air.

"You're still cold," he breathed, his lips brushing her shoulder.

"No."

"Ah, then I must soothe your concerns away." He put her hands on his chest, over the leather of his jerkin "Your turn."

Her mind blanked. "You mean...?"

He smiled. "Yes. You take them off me. How else are you to learn?"

How, indeed. She fumbled to unbuckle the jerkin, with Steffan helping her, then tugged the shirt from his trousers. She was not tall enough to lift it over his head, so Steffan shrugged out of it and dropped it to one side.

Anwen's trembling increased. She reached out to touch his flesh, the rounded mounds and dips, where the muscles ended. "May I?" she asked.

Steffan seemed to know what she meant. He reached for her hand and found it, then drew it to him and pressed her palm against his chest. He drew in a breath. "Your hand is hot against me."

Anwen smoothed her fingers over his skin, enjoying the

warmth and softness. Then, driven by an impulse she didn't understand but obeyed anyway, she pressed her lips against his flesh, right over his heart.

He drew in a rough breath. She could feel his heart working, just below her lips. The sound of its fast beating made her own leap even higher. She reached for the fastenings of his trousers. She had never unfastened trousers before, although she had made many pairs and knew how they worked. Only, her fingers felt stiff and uncooperative. The flesh tingled because of the proximity to his body, to *there.*

"Let me," he said, his voice hoarse. He stripped the garment away and she saw for the first time the proud flesh.

Steffan drew her to the cloak he had spread upon the straw and laid her down and kissed her. His lips moved to her chin, then her throat and farther.

Anwen's understanding of the pleasures of the flesh blossomed as Steffan's mouth and hands explored her body. She reacted, her thoughts fragmenting, as every nerve and sinew grew taut and tingled, sensitized to every single touch, from the brush of his breath over her skin, to the touch of his hair and the sweep of his fingers. The heat of his body against hers was ferocious. His scent was a goad, making her nerves quiver.

His hand cupped her breast, stealing her breath with delight. How sweet the touch was! Then his mouth replaced his hand and her thoughts scattered once more.

"You are such a slight thing," he breathed as he drew her beneath him.

"Skinny, you mean." She had heard all the words before, either whispered or jeered. *Skinny, shapeless, boyish.* And more.

"Slender," he corrected and kissed her. "All flesh and joy," he added.

His taking of her was just as slow and gentle. She felt little pain, even though she had been braced for it. The small discomfort evaporated as he moved against her. Pleasure swirled and seemed to rise through her, promising something she did not yet know.

The first coupling unraveled the last of the mysteries in her mind except one. The pleasure she had glimpsed was not fully delivered.

As Steffan laid beside her, breathing hard, she rested her hand against his chest, a thrill running through her that she could do it. "Show me more."

Steffen's smile was heated. Even his eyes seemed to dance with warmth and knowledge. "What makes you think there is more?"

She pressed against his shoulder. He let her push him onto his back and she lifted herself up so she laid on his chest. "I've heard much about this matter over the years. Nothing you have done demonstrates why a woman would want to do it a second time, when a great many women *do* want to do it, very often."

"Ah…" His smile broadened. His hands came around her waist. He flipped her onto her back once more. "Then let me demonstrate."

And he did.

While her body recovered from the intense peak of excitement he created in her, Steffan drew her cloak over them, trapping the warm air. His hand settled over her waist. His fingers stroked. "I was right. Your flesh *is* soft and sweet."

She could feel her body warm at the compliment. "Which no one else sees," she whispered, trailing her own hands over him, tracing the size and power of his body.

The leisurely stroking ignited more flames. This time, Anwen was an active participant, striving for the joyful end with him.

WHILE THE MUSIC PLAYED FAR away, they stayed in the stable. No one disturbed them there, for everyone in the village had been included in the feast.

As the weak winter sun lowered and the light faded, Steffan leaned over her and seemed to study her, as his fingers stroked her hair back from her forehead. "You're not golden brown anymore," he murmured.

"I'm not?"

"You're pure golden light, now."

Her heart gave a little lurch. "I think you really are blind when it comes to me."

"You think so?" He didn't seem offended. "Is Morguase not strawberry red?"

He had her there. "She is," Anwen admitted. Strawberry red described Morguase perfectly. "What color is Igraine?" she asked.

"The green of a deep, deep sea."

Anwen shivered. That, too, was Igraine.

She touched his jaw. "Morgan isn't lilac, though, is she?"

Steffan froze for a heartbeat. "You knew I lied?"

"You wouldn't look at her directly. I mean…you don't anyway, yet you *seem* to look at people when you talk to them, just as you're staring into my eyes right now. Only, when Morgan asked, you shifted your eyes away and told her she was lilac."

Steffan grimaced. "*You* see far too much," he breathed.

"What color was she?" Anwen pressed.

He hesitated. "Red," he said, his voice low. "The color of blood when it is first spilled."

Anwen shivered.

Steffan pulled her against him and kissed away the shivers.

GORLOIS ANNOUNCED THE NEXT MORNING that the Cornwall contingent, including Gorlois' standing army, had been given the King's permission to leave Amesbury and they would leave immediately.

They were not the only army decamping and returning home. Ban and Bors and their men were returning to Lesser Britain, too. Percival and Ector headed for their northern holds, among other petty kings and leaders taking their leave.

The makeshift camp which had been just outside the walls of Amesbury for nearly a year was breaking up.

Anwen was pressed into service, helping Igraine repack the trunks and chests with her gowns and accoutrements and returning them to the wagon. She was happy to have the work to do, for it kept her mind from wandering back to yesterday and speculating about what might happen now.

One thing she had learned from the gossiping women was that a man must be allowed to make up his own mind about such matters.

All too soon, Anwen was told to find a place in the cart which would carry the women. Igraine had cushions for her back and bottom, while everyone else folded their cloaks beneath them and wrapped them around tightly for warmth.

Anwen shook her head. "I will walk, for now."

The other women all gasped. "You cannot walk all the way

to Tintagel!" one said.

"Why not?" Anwen asked dryly. "The cart moves more slowly than I."

Igraine nodded. "It is a fine idea, walking. I may join you in a while, Anwen."

The captain at the head of the line shouted and the carts and horses all moved forward with a slow, plodding step and creak of wheels. There were many more carts in the long column which rolled across the stone bridge than had brought them here, for Gorlois, his men and their gear had swelled the ranks. Four hundred armed foot soldiers walked beside and between the carts, trailing the war horses at the head of the column.

Steffan would be on one of those carts.

STEFFAN KNEW FROM EXPERIENCE TO find a spot at the front of the cart, where he could let his legs hang, or else risk cramps from sitting with them bent for too long.

The mid-winter journey at least minimized the dust the horses at the front of the column kicked up. The air was fresh and cold against his face, although as the sun rose the air warmed a little and the sunlight baked away the worst of the chill.

At first, there was much chatter among the occupants of

the cart. They didn't include Steffan. Eventually, though, the ceaseless steady motion rocked them into sleep or introspection, leaving Steffan alone with his thoughts.

Those thoughts lingered upon the stable and the sweet moments he had enjoyed yesterday. Such unexpected pleasure, stolen from a day which might have ended far differently. It had been worth the risk.

Igraine was not a lady who allowed her women complete freedom in such matters. Igraine was Christian, devoutly so, and the Christians frowned upon couplings outside a marriage. Igraine expected her women to abide by the standards she set for herself.

Once they had returned to Tintagel, Steffan could not put Anwen at further risk of Igraine's wrath by seeking additional moments. It would be unkind.

Besides, there was another factor in play now.

Steffan let his thoughts return to the astonishing moment at the campfire, last night. He had not let himself consider it since it had happened, for doing so brought a great swell of feelings to his chest, and made it ache. Now was the time to carefully explore the possibilities.

After Anwen had dressed and returned to the room Igraine's women were using before she was missed, Steffan reluctantly dressed and returned to the square where the evening meal was being prepared. The dancing had ceased with the end of the day and the descending of the colder night air. Now, fires dotted the square. From the aromas which wafted to him as Steffan weaved between the men huddled around the fires, he judged there were tripods and cooking pots hanging over many of the fires.

With a few questions, he was directed to Cornwall's contingent, where he was given a bowl of stew. He found a flask of wine and asked for and received some bread. Then, because he was free to do so, he searched for firewood of his own and set up a fire where he and Anwen had danced a handful of hours ago. A burning log borrowed from another fire soon had his crackling merrily. He sat downwind of the flames, letting their warmth bathe him, and ate in happy solitude, contemplating where he might find a comfortable bed for the night. Returning to the stable seemed to offer the best opportunity.

The hand which landed on his shoulder to warn him of another's presence was heavy. "You drink alone, Steffan? That isn't like you."

It was Uther's voice, thick with wine.

"Join me, if you wish, my lord," Steffan said.

"For a moment, I will," Uther said. "I need to clear my head."

Steffan heard him settle heavily beside him. He held out the flask of wine he had been sipping.

"No, thank you," Uther said. "It isn't helping," he added dryly.

Steffan didn't ask what he was referring to. He could guess well enough. He let the silence grow.

Uther let out a heavy breath. "I thought, this morning, that you had not changed at all, but you have changed greatly."

"Have I?"

"You are comfortable with silence. The old Steffan, the one I knew, could not stand silence. Nor inactivity, either. Yet here you are, indulging in both."

"I am thinking," Steffan admitted. "That is not inactivity."

"Which proves my point," Uther said. "You did not think beyond the next battle and the next bed, once."

"Neither did you," Steffan added.

Uther sighed heavily again. "True enough. Now I am beset with problems which require thought."

Steffan did not ask him what problems he had. He suspected the night would wane while Uther listed them. Any king's list of problems would be long, and Uther was adjusting to the High King's chair, too. "Then you must stay and share my silence. Problems seem smaller when you can draw a peaceful breath."

Uther dropped another log on the fire, which hissed and crackled. "Is that what it takes?" he asked.

"Solitude helps," Steffan admitted. "I suspect solitary moments are rare for you."

Uther laughed. "So rare I cannot name the last."

"Well, then." Steffan let the silence grow. The next time he sipped, and held out the flask, Uther took it.

Uther fed two more logs to the fire before either of them spoke once more. He rearranged his cloak over his knees, which washed heated air from the fire over Steffan's face. "I have thousands of problems, yet I can only think of one."

"Ah." Steffan hesitated. "She is my lady, Uther. Loyalty requires I defend her position and honor."

"I am your High King."

"Not quite yet," Steffan pointed out. "And even if you were crowned, I would still be sworn to Gorlois and his wife. I point that out only to caution you in what you say. If Gorlois was to question me about this conversation, I would be truthful."

Uther made an impatient sound. "We once shared everything and it has remained between us since…or has it not?"

"I have spoken of those times with no one," Steffan assured him.

"Ah…those times!" Uther sighed. "They are moments far back in history now, it seems." He paused. "I have missed you as I have not missed many companions who have come and gone over the years, Steffan. I rue the day the Saxons stole your sight from you, for they stole a friend, too." His voice grew harsher. "It is one more insult they have added to the pile which makes me determined to rid this land of them. Here, take this before I finish it. I have had too much already. My tongue is loosened."

Steffan held out his hand and Uther thrust the flask back into it.

"You know that nothing you say here will travel," Steffan assured him. "No matter how loose your tongue."

"Except I cannot speak of the one thing I must," Uther said, his voice tight.

"No, you should not speak of that," Steffan said in agreement.

Uther made another harsh sound in the back of his throat. "You should leave Gorlois and come and serve me, Steffan. Then this silly problem would not exist."

Steffan held himself still, his heart thudding. "You would employ a useless blind man just to speak freely?"

"Why not?" Uther said, his voice still harsh. "I know Tintagel well from the times when I lodged there and spied upon Vortigern for Ambrosius. I know its bleakness. You must not be happy there, with the women and children. You were a warrior, Steffan. One of the finest despite your age. You cannot tell me you do not miss it. You and I are alike in that regard. I would hate any life but this one."

Steffan swallowed. His heart was doing more than thudding, now. It seemed to be lodged in the base of his throat, making his chest ache. "What could *I* do to serve you?"

Uther's voice was warm. "I recall at least two men rolling upon the cobbles just here, this morning. You must show me how you use that staff of yours, one day. It is an unexpected weapon, which are the very best kind."

"Dropping drunk fools is one thing," Steffan said, his voice hoarse. "I would be useless in a real battle."

"That is not why I ask you to join me," Uther said. There was a touch of the old impatience in his voice. "I don't think you realize how few people I can trust."

"You are surrounded by good men," Steffan said.

"All of them with lands and people of their own they must protect first, even against the High King's wishes. I know that. So do they. It layers every conversation, no matter how much we see eye to eye." Uther paused. "You have no lands," he added gently.

The tension in his chest and belly tightened even further. Steffan said carefully, "I thank you for the offer, my lord."

"My lord?" Uther chuckled. "That is an unsubtle reminder of the difference in our positions. You were less choosy, once."

"As were you, although you are to be High King, Uther. If I were to linger in your court with no visible use than as an ear for you to vent upon, then those who plot against you—and there will be such men, for every powerful man draws them—those men would know I am a weakness they can exploit to manipulate you."

Uther laughed. "You are not weak, Steffan. That was why I assumed you had not changed at all, this morning. You are anything but weak. You think I would make such an offer to anyone who was? I have learned a thing or two from my brother about vulnerabilities." He made another soft impatient sound. "Think about it," he urged Steffan. "Now is not the time to commit yourself. In the sober light of day, you can consider the idea."

"We return to Tintagel at first light, now you have released Gorlois," Steffan pointed out.

"I will be moving on tomorrow, too. The court will be in Venta Belgarum until spring. The coronation will be there and Gorlois must attend." He added softly, "No matter how reluctant he may now be."

Steffan listened to him get to his feet and rearrange the cloak around him. "Good night, Steffan."

"Good night, my lord."

Uther sighed.

Steffan added, "Sleep well, Uther."

"I doubt it," Uther muttered.

He had moved on, leaving Steffan alone at the fire with his racing thoughts and overworked heart. Steffan had finished the flask, trying to control the hot flare of hope and excitement. In the end, the only way he could clamp down on both was to dismiss the subject every time his thoughts returned to it.

Now, though, as the cart jolted over every rut and tussock, Steffan let himself reconsider Uther's suggestion.

What sort of friend would he be to Uther, if he accepted his offer? What sort of man would Steffan be to abandon Gorlois at the first opportunity? Gorlois had given Steffan a place and work, when he had been obliged to do neither. When Steffan's use as a soldier expired, Gorlois would have been perfectly in his rights to discard him and let him find his own way in the world. He had not, which spoke much about the man.

Steffan could not now desert him. He was serving a purpose. A small purpose, it was true, but not an insignificant one.

Yet, to serve Uther…to be part of the court and the army once more, in any capacity at all…! To be surrounded by the men Steffan admired—the leaders and loyal companions, the morally upright and good men Uther and Ambrosius before him had attracted… Steffan's heart thumped at the prospect.

It was the life he missed, that he had tried to explain to Anwen. And now he could reach out and have it once more.

Anwen…

He sighed.

Yesterday, the entire delightful day, must be the start and end of the matter. For her sake…and maybe for his, too.

A hand cupped his calf and squeezed. Steffan jumped. He had heard nothing above the creak of the cart and the wheels turning sluggishly.

Anwen's thin, long-fingered hand rested over his for a moment. She must be walking, to have approached so silently.

Then he realized there was something in her hand. He turned his over, so the object settled on his palm.

Anwen's hand lifted away. "Merry Christmas," she murmured, her voice drifting backward as she slowed her pace and fell back behind the cart.

The spherical object was warm in his hand. Steffan lifted it and sniffed. Rich, fruity sweetness with not a hint of bitterness.

It was an apricot.

Abruptly, Steffan was back to questioning the future, doubts tearing at him.

Chapter Fifteen

nwen did not have to search out Steffan from among the hundreds of people spread out between the trees. Everyone huddled about roaring camp-fires as last of the daylight disappeared and the cooking pots simmered. Or they carried food and furs and cushions from the carts or took care of the horses. The camp was a busy place.

Despite the frantic activity, Anwen's gaze was drawn to Steffan's tall figure as he carried a metal platter heaped with stew away from the fires, his staff waving in an arc over the ground ahead of him.

He was finding a private place to eat.

She watched him tap against the trunk of a mighty oak, carefully navigate over the roots and move around to the other side. That was all she saw, for Igraine's tent had been raised and the cushions and furs needed to be arranged inside before Igraine retired.

Igraine was pale from the day's uncomfortable travel. She was quiet, too. Her gaze would flicker toward Gorlois, who was eating with his officers. She ate little.

It was not Anwen's place to draw Igraine out. Anwen was the least favored and most frequently ignored of Igraine's companions. The women Igraine sought for company and gossip must tend to her preoccupation, instead.

The matter was straightforward enough in Anwen's mind. Igraine was married and a Christian. She would be breaking her own religious vows to take Uther as a lover, no matter how kindly she felt toward him. Gorlois would not like it, either. Even though Uther was the High King, and such a liaison would confer favor and power upon Cornwall *and* Gorlois, Gorlois was a family man. He loved his children and his affection for Igraine was immense. He was also a Christian and would be forced to defend Igraine and Cornwall, if Uther pressed his attentions upon her.

The liaison simply could not take place. Igraine must surely understand that. She was not a stupid woman.

Anwen sat alone on the chilly side of the fire, staring at the dancing flames as she ate, her thoughts shifting from Igraine to Steffan. He had not emerged from behind the oak. He clearly intended to stay there for the night.

He had not reacted to her Christmas gift. He had not sought her out to speak to her at all.

Such things happened between men and women, Anwen assured herself. She remembered now the gossip of the women, bewailing a man who moved on, discarding them after a single dalliance. It was the way of it. Men were not easily tethered.

Now Anwen could say she had been discarded, too. Upon reflection, it was to be expected. She had no dowry, her father was not a king or a lord. She had finally come to understand she would never be married. A continuing relationship with a man was even less likely. She simply did not have the womanly assets to hold a man. She was not pretty or young or accomplished in the way men appreciated in a wife. She sewed badly, the yarn she spun was always uneven and inclined to break. She could not weave good cloth, either. She would rather read books than tend plants and gather food…no, she would not make a good wife *or* companion.

It was therefore only reasonable that Steffan would not seek her out a second time. She had nothing to offer him.

Yet she found herself on her feet and moving across the campsite, anyway. She stepped around people and slipped through them, weaving a path toward the oak. The firelight played redly upon the wide trunk and she could see nothing but night shadows beyond it.

For the first time Anwen appreciated always being overlooked. No one would notice her cross the campsite, nor the direction she was heading. The gossips were blind to what she did now.

Trembling, Anwen moved around the oak.

Clearly, Steffan had spent his time since the carts had stopped collecting gear and bringing it here. He laid upon furs and more covered him. A small fire burned on the earth in front of him, and the oak guarded his back.

His staff rested against the tree, an arm's length away.

He looked up as Anwen's feet crunched on the frosty ground.

"It is only me," Anwen told him.

"Only you smell as you do," Steffan replied, sitting up.

Anwen settled on her knees in front of him, the fire warming her flank. "I will go if you want me to," she said softly, speaking hurriedly. "Only, it occurred to me that you would not find me among everyone, if you had a mind to. So I came to you, to save you the problem…if it is a problem you want solved, that is."

Her chest and throat hurt, and her heart pounded in her ears as she waited for Steffan to respond.

His sightless gaze met hers. How did he do that? It was as if he really could see her.

"The gods above…" he breathed. "You have such courage."

She swallowed and made herself say crisply, "I am merely being practical."

Steffan's mouth pressed against hers and she lost the air in her lungs with a soft gasp, as he kissed her.

Then he drew back. His gaze was steady. "I will not compromise your position any further than I have."

It hurt. It hurt more than she had braced herself for. Anwen let her eyes close and her mouth tremble. He would see none of her agony. She held her teeth together so she did not make a single sound which might betray her.

"Do you understand, Anwen?" Steffan added. "Igraine is Christian. She would not look upon—"

"Of course I understand," Anwen said, using the same crisp tone. She got to her feet. "I *said* I would go if you wanted me to, and so I shall. I apologize for disturbing your rest."

She hurried away, her heart throwing itself against her chest.

"Anwen!" Steffan called behind her.

She didn't stop. As soon as she was among the other people around the fires, he would never find her, for she would be invisible once more.

ILSA FOUND BAN AND HIS smaller company of men off to one side of the large royal host preparing to leave Amesbury at first light. Ban's normally handsome face was drawn in lines of weariness which had grown steadily deeper over the last few weeks.

He held Ilsa in a long, warm hold, then took her letters. "Of course I will deliver them to Elaine, and Evaine, too," he said, tucking them in his belt pouch. "It will be my great pleasure." His breath blew frost into the air.

Ilsa patted his arm. "It will do you good to go home," she said gently.

"Home…" he muttered. "It will be like starting all over again," he added, with a hint of bitterness.

"Will you tell Elaine about…" Ilsa hesitated. "The child?" she finished.

"I must," Ban said, his bitterness rising and twisting his voice. "If Elaine is not able to bear a child, then this bastard will be my heir." His mouth turned down.

A horn sounded, gathering the host, warning them to be ready to ride. Ilsa wrung her hands. "It has not all been wasted time," she told him quickly. "We have done great good here, Ban. Uther will not forget that. Britain will not. There is peace, the first in years and years. You can be proud of that. So can Elaine."

Ban scanned the company as men climbed onto their horses in response to the warning. "If this is what peace looks like…" He blew out his breath. "There was more glory in war," he said shortly.

"When your son and true-born heir sits upon your knee, at

your hearth, with Elaine by your side, you will appreciate peace," Ilsa assured him.

"I hope so." He swung up onto his horse. "We fought for seven years. There must be more we fought for than petty squabbling among bored kings."

The second horn sounded, forcing Ilsa to turn and run for her horse, before the company moved off. There was no time to say more. She wasn't sure there was anything she *could* say to counter Ban's disillusionment.

She could only hope that Elaine's arms would comfort him.

GORLOIS' LARGE COMPANY HAD BEEN on the road for several hours and the sun had burned off the last of the mist, when Igraine gathered her hems up in one arm and jumped from the cart while it was still moving.

Igraine dropped her gown and smoothed it down, waiting for Anwen to reach where she stood. She gave Anwen a small smile, her full lips turning up at the corners. "I thought I might walk for a while. It could not possibly be any more un-comfortable than another day upon the cart." She turned and matched Anwen's pace.

Anwen hid her mild irritation. She had been walking alone, which let her think. A night of heavy thinking had left her tired and still without hope. She was still dependent upon

Igraine's goodwill and always would be. Things had returned to exactly where they had been through all the long years.

"This ground is rather rough, isn't it?" Igraine commented.

Anwen glanced at Igraine's slippers. "We can walk on the grass at the edge of the road," she suggested.

"Yes, that might help."

They edged closer to the side of the road, which let Igraine walk on the softer growth, while Anwen continued on the dirt which had been compressed by traffic into a flat, frozen path. The sun had burned off the frost which had left it white and glistening. Now it was merely a dark, damp route through the trees.

Walking along the side of the road put them out of listening distance of anyone on the carts which moved beside them.

Igraine glanced at the cart she had been traveling in, which was now farther ahead than they. "What did you think of Amesbury, Anwen?"

"I didn't see much of it," Anwen admitted. "The standing stones are majestic, of course."

"A fitting tribute for Ambrosius, and for the leaders who died at Vortigern's hand."

"Indeed," Anwen said. "Did you meet Merlin, my lady?"

"I did."

"Is it true he is taller than any man alive? And his eyes spark fire?"

"You didn't see him at the standing stones?"

Anwen dropped her gaze to her feet. She hadn't been looking at the stones. "No," she admitted.

"Merlin is a normal man," Igraine said. "Although he is younger than I expected. He *is* tall, but no taller than any other man. Uther is just as tall…although they are blood kin."

"Then Merlin has red hair, too?"

Igraine shook her head. "Uther's cousin, Ilsa, has the same red hair, but no one else in their family." She glanced along the road, toward the head of the column. "Uther is the only man."

Anwen sensed Igraine was not speaking of hair color now. She said carefully, "Uther, the High King."

Igraine pressed her lips together. "Yes," she said, with a sigh.

"Of course, Gorlois has red hair, too," Anwen pointed out.

"It is fading now," Igraine said. "As he grows older."

Anwen hesitated. "As he is your husband, surely it does not matter? Gorlois has many admirable qualities. He is fiercely loyal to the High King."

Igraine flinched. She stopped walking, forcing Anwen to turn back to face her. Igraine's face worked. Her hands trembled. "God help me, Anwen," she breathed, so softly Anwen barely heard it. "I cannot stop thinking about him! Even now, all I can see is his face. His eyes. The…the passion there."

She put her hand on her belly, her fingers spread.

Anwen glanced around uneasily, to see who noticed that the Duchess had halted and appeared to be stressed. She took Igraine's arm. "Keep walking."

Igraine obeyed.

Their steps were slower than before, although they would not draw attention, now.

"You must let this go, my lady," Anwen said firmly. "You know that as well as I do. As a Christian…"

Igraine sighed. "I have prayed for guidance. None comes."

Anwen shook her head. "You need none. The facts are simple, my lady. If you indulge yourself in this, you will tear the kingdom apart, just when Ambrosius and Uther put it back together again."

"I know that," Igraine said. "I know it all too well. I am not a vapid woman, yearning for romance and adventure. I was raised to consider the political side of everything. I know it is impossible. Yet I cannot rid myself of the memory of him. It is as though, now I have seen him, I can see nothing else. If I was permitted by the Church to believe in magic, Anwen, I would say I have been bewitched."

She spoke quite seriously.

"You must keep that to yourself," Anwen said quickly. "There are many others who *do* believe in witchcraft and they would not look kindly upon a woman of your rank professing to be the victim of a spell."

Igraine chewed at her lip thoughtfully. Her gaze shifted to Anwen. "Of course, you are right."

Anwen relaxed. "I am sure Yvette and Mary told you the same thing, when you explained it to them." Yvette and Mary were Igraine's closest companions, the ones she trusted with everything.

Igraine shook her head. "I dare not tell them," she said, her voice low. "They have husbands, and an indiscrete word, perhaps to entertain their husband…it would be the ruin of me."

Anwen let out a deeper breath. At least Igraine had enough sense left to be cautious.

"Have you never yearned for a man, Anwen?" Igraine asked, her voice still soft. "Do you not know even a little of what I am feeling?"

"I do know, my lady," Anwen said stiffly. Truthfully.

"Ah…" Igraine said, sounding both surprised and satisfied.

Anwen's heart ached. She kept her gaze down.

"Then we have something in common, after all," Igraine added.

"Something *else*," Anwen corrected her.

"Oh?"

"Anwen! Anwen!" The cart which Morgan and Morguase rode upon had drawn level with Anwen and Igraine. Morgan waved fiercely. "Look at the rainbow, Anwen! See it! And it hasn't rained at all! It's just there!"

Anwen glanced at the rainbow on the horizon, painted up-on black clouds. "It means there is rain where the rainbow is, Morgan. Or mist or fog, or moisture in the air."

"I would not have known that," Igraine admitted. "All it takes is damp air?"

"And sunlight," Anwen added.

Morguase leaned against the side of the cart, her chin on her hands. "I'm bored," she said, pouting. "I want Steffan to give us a lesson."

"I don't know where Steffan is," Anwen told her.

"He's in the cart five up from ours," Morgan said instantly. "Tell him to come and teach us, please?"

Anwen smiled. "This is supposed to be a holiday for you, Morgan."

Morgan's smile was angelic. "Learning things *is* fun."

Morguase's pout deepened. "Mother, please tell Anwen to fetch Steffan. I want a story."

Igraine glanced at Anwen. "Perhaps, to distract them…?"

"There is no room on the cart for him," Anwen pointed out.

"He can walk alongside," Morguase said quickly.

"He cannot see where he is walking," Anwen said, hiding her impatience.

"He can keep one hand on the cart," Morguase said.

"Go and fetch him, Anwen," Igraine said, her tone firm.

She lifted her hems and hurried along the road to catch up with her cart, caught hold of the railing and jumped onto it with a graceful movement.

Anwen was left standing on the side of the road, alone as she had wished, only now the fragile acceptance she had formed was shattered.

THE DRIVER TAPPED STEFFAN'S SHOULDER to draw his attention. "There be a lady walking beside the cart," he said in a scratched voice. "On your right."

Steffan turned his head in that direction. People would not speak to him if he didn't appear to be looking at them.

"Oh!" the driver said, startled. "Oops! Careful there, lady."

"I'm fine, thank you," Anwen said breathlessly.

It sounded as though she was on the cart itself. Had she leapt on to it?

"Steffan, I'm sorry to intrude, only the girls and Lady Igraine are asking for you. Morguase wants a story and Morgan wishes to learn something. Can you jump off the cart without seeing? Or should the cart stop?"

Steffan frowned. Her voice. What was it about her voice? It stroked his spine with soft fingers.

"Steffan?" Anwen repeated.

He stirred. "A story?" he said, keeping his voice even. "I

can give them a story."

"I should stop the cart," the driver said, alarm building in his voice.

"There's no need," Steffan told him.

"You can't jump!" the driver cried.

Steffan pulled up his feet and got to them and reached for the side of the cart. It was hip-high, made of undressed timber, the bark dry and flaking. He swooped his hand toward the front end of the railing and gripped the edge. "Anwen?"

"I'm here."

"The road is flat here?"

"Flat enough," she assured him.

He nodded and tucked his staff under his arm, and swung himself out of the cart and sideways, onto the road. It was a heavy landing, because he didn't know where the ground was, exactly, although he had braced himself for the shock of it.

"Oh!" Anwen exclaimed, as he heard someone land beside him.

"You don't have to come with me," he told her. "Rest on the cart—sit where I was." The cart groaned and rumbled as it went past them.

"I will have to guide your hand to the side of the cart the girls are upon," Anwen said. Irritation colored her tone. "There is no room for you to sit upon it. You must walk beside them."

Steffan considered it. "Is there room on the road for me and the cart?"

"Yes." She gripped his wrist. "The cart comes. I will put your hand on the side." Her voice came from behind him now. How close was she? The soft fingers played upon his spine one more time.

She extended his hand.

"Steffan! Steffan!" Morgan's voice, excitement lifting it high.

All Steffan was aware of was her fingers upon his flesh. He thought he could feel the heat of her behind him. It might have been just the two of them, once more, twined upon the straw....

"Now," Anwen breathed, her voice low and something jumped in Steffan's middle.

She pulled on his arm and his fingers brushed wood railings. He had the sense to grip them and let himself be tugged into walking forward, his pace matching the cart, his heart climbing from his chest.

"You did it!" Morguase cried. She clapped her hands.

For a frightening moment of near panic, Steffan fought to stay on his feet and not be dragged along. Where was Anwen? Was she still behind him? Had she remained still and was now far behind?

Where was she?

Morgan patted Steffan's hand. "Breton today!" she demanded.

"No, Latin," Morguase insisted, for she was more familiar with Latin and didn't have to work so hard to understand it.

Just as the cart was pulling Steffan along, the girls' demands hauled his thoughts back to the mundane and the ordinary. He grabbed it and held on, making himself recall simple Latin phrases he could teach the girls, plus the stories which went with them.

This is as it will always be, he told himself as the lesson progressed. This simple life is all that is left for me.

And before the abject protests could properly form in his mind, he shoved them aside and concentrated on the lesson, instead.

Chapter Sixteen

here was no warning. No fumbling at the door, no tap of a staff along the cold stone corridors. Anwen only realized he was there when the door opened silently to avoid raising the alarm.

She was awake, even though it was late. It was the first night of their return to Tintagel. After days on the road, her bed was far too soft and warm. As the fortress grew silent, as the corridors emptied and everyone slept, her thoughts chased themselves in endless circles.

Even though her room was on the courtyard side of the tower, Tintagel was so silent and still she could hear and feel the waves crashing against the cliff the fortress was built upon.

The restlessness of the water matched her innards.

When the door eased open, Anwen sat up instantly. Her heart, which had not slowed for sleep at all, now accelerated beyond reason, hurting her chest with its wild beating.

In the moonlight, Steffan's face was pale. He shut the door and leaned against it. "I shouldn't be here," he breathed.

"Yet you are."

"I couldn't...I should stay away."

"If you think you must because of me, then you are wrong."

He grew still. "Why do you say that?"

Anwen moved to where he stood. She didn't touch him. Not yet, even though he was warm and her fingers tingled in anticipation of stroking his flesh. "No one cares about either of us, except for the letters I teach and the stories you tell. Why should we care what they think?"

"Igraine would not approve and we both must preserve her good will."

Anwen could resist no longer. She pressed her hand against his chest, over the warm leather which covered it. "Then we will fail to inform her."

Still, he did not move. "I feel..." She saw his throat work in the moonlight which spilled through the narrow window. "I'm being torn in two," he breathed.

"Go, then," she whispered. "Go on. Open the door and step out. I won't stop you."

He let out a soft exhalation and remained where he was. "I don't know why I came here."

"Yes, you do," she breathed and kissed him.

His staff clattered as it came to rest in the corner of the

room. He pulled her against him. His arm was a strong band around her, keeping her there. He held her face and took control of the kiss, making it deeper.

When he drew her to the bed, she went willingly, wanting the tiny sliver of happiness it provided.

AFTERWARD, WHEN THEIR HEARTS HAD calmed and their breath, too, Steffan raised above her, his gaze upon her face.

"You are in moonlight," he breathed.

Her heart jumped. "How did you know?"

"I can...*almost* see you," he breathed. His voice was hoarse with excitement, even pleasure.

Panic touched her. Anwen brought her hand to her face, shielding it. She tried to roll out of the light. He held her in place.

"No, don't move!" he begged. "Let me see. Stay still."

Anwen shoved against his shoulder. "No!" She sat up, sliding out of the silvery glimmer and out of his hold, pushing herself into the dark corner of the bed. She wrapped her arms around her and shivered.

Steffan didn't move. He didn't try to pull her back into the light. Because his back was to the window, she could not see anything but the stark plains of his cheeks and the shadowed hollows of his eyes. His jaw flexed. "*That* terrifies you..." he breathed.

Anwen tightened her arms. "I would rather you go on see-ing me as you have painted me in your mind."

"Why? You are not ugly."

"I am!"

He shook his head. "I have explored every tiny part of your face. I have tasted it. I have run my hands over every inch of your body and felt you beneath me. You are soft and supple and warm, and nothing about your face would make any man look askance."

"Not that any man looks in the first place." Her voice was as strained as his had been a moment ago. "And do not say it is their misfortune. I know what I am."

Steffan reached for her. His fingers swept over her elbow, then down her arm to her wrist. He took her wrist and pulled. Gently. "You can relax. The moment of clarity has gone. Even if you were in full moonlight, I would see nothing but the golden shadow that is you, now." The bitterness in his voice surprised her enough that she allowed him to draw across the bed, and up against him.

"I'm sorry," she breathed.

He shook his head. "It is not my lot to see. These moments of clarity are provided to remind me of what I have lost, so I don't grow complacent or content."

"Why should you not be content?" she whispered.

"I suppose…to remind me of my place," he breathed and kissed her. "I need the reminder, for when you are in my arms, humility is the last thing I feel."

She thumped his shoulder. "Do not jest like that. It is the worst sort of teasing."

"I wasn't teasing." He kissed her again, stealing her response, making her forget the last few moments and the fear which had swamped her. She followed Steffan's lead and let herself believe she was worthy of this simple happiness and joy.

In his arms, she was beautiful—as long as he could not see her.

THE LARGE GROUP OF ROBBERS had been desperate indeed to attack a well-armed and large contingent of King's men. Hunger drove them to a vicious offensive only hours after Uther's company had left Amesbury.

The robbers fell upon the middle of the column, where the carts hauling food and supplies were, taking on anyone who stood between them and the carts. Ilsa had drawn her short sword instinctively, even though she wore no armor and was not upon her war horse. She had been riding upon a cart with Alun, Eren and Arawn Uther. She had learned that when the company traveled, it was always a good opportunity to spend time with the three.

While her children hid in the corner of the cart, Ilsa rose to her feet, drawing her sword. The first brigand was easily dealt with because he wasn't expecting resistance or weapons from a woman. She brought the sword flashing from between the folds of her gown, to pierce his heart and stop him in his tracks even before his ax was fully raised.

He fell back soundlessly. Already another robber climbed onto the cart behind him. The man wore rags and his teeth were black stumps. The fury in his eyes at being challenged made him dangerous. Ilsa brought the sword up to the ready position.

Around her, she could hear the clash of sword against sword and other weapons, the cries of men and women. There were few women left in Uther's entourage.

Ilsa ignored them. She did not wonder where Arawn was or how he fared. After eight years of campaigning, she had learned to starve her imagination until the fighting was done.

The man leapt at her. She could not afford to side-step him and deliver a blow that way, for the children cowered behind her. Instead, she angled the sword upward and as he moved into range, it was easy to punch the sharp tip in under his chin. His impetus drove the sword into his skull.

He grunted and twitched.

A third man she had not seen reached around the second

and slammed his dagger into her belly.

The second man had sacrificed himself to secure her blade so the third could attack with impunity. She could not withdraw her sword easily.

She could withdraw the knife, though, for the fool had let go of the handle, grinning victoriously.

Ilsa gripped the hilt and pulled it out. The pain the movement caused was enough to snap her fully alert and aware, shaking off the shock of the blow. She flipped the knife and rammed it into his chest, just beneath the ribs, angling upward. After so many years of practice, she knew exactly where to aim.

Surprise showed in the man's face. Then his surprise faded. So did his life. His eyes turned glassy as she watched.

Both bodies dropped, pulling her arms down. Pulling *her* down. For the first time, Ilsa was afraid. She was injured and unable to fight. Who would protect the food now? Who would protect her children?

She was already falling and couldn't halt it. She had no strength left.

She folded with a sigh, sinking to the floor of the cart, her eyes closing. That was the last of the skirmish she remembered.

She returned to consciousness some time later—she didn't know how long, although it was long enough for Merlin to have tended her wound. He was still bent over her, stitching the last of it, when she opened her eyes and groaned at the agony.

Merlin's black-eyed gaze shifted to her face, then back to what he was doing. "Arawn is untouched. So are your children. You took out their leader. The fight ceased after that."

Relief was a warm, expanding bubble in her chest. "And me?" she asked, her voice not much more than a whisper.

"You'll live," Merlin said, his tone dry.

A tent had been built quickly for Merlin to treat her—the walls sagged and daylight showed between the roof and the walls. It gave her privacy, though. She was grateful for that.

"You took on three of them, Ilsa?" Merlin shook his head. "Uther laughed when we told him. Even he only dealt with two."

"I had no choice." She hissed as pain flared in her belly. "I really will survive?"

Merlin hesitated. "Yes," he said, his tone flat.

"What is it you will not speak of?" she insisted, for she knew that tone of his. Most mistook the tone for one of arrogance and authority. She knew Merlin used it to hide uncertainty.

Merlin picked up shears and snipped the thread. He dropped the sheers into a bowl and straightened. His gaze met hers. "You *will* live," he assured her. "Only...there will be no more children, Ilsa."

Ilsa's thoughts floundered. Until that moment, she would have said she was quite content with the three children which fate had given her. Now, though, she felt the loss of other children she would never know. "Oh…" she breathed.

Merlin rested his hand on her shoulder. He squeezed gently. "Arawn waits to see you. Are you ready?"

She tried to sit up. His hand kept her still. "No, you must remain this way for a few days, to give the wound time to seal. No bending or stretching."

"We're travelling! I cannot stay here!" Ilsa thought of Uther's drive to reach Venta Belgarum and permanent quarters for his army. He would be irritated if a wounded woman forced him to remain by the side of the road for days. "Uther will be mad," she whispered.

Merlin's smile was small. "I will deal with Uther." He rolled down his sleeves. "I'll send Arawn in."

That had been three days ago. Ilsa had spent the night in the tent, with Arawn at her side. She didn't know what Merlin said to Uther. There was no explosion of curses heard across the camp, which normally alerted everyone to Uther's irritability.

On the second day, as soon as it was fully light, the tent was struck around her. She was lifted onto a pallet on the back of a cart. The day of travel was extraordinarily taxing even though she did nothing but sleep and rest. The jolting of the cart made her body throb and pulse.

Merlin checked her that evening, once the men had built the tent around her once more. He looked grave. "This day of travel has not done you any favors," he said mildly.

Ilsa already knew that, for the throbbing had not faded.

Merlin shook his head. "Complete rest it must be. I will speak to Uther again."

This time, Ilsa heard Uther's bawled complaints when Merlin broke the news. They were too far away from the tent for her to distinguish words among the explosion, although hearing Uther's irritation told her the matter was a minor one. If she had been in grave peril, she suspected Uther's temper would not have been roused at the prospect of delaying the journey for days.

It allowed her to sleep.

She woke to find Arawn sleeping next to her and her children ranged on the other side of the tent. Content, she returned to sleep.

The next day had passed in sleep, too. Merlin made her drink concoctions that let her drift, her thoughts unanchored by day-to-day concerns.

This morning, though, she was properly awake. Everything hurt...only now, the injury did not hurt as much as it had at first. The deep throbbing had gone.

The sound of strident commands outside the hastily erected tent stirred Ilsa with a jerk.

Arawn's hand tightened about hers. "It's only Uther. He insists upon seeing you," he said, smoothing her hair back.

"Oh…" she whispered. Even that much movement hurt.

Arawn got to his feet. He pulled the furs and blankets he had been using out of the way, as the tent flap opened.

Uther ducked under it and straightened. He nodded at Arawn and stood over Ilsa, peering down at her.

Ilsa met his gaze. "It wasn't done to spite you, my lord."

Uther's mouth quirked up. "No, you have far more effective ways of putting me in my place, madam." He crouched, bringing himself closer. "Arawn has argued that I should leave you here and move the army on to Venta Belgarum. We could be there by nightfall if we start at once."

Ilsa glanced at Arawn, startled. Arawn's gaze was steady. "My men would stay with us," Arawn said. "They are numerous enough to keep us secure. After dealing with the last band, word will have passed up and down the road. No one else will bother us."

"Merlin insists you not travel for at least five days more," Uther added. "I can see from your pallor that he is not exaggerating. As much as it pains me to deprive myself of one of my best and most able contingents of men and their leaders, I will agree with Arawn's suggestion."

He glanced at Arawn. "I will leave Merlin here to tend Ilsa until she can travel. Merlin has no fear of traveling alone—he can hide in plain view and no one would dare attack a magician, anyway." His eyes rolled. "He can join me in Venta Belgarum once you can travel again."

Arawn nodded. "Thank you, my lord." His tone was one of deep gratitude.

"*We* join you in Venta Belgarum," Ilsa amended.

"No, Ilsa," Arawn said quietly.

Uther's brows came together. "Arawn has argued strenuously that this is a sign that his service to me and to Britain is at an end."

Ilsa caught her breath. "My lord?"

"We have not seen Lorient in eight years, Ilsa," Arawn said softly. "Our children have never seen it."

Uther glanced at him. "I, too, have not seen Lesser Britain in all that time," he said mildly.

"It was only ever a place of retreat for you," Arawn said, his voice growing strident. "It is my home."

Uther lifted his hand. "Enough, Arawn. You convinced me last night. You and Ilsa should return home." His tone turned bitter. "Just as Ban and Bors and Ector and Pellinore have."

"Britain is peaceful, Uther. You don't need us," Arawn said.

"Britain's High King does not need the King of Brocéliande, his mighty queen and his men, that is true. I, though, will miss your friendship and your counsel." Uther drew in a breath and let it out. "I would have liked to have you there for the coronation, although I will not put Ilsa at greater risk simply to soothe my feelings."

He turned to her, then bent and touched her forehead. "I remember you covered in mud, arguing your claim to a deer was stronger than a king's. We have come a long way, have we not?"

Ilsa's eyes prickled with tears. "You will make a great king, Uther. Ambrosius would be proud of you."

Uther nodded. "Until we meet again, then." He straightened and gripped Arawn's hand. "Fare well."

Then with a whirl of his cloak, Uther turned and strode from the tent.

Chapter Seventeen

Tintagel Fortress, Duchy of Cornwall, 465 C.E. Spring.

ong ago, Steffan had learned to think of winter as a time of rest. Wars were rarely waged in the depth of winter. Instead, fighting men clung to the home hearth, staying warm. The frantic household tasks of summer halted. Fields could not be tended, nothing grew and the days were short.

As Steffan climbed to the top of the tower, he reflected that this winter had not been one of rest, but one of waiting. The expectation of events to come filled the fortress with tension.

Now the events were nearly upon them. Igraine's orchestration of the household in preparation for the High King's coronation at Easter had the entire fortress in an uproar. As they had for Ambrosius' funeral, every able body would travel to Venta Belgarum for Easter.

This time, though, Igraine had the balance of winter to plan, instead of a mere two days. "No more jolting about in carts like sacks of grain," she told her ladies. "No plain mourning for us, either. We will honor the new king with elegance and embellishment."

Igraine's plans kept every woman in the keep sewing frantically by lamplight for weeks, while every man in the household burnished blades, finished armor and polished shields. They turned their hands to unexpected tasks such as building wagons with cushioned benches and roofs.

Trunks were filled. Food was prepared for the journey.

Complaints were frequent, for Igraine maintained a frantic pace, insisting upon more and more. Her focus upon minute details was beyond reason, although no one had the courage to complain where Igraine or Gorlois could hear them.

Steffan and Anwen heard every complaint, eventually. No one paid either of them any notice. They sat in the corner of workrooms and heard every frank opinion and grievance.

Igraine worked Anwen as hard as any of her other companions. Anwen was not a strong seamstress, although basic seams were within her capabilities. The mound of garments at the end of the table waiting to be stitched when Anwen had completed her normal duties rose higher every day. They claimed more space, while Morgan and Morguase squeezed themselves in at the other end.

Anwen spent hours at the table after the evening meal until Steffan snuffed out the lamp, told her she had done enough for the day and drew her to bed.

For a season of tense waiting, Steffan thought he should be more irritable. He had been bored at Dimilioc, which had caused everyone to describe him as angry. Here at Tintagel, while waiting for the journey to Venta Belgarum to begin, he expected the tension would make his temper even more uncertain, but it had not.

He could not forget Uther's offer to take him into service. It lived like a solitary standing stone upon an open plain in his mind. Even when he was occupied with the stitching of leather armor, which he could do by touch, or even while instructing the girls, the stone was there, visible from miles away.

At Venta Belgarum, at Easter, the decision would be made. He would remain in Venta Belgarum at Uther's side. Or he would return here.

He'd thought a season of reflection would bring him closer to a decision. The passing of time, though, had muddied the water, not clarified it. He was further from a clear decision than before. The uncertainty should have added to his temper, too.

Yet this winter of waiting had been placid.

As they climbed to Igraine's antechamber to answer her summons, Steffan recalled the fury which had gripped him the first time he had come here. How differently he felt now!

Days of peace left their mark, as did days of war. He had always considered peace as merely the rare absence of war, although now he understood the healing such peaceful times imparted. They were restorative, just as war was destructive.

Peace was in his heart, despite his dithering over Uther's offer.

Anwen's hand rested on the back of his shoulder. "Two more steps," she warned in an undertone.

He took the two steps and moved into the antechamber, grateful for her warning. She never forgot. It saved him from jarring his knees when he reached the top and his foot did not find a higher level.

Light filled the antechamber. It was a bright day outside and sun-warmed air blew through the large window. Steffan could see the edges of the window, for they were dark against the light beyond.

He could see clouds!

His heart strummed. Steffan halted, gripping his staff tightly.

Yes, thick white clouds which looked dense enough to reach out and pluck them from the sky. The sky was a clear blue. And there, floating on the winds off the cliff, was a merlin. The bird had its wings stretched, the feathers at the tips ruffling as air streamed through them. It hovered, its gaze on the sea below.

What did it see there?

Steffan's throat tightened. How long would this moment last? He was afraid to move, in case movement destroyed it.

"Steffan?" Anwen murmured. His stillness had puzzled her.

Anwen. Steffan drew in a sharp breath, his heart leaping high. Anticipation sizzled in his veins. He spun on his heel to face her and to look at her.

The bright light blurred as he turned. He blinked, holding his breath, only the shapes in his vision did not sharpen their focus. They remained hazy colors, less distinct than the clouds he had just seen.

There was only the golden shape which was Anwen.

Steffan closed his eyes, bitter disappointment tearing at his chest. "No…" he breathed.

"Steffan, what is wrong?" Anwen murmured. "The Duchess comes. You must move out of the way." She tugged on his sleeve. "This way."

Steffan tore his arm out of her grasp. "Don't do that! I am not a sheep!"

He could feel her surprise in her silence but barely acknowledged it in his mind. His heart thudded, each beat hurting.

"She comes…" Anwen said, her tone tense.

Steffan couldn't abide the thought of attending Gorlois and

Igraine, of listening and obeying. He wanted to be alone. He needed to shore his defenses after this last disappointment.

He needed to think. He had spent far too long this winter letting himself drift, avoiding thought and decision. Now he had been reminded.

Steffan turned and strode toward the stairs. He did not use his staff to check the way ahead was clear. Let everyone step aside for him, for once. By the time he reached them, he was nearly running. He pressed his hand against the wall to brake his speed, yet nearly tumbled down the steps. His heels slipped, jarring him and making his heart work even harder.

Now the anger was building. It had been there all along, buried under the balm of warm arms and lips.

Peace was as fragmentary as his vision, and just as unreliable.

As soon as Igraine dismissed everyone, Anwen hurried down the stairs, cannoning into those ahead of her and rattling down them faster than was safe. Her heart worked frantically and not purely because of the neck-risking speed of her descent.

She suspected that Steffan had for a moment been able to see. She had puzzled it out while standing in her usual position on the edge of the room. He had come to a halt, his chin up, facing the big, unshuttered window. Had he seen the sea beyond?

Then he had spun to face her.

He had been turning to see *her*, she was sure of it. Only, by the time he faced her, his vision had faded once more.

Her heart gave an extra thud as she pushed through the people lingering at the bottom of the steps. She hurried down the corridor. There was a door into the yard, farther down. If Steffan followed his usual pattern, he would retreat to the stables to be alone.

Men working stripped to their shirts in the mild spring day filled the yard. Smithies and groomsmen, carpenters and wheel-makers and all manner of craftsmen went about their noisy business. Anwen side-stepped and skipped around a dozen of them before she reached the big door into the primary stable and stepped inside.

The stalls were full of horses and empty of people. She moved through them to the tack rooms beyond.

Steffan stood at a high workbench in the middle of the main room, ramming a shirt she had made him into a saddle bag.

Her heart skipped a beat, hurting.

A young page stood at the end of the workbench, watching Steffan with a wary expression. He saw Anwen and relief painted itself on his face.

She jerked her head. He left, looking pleased.

"Ralph, come back!" Steffan yelled. The boy's steps had told him of Ralph's escape.

"You're leaving?" Anwen asked.

Steffan grew still. Then, with a tiny shrug of his shoulders, he closed the flap of the bag and buckled it.

"You are, then…" She moved closer. "Where are you going?"

"Venta Belgarum."

She drew in a breath, to steady herself. "All of Tintagel leaves for Venta Belgarum in three days."

He shook his head. "I cannot wait that long." He sought for the second buckle.

"Why not? Does a moment of vision make you so humble you must escape everyone here?"

He paused. "You know, then."

"I guessed," she admitted. "You cannot travel alone, Steffan. It is risky for anyone, but for you—"

He rounded on her, his face working with a fury she had not noticed until now. "Do not dare tell me I cannot because I am blind!" he roared.

Anwen stepped back, a gasp escaping her.

Steffan slapped the table. "There was a time where I could ride wherever I wanted. No one would dare try to stop or attack me. I could go *anywhere.*" His jaw flexed. "Now I am confined to a stone fortress on a spit of land surrounded by sea."

"You can still go where you want." Anwen kept her voice soft and even. "No one says you cannot. Only, how will you know you are even upon the right road?"

He rolled his eyes. "I know the way to Isca well enough. The entire country is heading for Venta Belgarum right now. There will be a party in Isca who will let me ride with them."

"You could travel with us," she said quickly. *With me*, she added only in her mind. "Steffan—"

"Uther asked me to serve him," Steffan said, interrupting her. He spoke as if the words were pushed from him unwillingly, as if something drove him to it. It was as if she had not spoken at all.

Anwen pressed her clenched fist against her heart. "Uther?"

"In Amesbury, after the funeral," Steffan added. "He wants me. He has need of my services."

Anwen could barely breathe for the tight band constricting her chest and her throat. "He wants you to fight for him?"

"He wants me to help him. To listen. To talk." He turned back to fastening the last buckle.

"You can go back to your world..." she whispered.

Steffan picked up the saddle bag and moved around the workbench toward the door. He knew the way well enough that he didn't need his staff, which was propped against the door. He picked up the staff and turned his head, as if he looked at her. "I'm needed there. *Me.* Not a makeshift tutor."

Anwen forced herself to speak despite the painful knot in her throat. "Then you should go, of course."

His eyes widened. He hesitated. His knuckles where he gripped the staff whitened.

"Go," she whispered.

He bent and pressed his lips to hers. The kiss did not rouse her senses as it might normally. Even though Steffan seemed to be trying to say so much with the simple gesture, she was too numb to understand.

He let her go and strode through the stable and was gone, leaving only an after image of his silhouette framed by the big door burned upon her mind.

Even when she closed her eyes, she could see him still.

Chapter Eighteen

It was a relief to step into the great keep, out of the noise and bustle of the busy streets of the great city. Although, even here, haste and activity battered Steffan's ears, making it hard to distinguish voices.

"This way," the boy said cheerfully.

"*Which* way?" Steffan asked.

"Oh, right." The boy gripped his staff. "Here." He tugged.

Steffan held in his protest and allowed the boy to lead him through the stuffed corridors and passages. Up two flights of stairs. Everywhere, there were people. Venta Belgarum was a city in the throes of celebration and the fortress was the beating heart of the preparations.

The boy opened another door and came to a halt three paces inside. "Steffan of Durnovaria," he announced.

"I'll let the King know," someone murmured.

Steffan heard an inner door open and close.

"Steffan. It's Merlin." The hand on his shoulder was friendly enough. "Has Gorlois arrived, then?"

"He and his household are at least three days behind me," Steffan said. He paused. "I'm no longer in the Duke's service," he added.

"Uther's, then?" Merlin's tone made it sound as though he was smiling. Steffan remembered the black-haired and black-eyed young man from Doward. He had rarely smiled.

"If Uther will have me. He asked, in Amesbury."

Another voice said, "The King wants to see you right now. This way."

Merlin turned Steffan's shoulder with a slight pressure. "Straight ahead," he murmured. "We can speak, afterwards."

Steffan found the door with the tip of his staff and felt it was open. He moved forward warily. Thick furs came under his feet.

"Steffan," Uther said. "You traveled alone, all the way from Cornwall?" His voice grew nearer. "I'm pleased you are here. Give me your hand."

Steffan lifted his hand and Uther gripped it firmly.

"I am here to serve, as you asked me to, in Amesbury," Steffan said.

"I hoped you would change your mind." Uther let his hand go. "These last few months have been trying indeed. Arawn returned to Brittany just after mid-winter, which left me with damn few men I trust. More than half the faces around me these days are those of strangers, sent by kings from afar to have an ear in my court."

"I heard a dozen different languages on the way from the gates to the castle," Steffan said. "Most of them I've never heard before."

"There is even a man here from the Emperor of Eastern Rome," Uther said. His voice was strained. "He's demanding fealty, as if Britain is still a province of Rome. I've sent him packing twice, yet he keeps returning."

"You sound tired."

"More than tired," Uther admitted. "Ah, there is still a thousand things to see to before this madness is over."

Steffan wondered if the madness which strained Uther would end once he was confirmed as High King. He said, instead, "What can I do to help?"

Uther's hand settled on Steffan's shoulder. "Being here is help enough. For now, Steffan, I must meet with an eastern potentate, I'm told. Have my steward find you a room and a soft bed and recover from your travels. I will send for you as soon as I have need of you."

Steffan bowed. "Thank you, my lord." He turned and found the door once more. It was closed again. He fumbled with the latch until it opened and stepped out.

The conversation in the antechamber ceased when he appeared. Then even more quiet whispers broke out.

"Merlin?" Steffan called.

A hand on his arm. "Here," Merlin said.

"I'm to find a room."

"I know one you can use. It's beside mine. Come. I'll show you the way." Instead of gripping Steffan's sleeve and tugging, Merlin picked up his left wrist and curled his fingers around Merlin's arm.

"You must hold on," Merlin said, his tone even softer. "There are too many rugs and furs and clutter for you to trip upon. Keep your staff out."

Steffan appreciated both the warning and the way Merlin guided him. It took the sting out of being led.

He waited until they had moved out of the antechamber and were traversing the passage beyond it. The passage felt wide yet muffled. Furs and rugs, Steffan presumed, for it was not unforgiving stone beneath his feet.

"Uther sounds strained," he murmured.

Merlin's tone was light. "Politics is not Uther's greatest strength, as we both know." He paused, as they turned into another corridor. A narrower one, this time, and there were no rugs. "If you are here to help, that is where you can help him, for I will not always be here."

"You help Uther with politics? I thought magic and medicine were your forte."

"What is magic and healing, if they are not other forms of

power?"

Steffan considered it. "I see, yes." It was his turn to hesitate. "I am a fighter, Merlin. Politics is not my forte, either."

"You *were* a fighter, which is why Uther trusts you. You're much more than that, now." Merlin's tone was sincere.

Startled, Steffan could find no response.

Merlin did not seem to need one. He continued. "Uther commands the loyalty of fighting men. You know that. You've seen it at work. He makes men willing to follow him anywhere, including into death."

"I have seen it," Steffan said. "I have felt it," he added.

"What he does not know is how to win the hearts and minds of ordinary people," Merlin finished. "Here we are." A door opened and Merlin moved through it.

Steffan tapped out the doorway and stepped through, too. The room was airy and felt large. He would explore it later. He turned back to where he presumed Merlin was standing. "Why does Uther not know how to deal with ordinary people?" he demanded. "It is simple enough. By being a good man, who lives according to his values, Uther will win over anyone."

"You're thinking of Gorlois, of course," Merlin said.

"The perfect example," Steffan said.

"Yes," Merlin said. "Although it is odd to have you of all people say it."

"Why?"

"You and Uther were much alike when we first met."

Steffan was startled. "Are we not still alike?"

"Not at all," Merlin said. "You have not changed physically. That is the only way you have not changed." He paused. "You studied the eastern philosophers in your search for answers, did you not?"

"How did you know that?"

"I have spoken to Cador at length. The values you instilled in him shine through everything he says. I recognized their roots."

"Cador is well, then?" Cador had remained behind with Uther's company when Gorlois had returned to Cornwall.

"He flourishes," Merlin said. Then he added, his voice rising, "You want something, Madog?"

A soft sound behind Steffan made him turn.

"The eunuch," Madog said. "I heard you were visiting. I had to come and see for myself. And I find you in the company of the black bastard. How fitting."

Steffan held his face immobile.

"Madog, you've been misinformed," Merlin said, his tone light. Nothing in his voice revealed how he felt about the epithet Madog had used for him. "Steffan is not visiting. He is Uther's man, now."

Madog made a choked sound.

"What was that?" Merlin asked.

"Just stay out of my way, eunuch," Madog snarled.

"Done," Steffan said flatly. "Unless…do you spend your time in the King's chamber?"

"From the smell of it, I'd say no," Merlin said. "The field by the cow barn, Madog?"

Madog made another straggled sound. His footsteps receded.

Merlin laughed.

"*Please* tell me what his expression was when you told him I was here to stay," Steffan begged.

Merlin did, in satisfying detail.

VENTA BELGARUM WAS OVERWHELMING IN its size and grandeur. Anwen had never seen a city before and the scale and the people were hard to adjust to. She was grateful that today she had been permitted to ride in one of the covered wagons instead walking or riding one of the geldings brought for the ladies to use. While in the wagon, she didn't have to watch her footing or control a mount. She could peer through the window, instead, letting her gaze sweep back and forth as she took in the marvelous pageantry and sights.

Everywhere, there was color—in the pennants fluttering from the walls of the city, in the drapes at the windows, to the

astonishing range and variation of gowns and accessories upon the women in the streets. Even the men wore colorful
cloaks and tunics.

The buildings were painted in gay colors, too, and the
paint looked fresh.

The streets were narrow, taking up minimal space so as
many buildings could be squeezed behind the walls as possible. The horses clopped on the cobbles, although the sound
was barely discernable over the shouts and calls and noise so
many people made.

Anwen brushed at the good, new cloth of her gown. Like
all Igraine's ladies, she had been given new clothes for the
journey and a lovely gown with gold embroidery for the coronation itself and the feast, afterwards. She had considered the
garments to be far too sophisticated. Now the gown she wore
felt plain in comparison to the multi-colored, many layered
ensembles she could see upon the street.

Igraine had anticipated this grandeur. Anwen recalled
Igraine's manic preparations for the journey and her strident
demands for more and better quality everything. Only now did
Anwen appreciated that foresight. Cornwall's arrival matched
the great city's shining welcome. They were not the poor kingdom in the south.

By emptying Tintagel and most of Dimilioc of the people
there, Igraine had swelled the Cornwall contingent to a com-

pany of over one thousand. Everyone was on horseback, or rode in a cart, or the new wagons. Everyone wore smart new clothes. The horses had new saddlecloths and bridles. The Cornwall emblem was upon shining shields and tunics and flew from the banner at the head of the company, where Gorlois sat upon his white stallion, tall and straight.

Heads swiveled as the company passed by. Pedestrians turned to one another and whispered behind hands or murmured, their gazes upon the newly arrived travelers.

A great house had been put aside for Cornwall and his people, although not everyone could be accommodated there. The rest of the Cornish company were spread out among neighboring houses and stables. Venta Belgarum was filled to bursting point for the coming coronation, and many more people were sleeping in the fields beyond the walls, guarded by Uther's men.

Anwen presumed she would be one of those to sleep in the fields. Igraine frowned when she saw Anwen carrying her sack of clothing and a bundle of furs toward the door. "No, you are to stay here," Igraine said.

"I?" Anwen asked, startled.

"Find a bed or a bench, I don't care," Igraine said. "I want you within reach, Anwen. Morgan and Morguase need monitoring."

Anwen held in her first response and said meekly, "Yes, my

lady." She recognized that Igraine was using the care of her daughters as a pretext to keep Anwen nearby. The girls had a nurse, Elen, who had been caring for them since infancy and Elen was a part of the Cornish entourage.

So Anwen found a narrow bench beneath a window which was wide enough for her to repose comfortably and spread her furs upon it. She removed the other plain gown from the sack, for the one she wore was stained from travel. As she was washing, the news swept through the big house, passed from mouth to mouth, that the King expected Cornwall at his dinner table that night.

The preparations to attend the fortress took on a hasty air for the sun was sinking.

The room where Anwen's bench was located was within hailing distance of Igraine's large chamber. When Igraine swept out from her room just as the sun was setting, Anwen hurried to the door to accompany her and paused.

Anwen knew the golden yellow gown Igraine intended to wear for the coronation. Its richness of thread and beads was overwhelming. The coronation was two days away, though. The blue gown Igraine wore now was simple in embellishments. A fine gold thread ran around the hem and the edges of the sleeve. The gown outlined her figure to perfection and the white belt she wore over it emphasized her trim waist. Jewelry blazed and glittered at her throat and ears, also silvery white. Her hair tumbled down between her shoulders in rich, thick waves.

Igraine glowed.

Gorlois smiled when he saw her. He wore one of the new tunics Igraine had arranged for him, and was a strong, upright figure beside her. He held out his hand and Igraine took it. "You do Cornwell proud," he told her. "Thank you."

Anwen fell in behind them, lifting the hem of her new gown, safe in the knowledge that no one would see her there. Igraine would draw all the attention.

They walked to the fortress, which sat high above the street, overlooking the city and the well-tilled fields which surrounded it. The air was cool, not cold. Everyone arrived with cheeks tinged pink.

Gorlois was familiar with the fortress. "Ambrosius thought he would use this place as his primary residence, once peace was established," he said, with a wistful note.

He led Igraine and the Cornish company into a massive hall, with a vaulted roof which soared many times the height of a man overhead. Windows with colored glass shed the last of the daylight at the end of the hall, while hundreds of lamps illuminated the hall and the many tables set there.

The King's long table was empty and would remain so until all the guests had assembled and stood waiting for the King. It seemed to Anwen that everyone was already waiting. The

258

long table the page led them to was the only empty one in the huge hall.

Anwen found room on the bench at the end away from the King's table, while Gorlois and Igraine sat at the end closest to the head table.

Almost as soon as they stood ready, the King arrived.

Anwen turned to watch Uther enter the hall from the private door at the back. His men filed in behind him. Merlin was the first of them, dressed in black as usual.

She had forgotten how tall Uther was, although she had not forgotten the power of his blue eyes to intimidate and draw the eye. Even from a distance, his gaze caught her attention, until she saw Steffan.

Steffan was at the end of the line of men who took their places at the table. Startled, Anwen studied him. Surely, he would not sit at the table with the King? He hated eating in public and having everyone see him finger his food like a baby. This would be torture for him.

Yet he took the last chair at the far end of the table and waited for the King to sit, then sat as everyone else was doing. Belatedly, Anwen stepped over the bench and seated herself, too.

She had been hungry on the walk to the fortress. Now she had no appetite at all. She glanced around the table as the Cornwall people reached for the loaves of bread in the center and broke them open and tore hunks from them. *They* were hungry.

Anwen sat opposite Igraine and at the other far corner, so she could see Igraine's face and only the top of Gorlois' pale red hair. Igraine sat unmoving, her gaze upon the King's table.

Anwen glanced up and drew in a startled breath.

Uther stared at Igraine. He made no move to reach for bread, or to pick up any of the food which had been laid upon his plate first.

The hall grew still as everyone realized the King had not begun his meal and that they should wait. Heads turned.

Hectic red streaks appeared high on Igraine's cheeks. She tore her gaze away from the King and brought it to her empty plate. Her chest rose and fell quickly, making the white necklace glitter.

A servant brought the wine flagon over to Uther and prepared to pour into the jeweled cup. Uther covered the cup and shook his head. He murmured to the servant.

The man's eyes widened almost comically. He swallowed.

Uther waved him away. "Do as I say," he said, his voice loud enough to carry across the silent hall.

The servant walked around the head table and came over to where Gorlois and Igraine sat. He gave a jerky bow. "My lady," he said, his voice high and strained.

The whole room whispered and murmured in dismay and surprise.

Igraine pressed her lips together, hiding her reaction. With an infinitesimal movement, she nodded. Now her entire face was pink.

Anwen leaned forward to check Gorlois' reaction, her heart thudding.

Gorlois said something to the servant, who nodded with alacrity. He stepped over to Gorlois' side of the table, and filled his cup, too.

Gorlois picked up the mug and got to his feet, the bench scraping loudly in the stunned room. He turned to face Uther and raised the cup. "I toast High King Uther, who never fails to acknowledge the great friendship and regard he has for Cornwall." He paused. "The High King."

Everyone scrambled to their feet, reaching for cups which had not been filled, to raise them and repeat the oath, then pretend to drink.

Anwen sat down again, relief touching her. Gorlois had turned the moment and made it a compliment to Cornwall, not an insult to Cornwall's Duke.

The crackling tension in the room lessened. Everyone waited as the servant poured wine into Uther's cup. Uther lifted it and drank.

Sighs of relief sounded around the room.

Uther waved to the room. "Eat. All of you. I insist."

While he sat drinking, everyone returned to their meals. Slowly, conversations began and grew louder.

Anwen's appetite did not return. She accepted a small amount of venison and did not finish it. She sipped the wine yet did not finish that either. Her heart would not steady and slow. It swung wildly from high and fast to hard and heavy. It did not help that she only had to lift her head and look toward the end of the table, to see Steffan at the end of the other.

He was not eating, either. His face was pale, his gaze thoughtful as he sipped his wine. He did not speak to the diner beside him. He stared sightlessly ahead, alone with his thoughts.

Igraine also ate little. She drank nothing. Her cheeks had lost the slashes of color and now she was too pale. She kept her gaze upon the platter in front of her, not even looking up at her husband.

Gorlois ate steadily and mechanically. As soon as Uther got to his feet and left, so did Gorlois. He held out his hand to his wife and swept from the room, leaving the rest of the Cornish contingent to scramble from their benches and follow.

The night air was considerably colder as they walked back to the great house. Anwen welcomed the chilly touch. Just being away from the great hall was a relief of its own.

When they reached the house, Igraine turned to look behind her. "Anwen, help me prepare for bed."

Surprised, Anwen threaded through those who had not yet hurried for their billets to reach Igraine. "My lady."

Igraine turned to Gorlois. "With your consent, my lord, I will retire."

Gorlois was no longer smiling. He nodded shortly, then turned and stalked away, calling for the pot boy.

Igraine did not react to Gorlois' dark mood. She turned, too, lifted her hems and hurried through the house, with Anwen behind her.

Anwen shut the heavy door of the inner chamber behind them and only then did Igraine release her control. She sank onto the bench beside the big bed and raised her hand to her forehead. Her hand trembled. Her deep blue eyes glittered. "Mother Mary, help me," she murmured.

Anwen moved closer. "My lady?"

Igraine looked up at her. Her eyes glittered because tears were building there. "He has lost all sense," she breathed.

"The King, my lady?"

Igraine pressed her fingertips into her temples. "He looked like a man driven to the edge of reason. Did you see his eyes?"

Anwen threaded her hands together. "You were closer to the King than I."

Igraine laughed. It was a shaky sound. "Yes, and why was Cornwall so close to the King's chair? Mabon is just as faithful, just as stalwart." She closed her eyes. "Ah, god, Anwen, what am I to do? There will be no peace if what happened tonight happens again and peace *must* be kept!"

Anwen's heart hurried. "Do you truly ask for my advice, my lady?" Her voice trembled.

Igraine dropped her hands and looked at Anwen. "Yes," she said simply. "I cannot think properly, Anwen. I need another clear head and you have always been sensible and discreet."

Anwen wiped her damp palms on her gown. "As a true and faithful wife, my lady, you are within your rights to send a note to the King, thanking him for his attention and discouraging him from further flattery. Tell him you are devoted to your husband."

Igraine pressed her full lips together, hiding their pillowy softness. "Such a note would be read by every person who handles it between here and the fortress."

"Yes, my lady. If it is the truth, what does it matter?"

Igraine's gaze met Anwen's. Then it slid away. Igraine got to her feet and went to the unglazed window and pulled the heavy curtain aside.

"I see," Anwen said.

Igraine leaned her forehead against the cool stone walls and closed her eyes. "I am a wicked woman," she breathed. "I cannot stop thinking about him."

"It does not prevent you from writing such a note. Even if it is not the full truth, you must remain loyal to Gorlois to keep the peace."

"Not yet, Anwen. I cannot compose such a final note as that just yet. I need time." Igraine's tone was pleading. She wrapped her arms around herself and shivered yet did not move away from the window. "Time to bring myself to it," she added.

Anwen understood. "If not for Gorlois, you would go to him…"

Igraine sighed. "It cannot be, no matter how much my heart wills it so."

"I know something of that state, my lady," Anwen told her.

Igraine glanced at her, surprise building in her eyes. "You?"

Anwen couldn't meet Igraine's eyes. She had been indiscreet enough. "Please forget I spoke, my lady."

"Anwen, look at me," Igraine commanded.

Anwen reluctantly lifted her chin once more.

Igraine's expression was kind. "Who was he?" she asked.

"It doesn't matter, my lady," Anwen assured her. "It cannot be, just as you said." Her heart swooped sickeningly as she recalled Steffan's face in the great hall.

Anwen pressed her hand to her middle to halt the dizzy sensations. It gave her an idea. "My lady, tomorrow you must be ill and take to your bed." It was a perfect solution, for it did not commit Igraine to one action or another, and she could avoid any interactions with the King, too.

Igraine drew in a slow breath, considering it. Then, with a small smile, she nodded.

Chapter Nineteen

In three days, Steffan had learned that when Uther demanded his presence, it was because he felt uncertain. As a new king should appear decisive lest his subjects lose faith in his leadership, there were few people in the kingdom before whom Uther dared reveal his doubts. That was the real service Steffan could provide.

The morning after the disastrous supper, Uther sent for him. Steffan could guess why. He presented himself in the antechamber and the steward opened the door for him.

"What took you so long?" Uther demanded as the door closed behind Steffan.

"I came immediately," Steffan pointed out. "If you want me to appear faster, then you must ask Merlin to cast a spell which will let me walk through walls."

Uther snorted. "Merlin," he muttered.

Liquid trickled into a cup.

"Wine, Steffan?"

"Mulled?"

"Gods, no," Uther replied.

"Then yes, thank you."

"Ha!" Uther said, sounding pleased. "Here." A cup was pressed into Steffan's hand.

Steffan drank. He needed the fortification. Uther's temper had grown chancy, the last few days. "You sent for me," he reminded Uther.

A swirl of heavy cloth sounded. Uther was pacing. "She's ill, Steffan. She did not rise from her bed this morning. This is my doing!"

Steffan lowered his cup. "The lady Igraine?" he asked carefully.

Uther sighed. "Who else?"

Who else, indeed. "Are you spying upon her, my lord?"

"I spy on everyone," Uther said. "My brother died from poisoning. I trust no one. I prefer to see the knife coming."

"I thought…was not the poison a Saxon device?" Steffan asked.

"They say so," Uther said dismissively. "The lady Igraine…" Then he gasped.

Steffan braced himself. "What is wrong?" he asked sharply.

Uther's hands gripped his arms and squeezed. "Nothing at all. You said something a moment ago which just told me what I must do."

"About the lady Igraine?" Steffan asked.

"Walk through walls, you said," Uther replied and Steffan heard him pouring more wine. "That is what I will do. I will walk through walls to speak to her."

Coldness settled in Steffan's chest. "You would defy Gorlois and the peace of this country to speak to a woman?"

"Not if Merlin casts a spell," Uther said bluntly. "Find him, Steffan. Bring him here at once."

"Merlin?"

"Merlin," Uther said flatly. "Try not to dawdle this time."

Steffan held out his cup. "I still don't know where the table is," he said apologetically.

Uther chuckled. "They move, anyway," he said, taking the cup. "Hurry, man!"

Steffan hurried. He knew the way to Merlin's room well enough now to avoid the stumbling points. He hammered on Merlin's door. "Merlin, for the love of the gods, open!"

The door opened almost immediately. "Steffan, what ails you?"

"Not me. Uther. He commands you attend him at once."

Silence. "I see," Merlin said. "Move back, Steffan. I will come at once, as commanded."

Steffan stepped back and heard the door close. He gripped the staff. "You must talk Uther out of this madness, Merlin," he said, keeping his voice low.

"Walk with me," Merlin said, his voice just as low. "Igraine, you mean?"

"He wants you to use your magic and take him to her."

Three steps.

"Uther doesn't believe in magic," Merlin said flatly.

"He's not in his right mind," Steffan said. "His steward said he hasn't slept for days. Not properly. And he drinks all the time."

"Uther has never slept well," Merlin said, his voice remote. "He fills his bed so he is never alone…I presume his bed has been empty for the days he has not slept?"

"I didn't think to ask," Steffan admitted.

They turned into the antechamber and Steffan reached out for where he thought Merlin's arm would be. He found soft cloth. "You *must* halt this," he said, as softly as possible.

"Prince Merlin," the steward said heartily. "The King awaits you."

Merlin's finger closed over Steffan's wrist. "You must come with me."

Steffan followed Merlin into the King's chamber and found his way over to the warm corner where he would not trip Uther up or be in the way.

"My lord King," Merlin said, his tone grave.

Uther hissed. "Nephew."

"You need my help with something, I believe?" Merlin's

270

voice shifted as he sat. Then he added, "A sleeping potion, I would guess from your appearance. You would not have me attend you for a silly love potion."

Uther's tone was flat. "You know why I summoned you. If Steffan told you, or if he did not, you still know."

"I do," Merlin said. His voice was low.

When he said nothing else, Uther made a soft sound of irritation. "We have never agreed completely, you and I, yet we both served my brother well enough. I ask you to serve me now, as High King, if not as your last remaining relative. You have heard the rumors, you saw what happened last night. A fever grips me, Merlin, such as I have never felt. I will not sleep or eat until she is mine. For the sake of this country, you must help me in this before I tear it asunder in my need."

"She is not yours to have, Uther," Merlin said, his tone sharp.

Uther gave the same hissing sound. "I know women, Merlin, as you do not. I understand their hearts and minds. She is not indifferent to me, even though she is afraid to raise her eyes in public."

"You would insult your greatest ally to have your way?" Merlin asked.

"Of course not!" Uther cried. "Why do you think this has not gone beyond foolishness yet? If I cared nothing for Gorlois' enmity, I would have had my fill of her months ago, then laid siege to his fortress and razed it to the ground. My brother did not work his entire life to forge this peace only for me to destroy it in a night of pure folly."

Steffan relaxed a little. Strained, Uther might be, yet he was clinging to reason despite it.

"I know you, Merlin," Uther said. "I see how you work, how your mind turns. You and I come at life differently. Yet I have watched you over the years arrange matters in ways which everyone calls magic. I saw you raise the standing stones with music and engineering. Yet everyone sings of the magic you cast to lift them with one hand. *That* is the magic I demand of you now. The magic you weave with your mind and your knowledge."

Merlin remained silent.

"I want you to bring her to me. Or take me to her. I am certain you can do this. You know the by ways, the secret paths, the hollow hills."

"It is no simple matter you ask for," Merlin said. "The risks—"

"I am *your king*!" Uther roared.

"It is not the King who asks me this favor," Merlin said sharply. "The King would know better than to risk everything for the sake of a woman. No, Uther, it is the man who begs me now to help him."

The little silence throbbed with tension. "You will hold a

lifetime of disregard against me, then."

"Your disregard plays no part in this," Merlin said.

"You say that, yet—"

"I have not said I would not help you." Merlin's voice rose above Uther's.

Steffan drew in a startled breath.

Uther did, too.

Then, his voice eager, Uther said. "You must speak to her. Tell her…no, I will write a letter—"

"No, Uther," Merlin said, with a snap in his voice. "If I am to help you, then it will be done my way."

Uther's silence was pensive. "And what will this cost me?" he asked, a wise note in his voice.

"Nothing," Merlin said. "I do not do this for you. There will be a child—"

"There is always risk of that," Uther said dismissively.

"There will be a child," Merlin repeated firmly. "I want the boy given to me to raise."

"A bastard for a bastard?" Uther said. There was a hard note in his voice. "If there is indeed a child, then it will not be raised in my court, as a threat to my legitimate sons."

"There will be no other sons, Uther. This son will become your heir whether you wish it or not."

The silence crackled. "Do you have any idea who you are speaking to?" Uther asked. He sounded amused.

"I do," Merlin said evenly. "You, apparently, have forgotten who *you* are speaking to."

"I do not believe your visions of the future, Merlin. I never have."

"You are too much of the earth," Merlin said, his tone one of agreement. "The child, Uther. Yes or no?"

Uther hesitated. "If there is a child, you will have it with my blessing," he said heavily. "Now…" His tone was expectant.

Steffan heard Merlin get to his feet. "I will have a sleeping draught made for you. You must sleep before tomorrow, Uther. Your judgment is adrift while you are in this state. Tomorrow, you must move through the coronation ceremony and the feast which follows and offend no one."

"That is all?" Uther demanded.

Merlin's voice came from farther away, by the door. "I will give you more instructions once the arrangements have been made." The door opened.

Steffen gripped his staff. "My lord, do you have any need of me?"

Uther's tone was distant. Drained. "No, Steffan. Not anymore."

Steffan escaped the room. He walked faster than was wise when there were usually many people in the antechamber waiting to speak to the King, yet no one tripped him up or collided with him. Steffan moved to the outside corridor.

When he felt tapestry beneath his feet, he halted.

"Merlin!"

No answer.

The man was fast.

Steffan made his way to Merlin's borrowed room and used his staff to rattle the door.

It opened. "You'd better come in, then," Merlin said.

Steffan barely waited for the door to close behind him. "How can you think of helping him in this?" he demanded.

"I'm not helping him." The sound of glass tapping on glass came softly.

Steffan hissed. It was the same impatient sound Uther had made.

Merlin's voice came closer. "It only looks as though I am giving Uther what he wants. For this one moment in time, his desire and my work coincide."

"Your work?"

"Destiny is an overwhelming force, Steffan. I warned you I am a politician. This is my power. By giving Uther what he wants I am serving *my* master."

Steffan frowned. "Fate," he concluded. "You are serving the future."

"Very good." Merlin's voice was far away again. There were more soft clinks and taps. The flap of cloth.

"The child…" Steffan breathed. "You care about none of

this but the child to come."

"Not just a child," Merlin said. "A king. The greatest king of this age, Steffan."

"Greater than Ambrosius?" Steffan asked, astounded. It was uncomfortable relegating Ambrosius to a lesser rank. "Ambrosius brought peace to Britain."

"It won't last," Merlin said. "Now my father is dead, the Saxons are already preparing. Next summer, or the one after, they will spill into Britain by the thousands. It will be the Flood Years all over again."

"You cannot know that. How could you?"

Merlin didn't answer at once. When he did speak, there was a thread of amusement in his voice. "I could tell you I saw the Saxon invasions in a vision, or in the stars, but I will not. It is nothing but common sense, Steffan. I have spent my life studying my father's enemies and I am wise as to how they think. They will test Uther's strength and find it less than Ambrosius'. Uther is a soldiers' king, yet he needs the people behind him, too. They do not understand him as the soldiers do, so their support will be wary. The Saxons will use that wedge to drive themselves into the heart of Britain."

Steffan shuddered. "And Uther's son?" he breathed.

"He will rid all Britain of them," Merlin said. "That, I *have* seen in the stars. He will forge a lasting peace, Steffan. One which will serve a generation, at least. His ideals—the ideals I

276

will teach him—will last forever, in song and poem."

"How can a king born of such wrongness be so great?"

"The kind who wants to put things right. A man who knows what right is. A man like you, Steffan."

Steffan shook his head. "There must be another way than this…dishonesty you are undertaking."

"There is not."

"How can you condone it? You are a thinking man!"

"I can see farther ahead than you," Merlin said. He came much closer—Steffan could sense him standing just in front of him. "Consider what will happen if Uther does not get his way. It is a simple matter to predict. Go on."

Steffan swallowed. "Me? You are the politician, you said."

"And you are a learned man. If Uther were to avoid entanglements with lady Igraine, then what?"

Steffan frowned. "I suppose…he will become king and perhaps find a queen to create an heir."

"And before that could happen?" Merlin prompted.

"The Saxon flood," Steffan breathed. "It is coming no matter what happens, isn't it?"

"My father's death made it a certainty," Merlin said. "This is our one chance to find a way out of the dark years ahead, Steffan. I will do everything in my power to make sure it happens."

Cold, invisible fingers walked up his spine. Steffan shuddered. "I cannot see the future as you can," he told Merlin. "I can only act upon what I see before me and what I see is wrong."

"It *is* wrong," Merlin said. "Yet the King will achieve so much more through trying to rise above that ignoble beginning. Trust me, Steffan."

The soft rattle of metal against leather sounded.

"What are you doing?" Steffan asked.

"Packing."

"Are you not here to help Uther with this...seduction?" The word made his mouth twist.

"The matter will require me to travel," Merlin said. "While I am waiting, I am packing in anticipation."

"Waiting for what?"

A soft tapping sounded on the door.

"Ah," Merlin said. His voice shifted as he crossed the room to the door and opened it. "Good morning, Gorlois. Come in."

Steffan drew in a sharp breath.

Soft boot steps. Then, "Steffan!"

Steffan turned so he was facing in Gorlois' direction. "My lord Cornwall."

"You fare well, in the King's service? I saw you at the high table last night."

Steffan's mouth twisted into a grimace. "As with everything, my lord, it is both good and bad."

Gorlois cleared his throat. "Prince Merlin, forgive me for barging in. My wife, Igraine, is ill and we have no physician with us. Given the current circumstances, there are few men I would trust in this King's town. There is no love lost between you and Uther. I wonder…would you come and treat her? The coronation is tomorrow. She must be on her feet for that."

Steffan fought to keep his surprise and dismay from showing.

"I will come at once, Gorlois," Merlin said.

"You will? Thank you." The relief in Gorlois' voice was painful to listen to. "I must…I prefer to return to the house at once, do you mind? You know where we are lodged?"

"I do," Merlin said. "Here, let me get the door for you. I will be along shortly."

"Thank you again, Merlin. I trust you will help her. I am in your debt."

"My father considered you to be his greatest ally, Gorlois. Through him, my debt is greater. You owe me nothing. Go back to your wife. I will be there soon."

The door shut. The silence extended for long heartbeats.

"You could have spoken then, and exposed me," Merlin said. "If you are a man of conscience, as you say, then why did you remain silent?" He did not sound angry, merely curious.

Steffan gripped his staff. "Your talk of the future…of the

one light in the darkness…" He sighed. "You made me doubt."

"That is a good thing," Merlin assured him. "When you question what you believe about something, you find new wisdom."

"I was not yet finished with the old," Steffan muttered.

Merlin's laughter was deep and long.

Chapter Twenty

enny, one of Igraine's youngest companions, came to the room where Anwen was reading to Morgan and Morguase. "The Lady wants you," Jenny said, with a sniff of disdain.

"She is awake, then?" Anwen asked, letting the book roll up.

"Is Mother well again?" Morguase asked.

"Well enough to dispense orders everywhere," Jenny said.

Anwen glared at her. Jenny's bluntness would bother the girls.

Jenny stared back.

Anwen got to her feet. "Stay here with Morgan and Morguase," she told Jenny. "I'll find Elen and send her back."

Igraine's antechamber was full of people, which startled Anwen and made her pause inside the door. Most of the women standing in the room, whispering together, were Igraine's companions. A tall figure in black stood in the far corner, whom Anwen recognized. Prince Merlin.

He appeared to be waiting. When Anwen glanced at him, though, his gaze was steady upon her. He watched her?

Anwen cleared her throat and tugged her gown into position, then moved around the clusters of women to the inner door. She tapped and pushed it open, then stepped inside and shut it again.

The room was empty of anyone but Igraine. Igraine laid upon pillows. Her eyes opened the moment the door shut. She sat up. "You must stay here with me, Anwen."

Anwen moved closer to the door. "Merlin waits outside the door!" She kept her voice soft.

"That is why I sent for you." Igraine glanced at the door, her expression nervous. "Gorlois sent for him to examine me, so I may be well enough for tomorrow."

Anwen pushed on her shoulder. "Then you had best appear ill, my lady. Lie down."

Igraine settled on the pillows once more. Anwen considered her. She looked far too healthy. Perhaps the mention of a woman's concerns would be enough to deflect the wizard.

Anwen went to the door and opened it. "Prince Merlin?" she called.

The tall man moved passed her and over to the bed and stood looking down at Igraine, who had her eyes closed once more.

Anwen shut the door and moved to the foot of the big bed.

"You may stop pretending now, Igraine," Merlin said.

Igraine opened her eyes. "How did you know?"

Merlin stepped back a pace, giving her room. "It was easy enough to guess what ails you, given last night's supper."

Igraine sat and arranged the covers over her knees. "If you guessed that much, then why did you come? There is no treatment you can prescribe which will cure what ails me."

Merlin glanced at Anwen, measuring her with his gaze. Apparently, he approved of what he saw, for he shifted his attention back to Igraine. "Indirectly, I am here because Uther sent me."

Anwen drew in a long breath, riding out her shock. It was not her place to say anything.

Igraine's eyes opened. "Uther *sent you?*"

Merlin's eyes narrowed. "Your husband asked me to attend you and I welcomed the chance to speak with you." He gave a harsh smile. "The city talks of nothing but the King's attention toward you. No one breathes a word of your wrong-doing in this. They speak only of your piety and your devotion to your husband and Cornwall. I came to see for myself if this is true."

Igraine dropped her gaze to the furs over her knees. "I don't understand what you are asking me."

Merlin considered her for a long moment. "You have played

a careful game, Igraine, only now it is time to dispense with the masks. I cannot help you if I do not have your full measure. Tell me. Is Uther's certainty that you are not indifferent to him true?"

Igraine lifted her chin to look Merlin in the eye. She was a woman sitting in her bedchamber, while a prince stood over her, yet it might have been Igraine who was the royal one. Despite the slash of high color in her cheeks, her expression was haughty.

Merlin nodded. "Then we understand one another," he murmured. "It leaves just one more question." He hesitated. "If a way existed for you and Uther to be together, would you take it, Igraine?"

Anwen stared at the tall man, her horror building.

Igraine did not answer at once. The color remained in her cheeks as she spoke. "If no harm came to my husband or my children...indeed, if no harm came to Cornwall or Britain through such an indulgence then...perhaps...yes."

Merlin nodded briskly. "Then I will help you in this."

Igraine's eyes narrowed. "Why would you? I mean...forgive me, Prince Merlin. Everyone knows how little you and Uther like each other. Why would you help him in such an endeavor?"

"For reasons beyond your ken," he said, his tone short. "Now I am certain of your thoughts, I will make arrangements.

You will have your part to play in this, too. Your woman, there—you trust her?"

Anwen jumped, for Merlin's gaze was upon her once more.

"I do," Igraine said, her tone chilly. Merlin's peremptory tone did not sit well with her.

"Good. Do not let her leave your side until you return to Tintagel. Your appearance in public must be chaperoned at every moment. You must appear completely blameless."

"Return…?" Igraine said, startled. "We just arrived. If we miss the coronation—"

Merlin raised his hand, cutting her off. "Tell me about Tintagel. They say it cannot be taken by anyone. Is that true? There is not a single weakness to the fortress? No way to breach its walls? No way, say, for a loving husband to creep back into the fortress at night so he may visit his wife without the household laughing about his domestic devotion?"

Igraine didn't drop her gaze, yet her cheeks grew even warmer. "How did you know?"

Anwen stared at Igraine, astonished.

Merlin smiled. "When men sit about campfires at night and drink heavily, a great deal can be surmised from the stories they tell each other. The nightly absence of a leader, the happiness of his wife…"

Igraine smoothed the furs with her fingers. "There is a postern gate, on the seaward side of the tower. The way there is treacherous, yet manageable if the wind is not too high."

"And the stairs inside the gate lead directly to your chamber," Merlin finished.

Igraine nodded again.

Anwen had lived at Tintagel nearly all her life and had never once heard even a whisper of such an entrance. If one existed, then it would be a highly guarded secret, for it was a weakness in the fortress's impregnable defenses. Yet Igraine was sharing the secret willingly.

"There is a guard house, halfway up the stairs," Igraine added.

"Manned?" Merlin asked.

"Every night," Igraine said.

"I will take care of that," he said dismissively, his eyes narrowed. "What you must do is attend the coronation tomorrow. Stay at your husband's side and keep your eyes downcast as you have been doing. Afterward…" He paused once more. "Your wellbeing is important to Gorlois. You must tell him you are ill with the pressure the King is putting upon you with his public foolishness. Tell Gorlois you want to return to Cornwall at once, even before the feast. Use whatever charms you have, of which I am sure you have many—only you *must* convince Gorlois to leave immediately."

Igraine frowned. "To leave before the feast…the King will consider it an insult. He will be angry."

"He will appear to be angry, yes. The important thing is that he cannot slight his other guests by riding after you. He must stay for the feast and the formalities the next day, too. Until his guests have left, Uther must remain here in Venta Belgarum. In that time, you and your household will be installed in Tintagel. Gorlois will assemble troops in Dimilioc for the descent of the King upon Cornwall."

"I see," Igraine said slowly. "It will avoid violence upon the road."

"If you play your part, then it will avoid violence altogether," Merlin said. "For Uther will ride fast and arrive in Cornwall as his troops do and at least a day earlier than anyone might expect. The night before his troops should attack Dimilioc…" He paused. "That is the night he will come to you."

Anwen pressed her fist to her belly, which churned with illness. She could not speak, not while Merlin was in the room, only she didn't think she *could* speak right now.

Merlin straightened. "I will provide more detail once I have completed my plans. Do you read, madam?"

"No," Igraine replied. "Anwen does, though."

Merlin's gaze drilled into her. "Very well. Any letters you receive with the Pendragon seal you must make sure only Anwen opens."

Igraine held up a hand. "Swear to me, Merlin, that no harm will come to my family, that no lasting harm will be delivered upon Cornwall for this?"

Merlin's expression was impatient. "The High King himself has a stake in this and Uther is not a hypocrite. He will not smite Cornwall with one hand while taking its Duchess with the other."

"You have seen this?" Igraine insisted, keeping her chin high.

"I do not see the fate of every human upon this earth."

"You have seen mine?"

Merlin hesitated. "I have seen a child come from this union."

Igraine's expression softened. Her mouth curved up. "A child…!"

Merlin turned from the bed. "I will write," he said and strode to the door. Anwen jumped to open it for him and he nodded at her. "Do you read Latin?" he asked in a quiet tone.

"I do."

"Good. A further layer of security." He walked out of the chamber and moved through the ladies in the antechamber as if they were not there. Everyone stepped aside for him.

Anwen closed the door and turned to Igraine. "My lady, you cannot do this!"

Igraine threw the covers aside and leapt to her feet. "Why should I not? The High King himself wants me, Anwen. If nothing comes of this but a single child, then why not?"

"Because it is wrong, my lady." Anwen wrung her hands. "What of your husband? Your vows to him? Your church says they are inviolate."

Igraine frowned. Her lips pressed together. She moved over to the window and looked out upon Venta Belgarum, standing far enough away that no one would see her at the window. "I was seventeen when I married Gorlois. He was thirty-seven. I was in awe of him and he treated me gently, so I thought myself in love with him. I suppose, in a way, I did grow to love him." She sighed. "He is a good man. A kind man and a great leader. Yet, when I first saw Uther…" Igraine glanced at Anwen. Her eyes were filled with fiery energy. "I heard all the stories about Ambrosius' brother, the great war master. About his temper and ferocity, about his abilities as a fighter and leader of warriors. Who has not?"

Anwen nodded, for she had heard all the stories, too.

Igraine shook her head. "When I first saw Uther in Amesbury, he was not standing upon a tier, with heralds and banners and trumpets. He was an ordinary man, standing among ordinary men. Yet when his gaze met mine…" Igraine pressed her hand to her chest. "It made me realize Gorlois was merely the silvered, cold light of the moon. Uther is the sun. A blazing, bright sun which blinds one if they look too long." She turned, her gaze steady. "I cannot live without the sun."

Anwen shivered.

Igraine moved back to the bed and sat upon it. "I need food, Anwen. I cannot ask for it, not if I am to appear ill for the rest of the day. Go and beg some bread from the kitchen and bring it to me."

"Yes, my lady," Anwen said. She moved to the door, her heart pattering unsteadily.

"Some wine, too!" Igraine called.

Anwen shut the door and fled.

Chapter Twenty-One

The gate guards would not let Anwen into the fortress proper. They made her wait in the blockhouse while a message was sent. She perched upon the cold stone shelf, shivering, for there were no biers or fire pits in the blockhouse.

It seemed as if hours passed before she heard the sound she had been waiting for—the tap of a staff upon stone. Then his voice.

"I'm told someone wishes to speak to me?" Steffan murmured.

"In here, sir," the guard said.

Anwen got to her feet, her heart picking up speed.

Steffan's shadow filled the doorway. Then he moved into view and turned into the room, the staff swinging. Three steps, then he paused, his chin lifting.

Anwen opened her mouth to speak, to let him know she was there.

"Anwen?" he said, sounding startled.

Her lips parted in surprise. "Yes. I am here." She moved closer to him. "Do you know what Uther plans, Steffan? Do you?"

Steffan tilted his head. "Wait," he said softly. "There are too many people here and too many doors to listen at. Come with me." He held out his hand.

Anwen hesitated. Then she slid her hand into his. His touch was warm.

Steffan took her back through the blockhouse to a set of stone steps. "Up," he said.

She climbed beside him. The steps were a straight flight and at the top they emerged into bright sunlight. The wall of the outer perimeter curved around the fortress itself. They stood upon the top, which was five paces deep. The walkway was shielded by shoulder-high stone facing the city, and waist-high stone on the other side.

There were guards spread along the top of the wall, one every hundred paces. None of them turned to look at Anwen and Steffan as they emerged from the stairs.

"There are guards," Anwen warned Steffan.

"They won't look at us," Steffan said. "No one can hear us up here, if we move far enough away from the gatehouse. Pick a place, Anwen—somewhere between the guards."

She chose the best position and led Steffan along the wall

until they were standing between the two nearest guards, then turned to him. In the spring sunshine, Steffan's strong face showed signs of strain. "You are not well," Anwen said. "Are they treating you unkindly, here?"

"No more than anywhere else."

"They are making you eat in public," she pointed out.

"It was a just the one night." He paused. "You were there…!"

Anwen nodded, even though he could not see it. "I was. I saw it all." She dropped her voice even lower. "Steffan, this cannot be allowed to happen!"

He shook his head. "Speak plainly, Anwen. You always have."

"Uther and Igraine!" she whispered. "Merlin plots to bring them together. Surely, if you are Uther's man, you must be aware of this?"

Steffan sighed. "I am," he said heavily. "I cannot stop it, though. I'm not sure I even should."

Anwen stared at him, horrified. "I cannot believe you of all people would say such a thing. Of course it must be stopped! You were Gorlois' man for much longer than you have been Uther's. You understand the qualities of both men. How can you countenance Gorlois being cuckolded in this way?"

"There's more to this than you understand," Steffan said, his voice strained.

Anwen studied him, puzzled. "I do *not* understand," she said in agreement. "It is plain you disapprove, yet you will do nothing?"

Steffan reached out. His fingers touched her arm, then slid up to her face. He held it, his thumb stroking her cheek and making her skin sizzle. "Merlin has made me hesitate to interfere."

He told her of Merlin's predictions, about a king to surpass all others, of peace and prosperity. "If Merlin is right—and he has never once been wrong—then this is the only way Britain can be saved from the blackest of times to come."

"You do not believe in magic," Anwen said, her voice hoarse because her throat was so tight. "You have said so many times that reasoning and logic were the only truths. How can you possibly take Merlin's word for it?"

"Because it isn't magic he used to see it," Steffan replied. "It was logic and reason. Common sense says the Saxons will return and in greater numbers than ever before."

"Merlin told you what you wanted to hear," Anwen said. "He spoke to Igraine of a child—how could he infer that from logic and reason?"

"He didn't," Steffan said. "It could be what he calls his Sight or perhaps he is guessing."

"So you *do* believe in his powers?"

Steffan shook his head. "No."

"You won't try to stop Uther, though?"

"How can I possibly do anything?" Steffan asked, his tone reasonable.

Anwen gripped his sleeves and shook him. "Of course you can! You ride a horse like a sighted man. You made your own way to Venta Belgarum. You found your way back to the High King's service when everyone thought you should count yourself lucky to tutor little girls. I've seen you fight professional soldiers and win! How can you say you're helpless? You're the least helpless man I know!"

Steffan plucked her hand from his arm and held it. "That isn't what I meant. I swore to serve Uther, Anwen. I don't get to choose the manner of my service. Even if I disapprove of what Uther plans to do, what sort of man am I if I do not help him? He expects my loyalty. If I fail to give it to him, my disapproval would be hypocritical."

"Your values are stopping you?" Anwen breathed.

"Tell me yours are not," Steffan replied. "As you are aware of Uther's plans, Igraine must have asked you to help her with them. Will you refuse to help because it is wrong?"

Anwen tightened her grip on his hand. "I cannot refuse," she said. "I am sworn to serve her."

Steffan nodded. "You see?"

Anwen dropped her head. "That is why you cling to Merlin's predictions. It gives you hope where there was none before."

"If there *is* a king to be made from of this," Steffan said, "then perhaps it is as well he will be reared away from Uther's earthly impulses. Perhaps Merlin has the right of it there, too."

"Merlin is working for his higher power, only he is moving mere people about with his manipulations. Does he not see what he is condoning, with this?"

Steffan lifted his chin and turned his head, as if he was looking down at the city. "I think he knows perfectly well. I think he also knows the price which will be asked, too. He fails to tell the price to those of us caught up in it, for fear we might hesitate."

"The price?" Anwen repeated, her heart stirring uneasily.

"There is a price for everything. That is what I have learned." He lifted his hand toward his eyes. "I rose through the ranks to the highest there was, too young and too fast. I dined with kings and princes and leaders. I grew arrogant and far too sure of myself. I was convinced the world owed me everything I wanted. For my folly, my sight was lost."

"That was nothing but a Saxon hammer," Anwen said. "You did not ask to be blinded."

"In a way, I did. I grew careless on the battlefield, Anwen. I thought I was invincible. Fate made sure I learned I was not. Igraine and Uther, too, will pay for their treachery, one way or another."

Anwen shivered again, even though the sun was warm on her shoulders. "I must go back. I told no one, not even Igraine, I was coming here."

Steffan kissed her, stealing her breath and making her body thrum. "Thank you," he said, his lips brushing hers.

"For what?" she asked, struggling to keep her voice steady.

"For listening. For understanding. For being you." His thumb stroked over the back of her hand.

Anwen's eyes ached. She withdrew her hand. "As if being myself has such great benefit." She moved around Steffan, to head for the stairs once more and hesitated. "Shall I take you back to the blockhouse?"

"I can find the way from here," he told her, his back to her.

Anwen almost ran to the top of the steps down into the gatehouse, her heart swooping and spinning.

As she hurried through the busy streets of Venta Belgarum, she reflected that if there was a price attached to every decision one could make, then Steffan had failed to calculate what the price would be for himself and her, for their roles in Uther's conspiracy.

There was comfort in that idea. She had already lost everything it was possible to lose. She had nothing more for Fate to take from her but her life. Without Steffan in it, Anwen would give up that life without quibble.

PART THREE

Chapter Twenty-Two

Steffan could not eat at the feast. The tension in his chest was too tight. He listened to Uther bluster, cursing Gorlois and the day he was born, and any man who would betray their king. To Steffan's ears, Uther's complaints and threats sounded false and overly dramatic. No one else seemed to feel Uther was play-acting, though. His reputation for a high-flaring temper was sufficient for them to believe he meant every word he said.

When the pot boy filled Steffan's wine cup for the second time, Steffan murmured, "How much has the King had to drink?"

"Very little, sir," the boy whispered.

Uther sounded sober enough when Steffan hurried to his chamber after the feast. His voice shifted from place to place around the room as he stalked restlessly. "Another day of this will send me to the depths of madness," Uther seethed. "*When* can we leave?"

"Tomorrow afternoon, my lord," Steffan told him. "As soon as the assembly in the great hall is over."

Uther gave a strained laugh. "There may be some good come out of this, after all. Lot and Urien want to ride with me to Cornwall, to help me deal with Gorlois."

Steffan recalled the two northern leaders. Lot was a dour man with black hair, a thick beard and stark lines for a face. His beak of a nose was sharp, like his mind. Urien, his cousin, was as fair as Lot was dark, with a great beard and a half-shaved head, leaving long locks at the top, which he pulled back with silver rings. He was a ruthless fighter, Steffan remembered.

He said cautiously, "Do they wish to help, or watch? They are generally slow to commit themselves to any action."

"I don't care," Uther said. "They will ride beside me for two days on the way back. That is precious time to cement relationships I wouldn't have otherwise. Now, if only we could *start*," he finished with a growl. "I am the High King. I've a mind to outlaw all diplomacy for being insufferable."

"When you return from Cornwall, you can do what you like," Steffan reminded him. "First, you must get through tomorrow."

"I am running out of curses for Gorlois," Uther said. "And in truth, they leave a sour taste in my mouth."

"Then don't curse," Steffan suggested. "It would look natural for you to drop into dour silence tomorrow. Everyone will know why you simmer, without further insults to Cornwall."

"*That* is something I can do," Uther muttered. "By the way, where is Merlin? I did not see him at the table tonight."

"He has already left for Cornwall."

Uther completed another circle while Steffan listened to his rich coronation robes swish and flutter. "There is another thing which leaves a bad taste in my mouth," he muttered.

"Working with Merlin, my lord?"

"No, that damned sleeping potion he insists I must use."

"Does it work?" Steffan asked curiously.

"Too well. I wake and don't know if a night has passed or a year. I've never slept alone for so many nights in a row. Somewhere, Merlin is laughing at me!"

"READ THE LETTER AGAIN, ANWEN," Igraine insisted, as she settled in the cushioned chair by the window. Through the window, Anwen could see the restless green sea which washed endlessly against the Tintagel cliffs, and little else. The air was fresh and sweet, with just a touch of salt in it.

Anwen didn't reach for the letter. She had memorized the instructions from too many repetitions. Merlin's clear writing and phrases came back to her. Before she spoke, she glanced around the room once more. Igraine's bedchamber was empty of everyone but Igraine and Anwen.

"There is no one here," Igraine assured her. "From the silence, I judge everyone is sleeping."

Which was what Anwen wished she could do. The journey from Venta Belgarum to Tintagel had been a wild one, with the carts and wagons bouncing and rattling at a speed which threatened to break them apart or separate them from their wheels. At least a dozen horses were left behind as they grew lame or their riders too exhausted to continue.

Gorlois had set a cracking pace, driving the company deep into the night. They arrived at Tintagel at mid-afternoon on the second day—yesterday. The wagons were pushed into the courtyard and everyone streamed into the fortress, stretching and yawning and rubbing their eyes.

Gorlois swung Morgan and Morguase to the ground and kissed their cheeks, then kissed Igraine's hand. He swung into his stallion's saddle, turned the horse and clattered straight back through the gate. He and most of the men rode for Dimilioc. He left behind two dozen of his armed soldiers to defend Tintagel, if it was needed. Tintagel, though, was such a strong fortress only half that number could hold an entire army at bay.

Anwen had been more than ready to sleep, too, while Igraine crackled with energy and drive. Anwen had been forced to follow Igraine to the big chamber at the top of the tower, obeying Merlin's first instruction never to leave Igraine alone.

The other women all trailed Igraine into her room, as was usual. Igraine rounded on them. "Out, all of you! Leave me be!"

"My lady, we must protect you if the High King's army arrives here," Yvette objected.

"He will go to Dimilioc," Igraine told her. "Everyone knows my husband's army is quartered there. You can guard me in the audience chamber as well as you can here. I need to think. Out!"

The women had shuffled out, some of them sending Anwen looks of deep resentment and puzzlement.

As Igraine waited for the hot water she had requested, she made Anwen read Merlin's letter again. The letter had arrived at the house in Venta Belgarum before dawn and handed to Anwen, for she had slept across the door to Igraine's room that night.

Anwen read the letter slowly, translating from the Latin, while Igraine washed and changed her gown, then held out the comb and requested Anwen comb her hair.

While Anwen combed, they discussed the arrangements Merlin had requested. For the first time Igraine showed Anwen the hidden door. It was behind one of the ceiling-high wall hangings. When closed, it laid flush with the curved wall, with only a crack in the stonework to show where it was.

It was heavy to move, because the front of it bore the same stone as the walls around it. Igraine slipped her finger into a small hole and hauled with all her might until one edge emerged, then put both hands on the edge and pulled until the door creaked open.

Anwen looked down the curved stairs, which hugged the tower wall. They were dark and narrow, lit only by a small window high up by the roof.

"Beyond the curve is the guard room landing," Igraine said. She pushed the door closed once more. "They guard the outer door."

"There are guards there now?" Anwen whispered.

"As the outer door is unlocked, yes," Igraine said.

"Then you expect Gorlois to ride back tonight?" Anwen asked, alarmed.

Igraine grimaced. "I convinced him that guarding Dimilioc was the greater need."

Anwen twined her fingers together, her heart thudding unhappily. The lies were piling up, one upon the other.

That night she slept upon the narrow bench at the foot of Igraine's bed—if it could be called sleep at all. She was far too hot and restless even when she dropped the furs to the floor. The bench was too narrow even for her.

When daylight arrived, Anwen felt groggy, as if she had

drunk a cup too much wine. The feeling did not pass as the day marched on. She stayed hunched upon the footstool by Igraine's chair, as Igraine sent for dozens of people and requested all manner of work be completed, including a complete cleaning of her chamber, from ceiling to floor. The furs were taken and beaten, her mattress restuffed, the pillows cleaned and plumped.

As it was spring, this was normal work for the time of year. No one thought it was strange, although the timing—with the King's men about to descend upon Cornwall—made it a little odd.

Anwen listened to the women talking in the reception chamber as they restitched hems. They decided Igraine was merely keeping everyone busy so their thoughts would not linger upon what Uther and his men would do to them.

Late that afternoon, a goat herd sprinted across the land bridge and into the yard, his nervous goats following him, instead of the other way around. "King's men! The King's army is here!"

"Where? Where?" came the answering call from a dozen different throats.

Anwen stood by the high window on that side of the keep, listening. The goat herd dropped his voice to a murmur as the people surrounded him. Thoughtfully, she went back to Igraine's room.

"The King's army have arrived, my lady."

Igraine looked up from her embroidery. She ran the tip of her tongue over her lips. "This late in the afternoon, they will camp for the night. Gorlois will presume they will attack at first light." She dropped the linen back into the basket, as her other hand lifted to her throat. Her gaze met Anwen's.

Merlin's instructions had been clear. The night the army arrived would be the night Uther would visit.

Jenny ran into the room, breathless, her hand to her ribs. She paused, blowing hard.

"Where is the King's army?" Igraine asked her. Anyone might have thought Igraine was calm and controlled, except Anwen could see a pulse jumping at the base of Igraine's throat. She held her hands together not in elegant repose, but to hide their trembling.

Anwen wondered how often Igraine had hid nervousness or fear or any other strong emotion with this gauze of serenity. She had always presumed Igraine was a contained, sensible woman, with a natural control remarkable for a woman her age.

Jenny gathered her composure. Breathing hard, she said between gulps, "A mile north of Dimilioc, my lady. It is as Gorlois assumed—Uther plans to attack the army's fortress, not here."

Igraine did not glance at Anwen. She nodded instead.

"Thank you, Jenny. Please tell the steward to close the gates and bar them, just in case."

Jenny nodded and hurried away again, her hand at her side, her fingers digging into the flesh to relieve the stitch. Anwen heard her clatter down the stairs once more.

"And now we come to it," Anwen said.

Igraine put her face in her hands for a moment. Then she rose to her feet and moved to the window to look out upon the sea. "Yes, now the time is near," she said, her voice strained beyond recognition.

UTHER INSISTED STEFFAN RIDE WITH him to Cornwall. He gave Steffan his second war stallion, a great beast with a perfect stride, who followed Uther's mount like a shadow. Steffan had no need to direct the horse at all. He clung like a bur to the saddle and tried not to slow the pace of the small party which raced to catch the main army group, which had left Venta Belgarum a day ago.

They took little sleep. When they did, they dropped to the ground and pillowed their heads on their arms, their horses' reins beneath them.

Uther burned with an energy that showed no sign of waning. He spoke little in the long hours they rode. He was focused upon his inner thoughts. Merlin directed the men accompaning Uther, driving them through the night, along narrow tracks and unknown byways which took miles off their journey.

Merlin had returned to Venta Belgarum at the last moment to lead the group to where the main army camped in Cornwall to await Uther's arrival, which they expected in three days' time.

Thanks to Merlin's knowledge of the terrain and his relentless drive, they arrived at sunset at the main encampment a day before anyone expected them.

Steffan was glad to get off his horse. Merlin curled Steffan's hand around his arm, pulled his hood down low over his forehead and led him through the camp. Steffan could hear Uther's steps beside him, although Uther remained silent until they were inside a tent.

Warm air bathed Steffan's face.

"When do we leave?" Uther asked Merlin, his tone strained.

"As soon as you are ready. There are fresh horses waiting for us."

"Give me the tunic," Uther said.

"Here."

Steffan heard a distinctive slap of metal, one he recognized, and it had not come from Uther's direction. He reached for and found Merlin's arm. "You wear a sword?" he demanded.

"It is necessary to make men think they see who they expect to see," Merlin said curtly. "I am as tall as Brithael and my coloring is similar and I can speak the Cornish accent as easily as my own."

"This is your magic?" Steffan breathed. "Accents and tunics?"

"They are not the true magic which will happen tonight," Merlin said softly. There was a note in his voice, the call of a distant trumpet.

Steffan shook his arm. "Take off the sword," he said urgently. "You are no fighting man but if you carry a sword, any man can attack you with impunity."

"I know enough to defend myself. Let go, Steffan. I know what I am doing."

"Do you?" Steffan asked bleakly.

"Tonight, we must trust him," Uther said, from close by. His hand gripped Steffan's shoulder. "You can come no farther, friend. You and your staff are too well known in these lands."

Steffan nodded.

Uther patted his shoulder and was gone.

"Look for us at dawn," Merlin said.

"And when you do not appear by then?" Steffan asked, his voice a growl.

Merlin's laugh was soft. "I am in the lap of the gods tonight, Steffan. Their power strums in me like a harp. Fear not—this will happen as it should."

Then he left, too.

The tent suddenly felt too small and too warm. Steffan stepped out and from the west heard the fading beat of horses ridden fast. He made his way through the camp carefully, moving west, until he was upon the outskirts and beyond the hot, smoky air around the campfires. Cool, fresh air bathed his face.

His vision was completely dark. Not even colors played in his mind. It was what happened when his emotions had been held inside too tightly and for too long. Nothing would relieve that state until Uther returned at dawn, so Steffan wrapped his cloak around him and sat upon the soft spring grasses to wait.

IGRAINE REFUSED TO EAT AND Anwen had no appetite, either. The other women took their supper in the outer room, then got back to their sewing and spinning while the longer evening light held.

At Igraine's request, Anwen closed the chamber door.

Igraine washed and changed into a gossamer thin chemise which hid little of her lithe body. She slid her arms into a fur-lined robe with wide sleeves, a full collar and a single tie at the waist.

Anwen offered to comb her hair once more. Igraine refused.

Instead, she sat restlessly in her chair, watching the sun dip toward the sea. Anwen pulled the footstool to the other side of the window and sat upon it. She was tall enough she could just see over the stone sill.

Silently, they watched the sun touch the sea, then sink beneath it, painting the ocean a dull pink. When the sun had disappeared, pink clouds remained. The sky turned indigo, then black.

Stars appeared.

"Full night," Igraine whispered.

He will wait for the cover of full night, Merlin had written.

Anwen lit the lanterns.

They stayed by the window, even though nothing could be seen. Neither spoke. Anwen's heart beat rose, little by little, as she strained to hear any hint of noise which might warn them of an illicit approach.

From the other side of the wall hanging, a whisper of sound came. Voices, very low.

Her heart leaping, Anwen gripped the arm of Igraine's chair. "Is that…?"

Igraine nodded. Her eyes were wide.

Both rose to their feet and turned as one toward the secret

door. Igraine's fingers tangled with Anwen's. Igraine shook violently.

Anwen gave her hand a small squeeze. "I will open the door," she murmured.

Igraine nodded once more.

Glad to have something to do, Anwen pulled the hanging aside, then struggled to pull the door open, too. She managed it at last and stood at the top of the curved staircase and listened.

There was a lamp lit, somewhere farther around the curve. She could see the glow of the flame against the old stone walls. Footsteps sounded.

Then a voice, nervous and shaking. "My lord Gorlois! We...we did not expect you here tonight!"

Anwen whirled to look at Igraine, shock slithering through her.

Igraine raised her finger to her lips, then spread both her palms in a calming motion.

Anwen nodded. Pretend all is as it should be.

Another voice, louder than the rest, spoke. "It's cold as blazes out there. Let us in by the bier for pity's sake. You go ahead, my lord." Anwen thought she knew the voice and the accent. It was Gorlois' war commander, Brithael.

More footsteps. Climbing higher. On the wall, silhouettes crossed the lamplight. Then the figure came into view. Tall. A black, hooded cloak.

Anwen's breath halted. Thought halted. She watched the man take one step, then another. She saw the glimpse of metal beneath the cloak. A great sword. A flash of a white tunic.

Cornwall colors.

Then the man lifted his chin, to peer up the stairs to the door where she stood.

Uther.

His blue eyes glittered with ferocious concentration as he hurried up the stairs. The motion spread the fronts of the cloak and Anwen saw he wore a Cornwall tunic. He passed her with a nod.

She gripped the door and heaved, trying to shut it. Then it slid shut on its own, and she jumped out of the way.

Uther had one hand against the top of it.

"Thank you, lord Uther," Anwen murmured.

His eyes widened. "You knew it was me?" he breathed.

"Should I not?"

"Every Cornishman we have met tonight thought I was Gorlois and Merlin was Brithael. I had begun to believe in Merlin's magic." He pushed his hand through his thick, russet hair. His hand shook.

With a heavy breath, he turned to face Igraine.

Igraine stood transfixed in the middle of the room. She trembled.

Anwen picked up one of the lanterns and crept to the outer door. That one was easier to manage. She opened it only far enough to slip through the space and gripped the outer handle to draw it closed.

She paused as she glimpsed the pair once more.

Uther took a step toward Igraine. Then another. He reached out and brushed aside a skein of her hair, his gaze moving over her face. His fingers curled around her head, burying themselves in her hair as he pulled her toward him.

His head bent, his mouth reaching for hers, as Igraine wrapped her arms around his neck.

Anwen closed the door, then sat in front of it, her heart slowing as she studied the stone floor of the empty audience chamber, and the square of starlight which illuminated it through the big window behind Gorlois' chair. Igraine's women had retired for the night.

By every count, what Anwen had helped arrange tonight was wrong, yet the small glimpse she had caught of the two of them had felt natural and right. They were a pair, Igraine and Uther.

When her heart had fully calmed and her breath with it, Anwen got to her feet and pulled out the furs she had hidden behind the big chair earlier in the day. She unwrapped them and arranged them over her. She put her back to the door once more and closed her eyes.

She knew she would not sleep, although it would seem more natural to anyone who might come across her if she pretended to be bored and exhausted.

And so thinking, she slept.

Chapter Twenty-Three

nwen jerked awake when the screaming started.
She sat up, her heart racing. From the stairs came the distant sound of people murmuring in shock and surprise.

"What is that?"

"Little Morgan again. Another nightmare."

The screaming did not end. The note of terror in it sent a cold wave through Anwen. She gripped the furs. She could not go to the girl. Not now. She could not leave her post.

Her heart ached as she waited for someone to comfort Morgan and tell her the dream was not real.

The screaming did not cut off when someone woke Morgan. Instead, it died away, as if the girl had run out of breath. Sobs floated up the circular stairs, rending Anwen's heart and twisting her gut. The sobs were quieter than the screaming, which allowed her to hear distant thunder.

Horses. Many of them.

She glanced at the big window. The sky was lighter. Dawn was near.

The lamp, which had been lit when she fell asleep, had guttered and died and was now stone cold.

Anwen made her way through the pre-dawn gloom to the small window on the other side of the tower. The window overlooked the yard and the cliffs on the other side of the bridge.

The sky to the east was pale with light, although she didn't need the light to see the cavalry which approached. They carried torches which streamed flames as they rode at a great pace, sending up a cloud of dust which hung in the air behind them.

There were many torches, enough to light the two dozen horses and the men who rode them. They were still too far away for Anwen to see any detail except one.

They all wore white cloaks.

Anwen turned and stumbled across the chamber to the big door she had slept against and hammered her fist on it. "My lady!" she called as loudly as she dared. "It is I, Anwen. I must come in!"

She pushed the latch down and opened the door slowly. "My lady?"

Igraine stood at the courtyard window, wearing her fur-lined robe. She turned as Anwen entered. Her face was stricken.

Anwen stepped in and shut the door behind her.

A flash of movement and ruffle of cloth drew Anwen's attention to the other side of the room. The King swung the black, disguising cloak around his shoulders. His sharp gaze met Anwen's. "Cornwall men?"

She nodded.

The rattle of horse hooves across the land bridge was loud. A shout sounded from the guards on the gate as they demanded an explanation before they opened the gates.

Uther picked up his sword belt and buckled it around his waist, under the cloak.

"Hurry," Igraine urged him as the gates opened. Their heavy creak and thud was familiar.

Someone—a woman—screamed. More people babbled, their tones hysterical.

Anwen's gut clenched tighter. She hurried to the secret door and yanked it out enough to grip the edge, then hauled it open.

Uther came up behind her and peered down the stairs as he loosened his sword.

Anwen jumped as a loud thudding sounded, farther down the stairs and around the curve and out of sight.

Uther cursed and pulled his sword. He turned back to the room. "Igraine, come here."

Igraine moved to his side. He kissed her, the kiss hard and short.

The thudding at the bottom of the stairs halted and excited voices lifted.

Uther let Igraine go, turned and plunged down the stairs, his sword raised.

Anwen watched until he disappeared, then struggled to shut the door once more. Igraine leaned against it, too, helping her.

They were both breathing hard when it was shut at last. Anwen unhooked the wall hanging and let it fall. "Go back to bed," she whispered. "You've only just woken and are wondering what the fuss is about. Go on."

Igraine nodded and stripped the robe from her. She picked up the thin chemise from the floor beside the bed and struggled into it as she climbed into the high bed. She pulled the furs up around her. As she put her head on the cushion, the bed chamber door jumped and shivered as someone hammered on it.

Anwen hurried over to the door and opened it a crack. "What on earth?" she demanded in a harsh whisper. "You'll wake the lady!"

The soldier on the other side of the door was unshaved and splattered in blood. "We must speak with her! At once! There is grave news." Another armed man stood at his shoulder, looking just as gory.

"Where is Brithael?" Anwen demanded. "Why is he not bringing news?"

The man scowled. "Open the door, woman. It's not your place to delay this news."

"I think not," Anwen replied, even though she trembled at the man's impatience and irritation. Would he try to force the door open? "It *is* my place to protect my lady."

"It's all right, Anwen. I am awake," Igraine said, behind her. "Let the man in."

Anwen glanced behind her. Igraine stood calmly in the middle of the floor once more, the robe draped about her and firmly tied closed.

Anwen opened the door and stood out of the way. The two men stalked into the room, their hands on the hilts of their swords. They saw Igraine and halted. The first bowed. "My lady, I bring the gravest of news."

At the open door more people gathered, including Igraine's women who still wore sleeping robes. Some of them were crying.

Anwen's chest tightened. Her throat, too.

The man standing in front of Igraine licked his lips. "Earlier in the night, my lady, your lord husband directed us to sally forth and attack the King's army where it camped. He wanted to weaken the forces before the King arrived to lead them."

Igraine's face was already pale. Now it turned the color of whey. "Gorlois is dead?" she breathed.

Anwen hurried to Igraine's side and took her arm, to steady her.

"Yes, my lady. I'm sorry," the soldier said. He hesitated, as Igraine swayed.

"Get out," Anwen said. "You've brought your news. Give the lady some privacy. Go on. Out!"

The soldier flinched and bowed again, then hurried out of the room, collecting his companion with a jerk of his head.

The women tried to push their way into the room as soon as the soldiers passed. Anwen shook her head and they hesitated. She flung her hand at them, in a signal to remove themselves, as Igraine moaned softly beside her.

The door shut with a loud click of the latch. Anwen walked Igraine to the bed.

"No, no, not there…" Igraine protested.

Anwen took her, instead, to the great chair. Igraine sank into it, trembling violently. She gripped her hands together as if she would pray, but said in a choked voice, "Merlin lied to me! He said no one would suffer for this! He lied! Oh my dear God…" She rocked on the chair.

Anwen stood at the window, putting her back to Igraine to give the woman a little privacy, and watched the sky lighten. Far below, muffled by the boom of the waves against the cliffs, she thought she heard a hint of steel against steel, and wondered if she imagined it.

AS THE DAWN BIRDS BEGAN their twitter and chirping, Steffan detected the beat of a galloping horse approaching the camp from the west.

He put down the box of tools he had been carrying for the surgeon, while the man stitched and bandaged and otherwise treated the wounded soldiers. Instead, Steffan listened to the progress of the horse, while men moaned around him.

Cornwall and his men had struck an hour ago, while soldiers snored about their fires. It had been a short, sharp clash. Steffan listened to it, his staff at the ready, although the skirmish had not come near his position on the western edge of the camp.

Then the cry had gone up. "The Duke! The Duke is dead!"

Abruptly, the Cornish troops had withdrawn, taking their wounded and dead with them, including Gorlois.

The single horseman thundered into the camp, not stopping for the sentries.

"The King!" someone cried. "The King is here!"

Steffan felt his way through the wounded men, toward the King.

"Where is Steffan?" Uther shouted.

His heart skittering uneasily, Steffan turned his head. "Can someone guide me there?"

A hand gripped his sleeve. "This way," came the gruff growl.

He was led to where Uther stood.

"My lord?" Steffan said.

"I just heard," Uther said abruptly. He grasped Steffan's sleeve, too, and pulled him away from everyone else and lowered his voice. "Gorlois is dead. The stupid fool tried a surprise attack. Against *my* men!"

"I heard it happen," Steffan said. "A stray arrow caught him in the throat."

Uther made a growling sound. "This must be managed quietly now. No word of the night's adventure can escape."

For the first time, Steffan noticed the odor of fresh blood coming from Uther. "My lord, was there trouble at Tintagel?"

"Yes," Uther said flatly, anger making his voice tight. "Damn Merlin and his mighty schemes. If we had just waited a few hours more I could have claimed her..." He broke off. "You know the people in Tintagel, Steffan. You must go there—take my horse, it's fresh enough. Talk to those involved. Make sure they know to stop their tongues." As he spoke, Uther drew Steffan farther from the camp.

A horse snorted, close by. Steffan raised his hand and felt the stallions' neck beneath his fingers. He slid his hand up to the bridle and grasped for the reins. "Where is Merlin?" he asked.

"I know not and care less," Uther said. He was already moving away. "Ride, Steffan! The horse knows the way."

Steffan eased himself into the saddle and soothed the prancing stallion with pats and murmurs. He *was* fresh, for it was only two miles to the fortress from here. The scent of blood from the camp was unsettling him.

Steffan stowed his staff under the saddle cloth, against his knee. He grasped the reins and turned the horse to face west and the sea, which he could smell from here—even though no one believed he could. He kicked the beast forward. The stallion leapt eagerly into a great gallop.

The only warning Steffan had was a whistling sound. Something large—a branch the width of a man's wrist, most likely—slammed across his middle and knocked him out of the saddle. He landed heavily on his back, his breath shoved out of him by the impact. He tried to breathe as his stomach cramped and his back throbbed.

Thick, foul-smelling fingers gripped his throat. "Think you can just dance back into the King's favors, eunuch?" The fingers squeezed.

"Madog, wait…" Steffan croaked.

"It should be *me* running Uther's favors," Madog growled. "I know how to make women shut up, right enough."

Steffan tried to speak again, as alarm crashed through him. He scrambled at Madog's hand, trying to lift it away from his throat.

Madog gave a curse. A weight slammed into Steffan's temple and he knew no more.

Chapter Twenty-Four

While Igraine sat motionless upon the chair, her gaze turned inward and her hands locked together in silent prayer, Anwen fended the concerns of the household away from the Duchess' door. She had watched Igraine giving directions for years. It was simple enough to set in motion the things which needed to be done.

She asked that Elen prepare Morgan and Morguase and bring them to speak to their mother. Igraine would need to break the news to them.

Anwen also asked that the cooks prepare a hearty first meal, one which would help everyone recover from the shocking news. She asked that a portion of the meal be brought to Igraine's room—Anwen would feed it to her a spoonful at a time, if necessary.

As household members asked questions, Anwen answered them as best she could. In between the taps upon the door,

Anwen hovered by Igraine, unsure of how she might help the lady.

The first hint of a greater disaster came with cries of panic from the lower levels of the fortress. The screams were sharp and not the wailing of the bereaved…and they were coming closer.

Whatever was causing those screams was ascending the stairs to the top of the tower.

Fright tore through her. Anwen couldn't guess who was approaching. It might be anyone—Cador may have learned of his father's death and be exacting vengeance. Or the men at Dimilioc had gone mad. Or a lone robber or a whole band of them had set upon Tintagel while the gates were open and no one in their grief noticed their approach. There had been so many deceits and lies in the last few days, Anwen could not anticipate who might have learned of them and been roused by them.

She hurried back to Igraine, took her shoulders and shook her. "Igraine! Listen to me!"

Igraine blinked and looked up at Anwen.

"Someone comes with evil intent. You must bar the door behind me. Come. Get to your feet. Hurry!"

"To kill me?" Igraine asked, her voice bodiless.

"I don't know. Perhaps," Anwen said. "It is why you must bar the door and I must guard it. There are no soldiers here but the old guards. They all returned to Dimilioc to prepare Gorlois."

Another scream wound up from the stairs and the half-dozen women in the outer chamber screamed in panic, too.

Igraine's gaze snapped into focus. "My children!"

"Elen has them," Anwen said quickly. "She will hide them. Come now. Come over to the door." She pulled Igraine to her feet and this time the woman did not resist her. She moved over to the door.

Anwen picked up the heavy bar and put it in her arms. "Drop it into place as soon as I shut the door."

Igraine nodded, hefting the bar.

Anwen opened the door and slipped out, then pulled it shut behind her and heard the latch drop into place.

Then, the heavier thud of the bar settling into the brackets on either side of the door.

Relieved, Anwen looked toward the top of the stairs. People were backing up into the room, tripping over each other and shoving.

Anwen plucked her eating knife from her belt. It was a small blade, although it was sharp. She hefted it. Her skin was clammy and cold, and the touch of the sea breeze through the big open window made her shiver.

What manner of man came for them now? Why?

No answers glimmered, this morning. The world had become a confused and uncertain place.

Just below the top of the stairs, a man gave a dreadful snarl. The women screamed and stumbled across the room, colliding with the big work table they had set up for their sewing. They streamed around either side of the table and over to where the big chairs sat, crowding close to them and clutching each other, their expressions fearful.

The man who stepped into the chamber was familiar to Anwen. For a moment she did not remember his name. A mad light shone in his squinted eyes. The sword and long dagger he carried in each hand were both covered in fresh blood. Blood splattered his tunic, almost disguising the red Pendragon symbol on the breast.

He smiled. "*There* you all are. Crowded in the corner like a good little herd." He stalked toward the women. Behind him, another man covered in just as much blood stepped into the chamber from the top of the stairs. He hefted his sword, although he did not look as though he was enjoying himself.

Madog—that was the name of the man with the crease over his nose and mean eyes. Madog, who had tried to beat Steffan and failed.

Madog leapt with a happy cry and lunged with his dagger hand out. The women screamed and parted. He snagged one by the throat, the hilt of the dagger digging into her flesh.

It was Jenny, who struggled and clawed at his hand. He

looked her up and down and gave her a shake. Her shoes swept back and forth over the floor, for she hung from his grip.

"You're a lady's maid from your clothes. You know all about last night, I'd wager."

Anwen pressed her hand to her belly as she realized what was happening here. Anyone who knew of Uther's visit was being dealt with. Only Jenny didn't know…no one knew. Igraine had trusted only Anwen with the truth.

Madog carried Jenny over to the big window. The low sill only came up to his knees. He looked out and down to where the sea sucked and swelled against the cliffs, far below.

"Sorry, my lovely. Orders is orders," Madog told Jenny. He pushed the point of his sword into her chest, shoving hard.

Jenny choked, her eyes opening wide.

Then Madog tossed her over the sill.

The women didn't scream this time. They moaned and cried.

Anwen shoved at the nearest of them. "Go! Run! Around the table and down the stairs." She shoved another and another in that direction. All the women turned and bolted, moving around the table which stood between them and the second man, who made no move to capture any of them.

Anwen turned to face Madog. His face worked with fury as he watched the women run away.

"I am the one you want," she told him.

Madog's narrow gaze settled on her face. "I know you." He hefted the bloody sword. A smile formed. "My, my. The eunuch's woman!" His chuckle was low and joy-filled.

Anwen waited. Let the man crow. It would give the women more time to escape. If Igraine was of sufficient mind, she would open the secret door and also escape.

"Madog, we should wait a wee," the other man began.

"I told you what Uther said!" Madog screamed, his fury spilling over.

Anwen flinched and took a step backward, despite her determination to face down Madog. Her back came up against the other man's hand.

Madog dropped the dagger and leapt at Anwen, his bloody hand reaching for her throat, the sword swinging around to spear her in the middle as it had Jenny.

She couldn't move backward, so she stepped sideways. Madog, though, flicked his hand to the side with a snap of his wrist. His fingers gripped the front of her throat, cutting off her breath and preventing her from speaking.

Her heart tried to climb out of her body. Each beat hurt. She moaned, knowing Madog was seconds away from running the sword through her and tossing her through the window, too. She clawed at Madog's wrist and hand, trying to release his fingers.

A quiet thud sounded. The other man grunted. He dropped to the stones, his eyes rolling.

Steffan stood behind him, his staff raised in both hands. There was blood on his face, yet his eyes were alive and snapping with fury. "Let her go, Madog."

Madog screamed. It was a mad sound. His fingers tightened even harder. The pain brought tears to her eyes and stole Anwen's breath. Dark spots danced in front of her eyes.

Madog lifted the sword the same way he had with Jenny, aiming the point at Anwen's middle. "You can't stop me, you blind fool," he muttered and thrust the sword.

The end of Steffan's staff deflected the blow from Anwen, making the sword ring. Steffan jabbed the staff against Madog. It didn't seem like a hard blow, yet Madog staggered backward, his grip on Anwen's throat torn away.

She dropped to the floor and propped herself up, breathing noisily, her hand to her throat.

Steffan moved passed her. His foot landed on the cross guard of the other King's man's sword, which scraped across the stones.

Steffan dropped the staff and bent and picked up the sword and tested it.

"No, Steffan!" Anwen croaked.

"Oh, you shouldn't have done that," Madog said, sounding happy that he had. "Now I *will* kill you."

"You would have tried anyway," Steffan said. He gripped the hilt with both hands. "Anwen, if I'm looking north, where is he?"

Madog laughed, the sound bursting from him with maniacal glee. "You're blind! You think you can fight? Your soldiering days were over a long time ago, eunuch!"

He leapt as he finished, his sword raising up for a downward slash.

Anwen cried out a wordless warning.

Madog's mad laughter had given Steffan both direction and distance. Madog was heavy on his feet, too, and his breath pushed out of him as he leapt. It was all the information Steffan needed. He stepped to one side, leaned away as the blade whistled through the air, and brought his sword around in a fast counter.

The two swords clashed, metal ringing. Madog spun away, cursing.

"Northwest, two paces," Anwen cried.

Steffan leapt, bringing the sword down in the same style of slashing strike which Madog had just used. Madog scrambled backward, just barely avoiding the blade.

"West-northwest, five paces!"

Steffan jumped forward with both feet and lunged, driving the sword forward. The point skewered Madog's tunic with a ripping sound and he hissed and spun away again and looked down at his side, where blood oozed.

"You cut him," Anwen said, moving around the edge of the room to spot Madog. "North-north east, three paces."

Madog screamed his frustration as Steffan thrust once more. He whacked at Steffan's blade, all finesse evaporating. Metal clanged sourly.

"North east, four paces," Anwen cried.

Madog made a sound in his throat which was more wild animal than human. He lunged around Steffan's blade and lurched against the end of the heavy sewing table and shoved with all his might.

The table slammed into Anwen's hips and pushed her backward. Her legs rammed up against the low sill of the great window. She circled her arms, her fright tearing at the back of her throat, as her weight toppled backward.

The moment seemed to last forever as she fought to regain her footing and save herself. Surely, her life would not end so stupidly? So abruptly?

The battle was lost. She fell backward, turning in the air beyond the window. Frantically, she reached out for something, *anything*, to grab and break her fall.

Sharp rock scraped her fingertips. She turned her hand into a claw and dug her fingers in.

The grip held. She slammed into the unforgiving rock face and hung, dizzy. She moaned, as she willed herself not to let go. It was the only thought she could hold in her mind.

A mortal cry rang out above her, evoked by a death blow.

Anwen closed her eyes. Madog had been mad with fury and Steffan was blind. He could not possibly win against such a cruel man, for Madog would follow no rules.

She let the knowledge form and tried to accept it but could not.

The thought came to her. *Just let go.*

"Anwen!" Steffan's cry, from just above her.

Anwen looked up, her heart leaping.

Steffan leaned over the low sill of the window, his hands reaching out. "Speak to me!" he said, his voice hoarse.

"I'm here!"

His fingers groped. "Where?" he demanded.

"A hand-span lower and to your right."

"I can't reach any lower," he breathed. He pulled himself up and disappeared.

Anwen shuddered, while her hooked fingers grew numb.

Steffan reappeared and straddled the window. He pulled his staff through and lowered it down, tapping until the end nudged her forearm. "Softness. There you are. Take the staff."

"I can't, not with that hand."

"Turn yourself. Take it with your other hand. I'll bring you up."

Anwen rested her head against her burning arm and drew a

shuddering breath.

"Anwen," Steffan said, his voice low. "You've the courage. I have the strength. Let me help you. Take the staff."

She was afraid. Courage be damned—her fear, now she could see a way out of this, crowded all her thoughts. What if she twisted and the movement pulled her fingers away from the edge? What if she couldn't grip the staff tightly enough?

"Anwen," Steffan said. "Reach for the staff. If you won't do it for yourself, do it for me."

Her heart jolted. Her breath caught. Then, before she could imagine once more the many ways this might not work, she twisted herself around. She threw her free arm over and flailed for the end of the staff.

Her crooked fingers slid off the tiny crevasse. With a cry of abject terror, Anwen turned her gaze toward the staff, the one thing which could save her. She threw her other hand out one last time. Her fingers curled around the wood and she tightened them with fear-induced strength.

She hung from the end of the staff, her body trembling, her chest heaving.

Then she realized she was being drawn up.

Anwen lifted her head. The wide sill of the window was mere inches away.

Steffan closed his hand around her wrist and dropped the staff. "Use your feet," he said. "Push yourself up. I'll catch you."

"Oh, you can see me now?" she asked, her tone dry.

"You are the golden light in my life," he replied. "When you are there, I can't see anything else."

Her heart jolted again, this time for more than the peril of her situation. Anwen flailed with her feet until she found purchase on the rocks, her heart hammering the whole time. She pushed herself up, fear giving her legs strength.

Steffan's arm snapped around her waist and pulled her against him like an iron band. "Got you," he whispered. Then with a heave, he pulled her back inside…and tripped over his staff.

They both went down. Steffan twisted to take the fall on his back, with Anwen on top. They both groaned at the impact.

Steffan gave a soft curse. "At least no one saw that but you," he murmured and stroked her cheek.

Anwen lifted her head. Igraine stood just beyond the door to her room, her eyes wide. At the head of the stairs, three of her ladies clung to the door, leaning in to watch.

Steffan grew still. "We're not alone, are we?"

"No," Anwen whispered.

Igraine skirted around Madog's still body and the pool of blood spreading beneath it. "I don't think you need to be concerned, Steffan. All I saw was your gallant rescue of a lady. So did everyone else." She glanced toward the door. The women there all nodded.

"Although, if you are finished with the rescue," Igraine continued, "I do need Anwen back for a while."

"Not quite finished," Steffan said. He caught Anwen's face in his hands and kissed her, deeply and thoroughly.

Chapter Twenty-Five

espite everyone telling Morgan everything was all right, that there was nothing to fear, she knew they were lying. She knew her father was dead.

She had seen him in her dreams, rearing back off his horse, a great feathered arrow at his throat and the red, deadly spurt of blood. It was a true dream. She didn't have many of them. They were as different from normal dreams as day was from night. What she had seen was true.

Morgan had learned to let adults fuss around her while she pretended. It was easier that way. While old Elen tugged at her dress and untangled her hair with mutters and curses for active children, Morgan instead reached out for her father and found him. He laid on a wagon, covered with a white pall blanket. The wagon rattled and shook as it followed the worn ruts to Tintagel.

He was nearly here. The gatehouse was just ahead of the horses pulling the wagon. Now, Morgan could hear the wagon and the horses not just in her mind, but with her ears, too.

"Mercy sake! Someone else?" Elen muttered, glancing at the window slit.

Morgan went over to the window. She climbed onto the edge of her bed, then onto the high end of the leg and balanced herself so she could peer through the window. She didn't need to look out to see what happened next. Only, Elen would tell others she had seen without looking, if she didn't pretend to watch.

The wagon came through the open gates and stopped in the middle of the yard. The captain who accompanied it—not Brithael, for Merlin had dealt with him—but Dwyn, who would one day be a great warrior, stopped his horse beside the cart. Dwyn swung out of the saddle and walked to where Morgan's mother stood upon the steps into the keep.

Her mother raised her hand to her throat, her gaze upon the wagon.

The captain bowed low.

Her mother moved past him without acknowledgement. She went straight up to the cart and peered in. Then, with a hand which shook, she pulled the blanket aside and looked down at what remained of Morgan's father.

It was only an empty husk. The sight of it did not distress Morgan, for her father now walked in places where he no longer needed his body. Morgan's mother, though, gripped the side of the wagon, shaking so badly she could barely hold herself up.

Her women all hurried out of the keep and surrounded her and helped her back inside.

Morgan looked at old Elen. "The King will come for my mother, now," she said. "You had best get my good gown out of the chest."

Elen crossed herself, backing away.

ANWEN HAD NEVER BEFORE CLIMBED to the sentry ramp above the gates of Tintagel and looked out upon the breadth of Cornwall.

"They say you can see for ten miles, from here," Steffan said, tucking her in front of him, which blocked the cold breeze coming off the sea.

"*I* can see for ten miles, at least," Anwen said.

A guard glanced at her, startled, then at Steffan. He edged away, as if he expected an explosion.

Steffan chuckled and put his arm around her. "As long as one of us can," he breathed and pressed his lips to her temple.

She let herself lean against him. "Is there a reason you made me climb up here?" she asked.

"I wanted you to see a horizon which was farther than a mile away," he said.

"Or did you want me to see the spectacle which approaches?" Anwen asked, as she spotted the flash of metal and the dust of a large company of horses, far away.

The guards jerked to attention and shaded their eyes to see the approaching troop for themselves.

"That would be the King, I imagine," Steffan said, his tone empty of any inflection. "Earlier than even I expected."

"We should prepare for his arrival," Anwen said.

Steffan's arm tightened. "Not yet. I want to breathe this air for just a little longer."

"The air is the same down there," Anwen pointed out.

He shook his head. "No, it really isn't."

BY THE TIME STEFFAN LET Anwen climb down to the courtyard, the King's troop were nearly there. Steffan pulled Anwen over to the corner of the yard, well out of the way of the household as everyone spilled out into the yard to greet the King.

The horses slowed for the narrow land bridge, crossing one at a time. The first through the arched gates was Uther. He sat upon his horse, his back straight, his gaze straight ahead. He wore the rich, embellished clothing of royalty and his helm was crowned.

"He does appear every inch a king," Anwen said.

"It is a pity not every inch of him is kingly," Steffan replied.

Anwen glanced at him, startled.

Then the second rider came through the gate. This man was tall, with thick black, long hair and no war helmet. "Long black hair, a big nose and a sharp chin," Anwen said. "Black pennant. Do you know him, Steffan?"

Steffan sighed. "Lot of Orkney. The next man through the gate will be Urien, then. Blond hair, with silver rings, and eyes bluer than Uther's."

Anwen gasped, as a man matching Steffan's description trotted through the gate. He jumped down with a flex of his muscled body, smiling. His smile looked as though he might laugh at any second.

Both men joined Uther, who had removed his helmet. As they waited, more men arrived in the yard.

Igraine moved out into the yard. She wore her most elegant gown and jewels sparkled at her throat and ears and wrists. She was gloriously beautiful.

She sank into a deep curtsey before Uther and signaled to Morgan and Morguase, who stood behind her, do the same.

Everyone who had trailed out behind Igraine also sank down before the King.

Uther gestured for them to stand again.

Igraine rose, straight and slender.

Uther glanced at Lot and lifted his chin.

Lot's eyes narrowed. He was looking at Morguase.

Anwen drew in a breath which hurt. "No! He cannot. Morguase is barely thirteen…!"

Steffan caught her arm and held her on the spot. "Now we come to it," he said softly.

"Come to what? Steffan, he is giving her to Lot!"

"It will tie the northern lord to Uther," Steffan said. "It is politically expedient." His voice was the same implacable, inflectionless one he had used every time he had spoken of Uther. His fingers tightened. "Watch Igraine," he said softly.

Anwen peered at the Duchess.

Igraine's face was the same pasty gray color it had been when she had learned of Gorlois' death. Her chin trembled. Her eyes were large and glittered with unshed tears. Her chin remained up, though. She made not a murmur of protest.

"Oh, Steffan, poor Morguase! Lot is inspecting her now. He is actually walking around her, looking from all sides."

Steffan's jaw rippled. "That matches what I have heard about Lot over the years."

Anwen gasped again, for Urien had stepped forward and dropped down to speak to Morgan. He laughed up at her, cajoling her.

Morgan stared back at him. Then she moved backward and without looking, reached for her mother's hand and clung to it.

Anwen felt a fierce surge of pride in the little girl.

Urien laughed and got to his feet. He shrugged and patted Uther's shoulder.

Uther looked around the yard. The wagons and carts which had accompanied him were moving into the yard now. One of them turned in a full circle so it faced the gate once more. The back opened.

Uther waved toward it. It was a signal.

Two Christian sisters stepped down from the back of the wagon and walked over to where Morgan stood with her mother. One of them held her hand out to Morgan.

Anwen drew in a shaky, painful breath. "No, he would not…!"

"Tell me," Steffan breathed.

"Two sisters of the Church. They're here for Morgan. Uther is taking Morgan away from Igraine, too."

Morgan shrank back against her mother.

Igraine stood like a marble statue while her tears slid down her face. She said nothing.

Uther made a low comment.

The sisters bent and picked Morgan up, one with her arms around Morgan's waist, the other containing Morgan's kicking legs.

Morgan screamed and struggled. In that silent courtyard,

her screams were as piercing and heart-rending as they were when they sounded in the dead of the night.

Igraine took a half step forward. Uther's gaze met hers and she halted. Then she closed her eyes.

While Urien and Lot turned to watch the sisters overcome Morgan's struggles and push her inside the closed wagon, Uther stood with his gaze straight ahead. Anwen saw him swallow and with swooping sensation, she realized he liked this arrangement no more than Igraine.

Anwen turned and pressed her face against Steffan's shoulder, so she did not have to watch. Morgan continued to scream, even as the wagon rolled back through the gate and across the narrow bridge and Anwen shivered.

"This is Igraine's price," Steffan said, his voice reverberating in his chest, against Anwen's cheek. "This is the price she must pay for her choice—Gorlois and her daughters and the guilt she will carry for the rest of her life."

"It's our price, too," Anwen said, as hot, aching tears scalded her cheeks.

Steffan sighed. "Yes, ours, too."

ANWEN COULD NOT BEAR TO watch Uther take Igraine back inside the fortress where the rest of his entourage and the household would witness him publicly claim the Duchess of

Cornwall as his queen.

When Steffan made no move to follow everyone inside, she was grateful. Instead, he picked up her hand. "Come with me," he murmured and walked across the yard with his staff tucked under his arm. He knew Tintagel well enough he did not need to tap his way around, and Anwen would warn him of any out-of-place objects which might trip him up.

"The stables?" she asked, rolling her eyes.

"It seems appropriate," he said, his mouth turning up at the corners. His hand tightened on hers. "Uther can have his audience chamber. Once, I would have resented that such grandeur could not be mine. Now a stable with fresh straw and warm air seems as refreshing as the wind which blows in from the sea."

He put the staff against the door of the tack room and drew her into the room and over to the bench. He put his back to it and picked up both her hands. "I have been a complete fool, Anwen."

Her heart jumped. "You are the last man anyone could accuse of being foolish."

"Which makes my error all the more stupefying," he said.

Anwen drew in a shaky breath. "You were wrong about Uther?" she guessed.

He tilted his head and his eyes widened a little. "Yes. How did you know?"

"You have not cursed his name when you speak of him, yet the admiration in your voice is gone. Before, you yearned for everything Uther and his army had once given you."

He sighed. "That is where I was foolish. I wanted my old life back, Anwen. I wanted everything I had lost when the Saxons took my sight. I wanted the glory and the company of great men and everything I said when I stood here this day and told you I was leaving Tintagel."

"You're coming back again," she breathed, in a long sigh.

"Oh, I'm still leaving," he said.

Her heart jumped again.

"Only, you're leaving with me, this time," he added. "That is, if you will have me."

Her trembling made her voice shake. "Leave Tintagel? I've never lived anywhere else. Where would you go?"

"Where would *we* go," he amended. "Wherever we wanted," he added. "I have no stomach to serve the King anymore. If Uther follows the practice of most leaders, he will distance himself from everyone who had anything to do with last night. It means Igraine will dispense with your services, too."

Anwen frowned. "Both us did our duty even though we didn't want to! Why would they discard us?"

"Because every time they saw us, they would be reminded of their guilt. It is the way of it, Anwen. Be thankful it is so, for it will give you a freedom you've never had before. I have a mind to travel. To see…well, to visit, the places we have only read about, you and I."

"How would we live?"

"When I request I be released from his service, Uther will be overwhelmingly generous," Steffan said, his tone dry. "Igraine will do the same. We will have enough between us to travel far and wide. And when we have nothing left, we can teach or write letters and read them for those who cannot."

Anwen shivered. Steffan must have sensed it, for he pulled her against him. "I know it seems frightening for you, to leave the only place you know and move about a strange world. It is what I do every single day, Anwen. I must grope and explore. When I first lost my sight, I was terrified. Now, I can tell you it makes life interesting in a way you cannot understand just yet. You will, though." He lifted her chin and bent his head toward hers. "Say you will," he breathed, his lips brushing hers.

"I will," she whispered and pressed her lips against his.

The kiss lengthened and deepened, until Steffan let her go long enough to pick her up and carry her over to the fresh pile of straw.

ONCE THEY WERE AWAY FROM the fortress and no one could hear them, the nuns slapped Morgan's face every time she screamed, until her face was swollen and her throat raw. She knew, though, that to stop screaming would be the same as giving in to them. She continued to kick at them and scream, despite their blows, which grew heavier as the journey lengthened.

It was dark when the wagon stopped and the door was wrenched open. A huge man with a ring of iron keys on his belt reached in and plucked Morgan up by the arm. He thrust her under his monstrous one and clapped his filthy hand over her mouth.

He carried her into a stone building which was far bigger than Tintagel and far colder and darker. He walked for what seemed like miles, through corridors which echoed and down stairs to a room which dripped with dampness.

A single lamp burned fitfully and smelled of rancid pork.

The monster used the keys on his belt to unlock an oak door with bars in it. He tossed Morgan inside, onto old, moldy straw. There was nothing else in the tiny room but the straw. Not even a light.

He slammed the door shut and locked it. Then he peered through the bars. "Here yer stay, 'til you learn some humility." He brushed the keys across the bars, making unmusical notes.

As he left, he extinguished the lamp, plunging the cell into darkness.

Morgan pushed herself into the corner and wrapped her

arms around her and sat shivering. Her face throbbed where the nuns had slapped her. Her throat ached. It hurt to swallow.

That was not the greatest hurt. Oh, no.

Morgan rocked in the dark, toting up the offenses which had been delivered.

Lot, who had stolen her sister. Igraine, who had not fought to save her. Uther, who had delivered this upon her.

Oh, and the base cause of all her misery. "Arthur," she said softly to the dark.

Arthur, her bastard half-brother, who would be born at Christmas. Because of him, she had been brought here.

One day, she would deliver the same terror and pain upon him and his kin.

One day.

Chapter Twenty-Six

Steffan seemed to know everyone in Dimilioc. Or they seemed to know him. As he led Anwen through the fortress, every man they passed glanced at Steffan with a startled expression, then murmured a greeting as they hurried away.

Anwen recalled what Daveth had said of Steffan's time here, when he had reported to Igraine and asked her to deal with the blind man. No wonder everyone wanted to step around Steffan.

The surgery was still full of wounded soldiers from the skirmish at the King's camp two nights ago. As Uther had taken over Dimilioc upon the death of their Duke, both King's men and Cornish soldiers laid in the low beds. Three physicians examined and treated the wounded men.

Anwen saw the bed in the far corner, separated from the others by a thick drape which had been hastily nailed to the ceiling. She tugged on Steffan's hand. "Over here," she said, pulling him in that direction.

They moved around the curtain and stopped at the foot of the bed. It was not a bunk, but a full-sized bed with sheets and furs and cushions. In one respect it was the same as the bunks the soldiers laid upon—the occupant was grievously injured.

Merlin opened his eyes a sliver, then completely, when he saw them. He lifted his head, hissed in pain, and let it fall back upon the cushion.

"God's teeth," Anwen breathed.

Steffan moved around the side of the bed. "From her tone, I am guessing you do not look well, Merlin."

Anwen squeezed the end of the bed, her fingers digging in. "The surgeon said you were recovering."

"I am," Merlin said. He lifted his hand, which laid on the covers. It was wrapped in thick bandages. "My hand is broken in four places, although that is the worst of it. The rest is bruises and cuts, which will mend."

"Bruises are the worst," Steffan said. "You had to pick up a sword, didn't you?"

"I did," Merlin said calmly. "The gods ask for full payment when they deliver. This was mine, this time."

"Does Uther know?" Steffan asked.

"I have no idea," Merlin said, his tone light. "As soon as I can sit upon a horse, I am going home to Maridunum. I haven't seen the cave in five years, and it will be the last time for quite a few more." He frowned, his gaze upon Anwen. "You appear much changed from when I saw you last." He rolled his head to glance at Steffan. "I supposed that has something to do with you?"

Steffan smiled. "How does she look? Pretty?"

Merlin's gaze came back to Anwen. She plucked at her dress self-consciously.

"A blue gown, a white undergown and bronze combs in her hair. Yes, she looks pretty."

Anwen could feel her cheeks heating.

Merlin frowned. "You are both leaving Cornwall…" he said, as if he had just realized a fact which should have been obvious and was feeling stupid because of it.

Steffan's grip on his staff tightened. "There is no place for us here. Not now. We will remind the wrong people of the wrong things."

Merlin nodded. "There is a reason I am not returning to the court. It does not pay to give powerful men what they want. They are never grateful, after. Yet we were all creatures of the gods that night—no matter how much you roll your eyes, Steffan. However, there are other places than beside the High King's chair."

"Where?" Steffan said.

Merlin frowned. "My Sight has deserted me since that

night. I could no more tell you than fly. I can only speak as a man with a little wisdom." He paused, wincing. Then he said softly, "Uther is not the only High King you can serve."

Anwen started, surprised. Merlin had told Igraine there would be a child. He had not said the child would be a king.

"This great king of yours, Merlin?" Steffan said, his tone light.

"Yes," Merlin said flatly. "This great king who shall be."

Anwen shivered.

"I could use a man of your qualities, Steffan," Merlin added.

"Me?" Steffan said, his tone one of disbelief.

"Because of you, Cador will serve the next High King as a good and honest servant. He will instill those qualities in his sons, who will in turn…" Merlin paused. "It is of no matter right now," he added. "I don't like seeing a good man go to waste, or a good, strong woman, either."

Anwen dropped her gaze as Merlin's slid toward her.

"Don't you think you have both paid enough of a price for your choices?" Merlin asked.

She gasped and looked at him.

So did Steffan. "I thought you said your Sight had failed you?"

"I don't need the Sight to guess what is in your mind," Merlin said. "You have been ever mindful of consequences since you lost your Sight. You call it price, I call it the will of the gods…it doesn't matter what the name is. It is the toll taken for our choices. You have paid for your choices, Steffan. Anwen, too. Now you get a rare chance to choose again and this time you can choose well."

"Because you say this is the right choice," Steffan said flatly.

"Because if this King does not meet your expectations, you can make sure the next one does," Merlin replied calmly.

Steffan drew in a sharp breath. "I thought you would teach him…"

"If Prince Merlin was to set himself up as a tutor anywhere, the entire world will know where to search for the baby prince," Merlin said. "My role will be far less direct than that and I won't be teaching the boy his letters, either. That role is for someone else." His gaze moved to Anwen.

She scratched at the foot of the bed with her nail, her heart thrumming.

Merlin seemed to relent. He relaxed and smiled. "There is time, yet. The child must be born, first, and I am still not entirely certain Uther will abide by his agreement to give the boy to me to arrange his rearing."

"And what price has Uther paid in all this?" Steffan said, as if the thought had been troubling him while they talked.

Merlin's smile faded. "There is always a reckoning."

"He got what he wanted," Steffan ground out. "People died to give it to him. Now he will marry her and wash the affair clean. He has paid nothing."

Merlin sighed. "He will," he said softly. Sadly.

Lorient, Kingdom of Brocéliande. Brittany. January 466 CE. (Ten months later.)

ANWEN LOOKED AT THE SEALED letter and the familiar script on the front with some confusion. "For me, my lady?" she asked the red-headed woman in front of her. "I don't understand. We did not know we would travel this way. How could Merlin have left a letter for me?"

Queen Ilsa laughed and pushed the letter into Anwen's hand. "I can see you have not had much experience dealing with people with the Sight."

"You have?" Anwen asked, as she broke the seal.

"One of the most powerful of Merlin's kind lives in the forest of Brocéliande," Ilsa replied. "I have given up being surprised by how much the Lady of the Lake knows about my inner thoughts and what I will do in the future. It is easier that way. Merlin stopped by on his way to the east. He told me you two would be coming and all about you. We have expected you all this winter, especially once we heard the news about the queen."

"Her child was born?" Anwen asked sharply.

"A boy, at Christmas," Ilsa said.

"You had better read the letter," Steffan added. He sat on the other side of the table from Ilsa and Anwen. Arawn, the king, would return in a moment.

Anwen opened the letter and sighed.

"What is it?" Ilsa asked.

"He has written in Latin," Anwen said.

Steffan laughed.

Anwen scanned the lines of script, translating and composing. "Oh, Steffan…"

He sat up. "What does he say?"

"In five years' time, Count Ector of Galleva, in the north, will be in need of a tutor for his son, Cai, and his foster son, Arthur. We are to present ourselves to him with Merlin's recommendation. I am to teach the boys their letters and you are to teach them philosophy and languages—especially Saxon."

She put the letter down, feeling winded.

Ilsa smiled. "Merlin is like the Lady—things never work out if you don't simply do what he says."

Anwen touched her fingers to Steffan's hand. "It leaves at least four years for us to…goodness, what *do* we do?"

Ilsa picked up the pitcher of wine. "For a start, you can

spend the remainder of the winter here. Then you must meet the Lady, and Elaine and Evaine and Bors and Ban. By then, I am sure you will have a better idea of what you might do for the next few years."

Steffan rubbed his chin. "If we are to obey Merlin and live in the north, then perhaps we should spend time in the south before we present ourselves to Ector. Iberia is warm, I believe."

"There's lots of time to decide," Anwen said.

"Yes, there is, isn't there?" he said softly.

LATER, AS THEY LAID TOGETHER in the large bed in the even larger chamber which Ilsa had insisted they use for the duration of their stay in Lorient, Steffan returned again to Merlin's letter.

"I can understand why a king would need to understand languages, especially Saxon," he said, his fingers trailing over Anwen's arm, making her shiver. "Philosophy, though, is a useless subject."

"How can you say that?" Anwen asked him. "All the eastern masters you studied gave you the answers you so badly wanted, about why you were blinded and what was to become of you after that."

"They did not," Steffan said firmly, lifting himself over her.

"You, my lady wife, gave me more answers than any Greek orator who ever put ink to parchment."

Anwen slid her hands up his strong arms. "Now you're just teasing."

He shook his head. "Not about that. I cannot. You saved my life, Anwen."

She cupped his cheek. "I thought *you* did that."

He kissed her, his kiss growing languid and warm. Their bodies melded together in the dim room lit only by moonlight in the window high overhead.

Afterward, as their hearts slowed, he continued to stroke her face, not to stir her senses but to remain familiar with the shape of it.

Steffan's fingers paused. He blinked and his breath caught. "I see you," he whispered.

Anwen laughed. "The golden light?" she teased.

He touched her face again. His hand trembled. "No, I *see* you," he breathed. His eyes glittered in the moonlight, as tears gathered.

Anwen looked up at him, her heart hurting. "Truly?" she whispered. She looked at his eyes and realized with a swiftly building delight he was *looking* at her.

"How long will it last?" she breathed, as tears gathered in her own eyes.

"It doesn't matter how long," he said, his voice hoarse. He

brushed her hair from her forehead. "I've seen you now and I know you are exactly as I have always imagined you to be."

She brought her hands to her face, covering it. "Not pretty," she whispered.

Steffan took her hands away. "What I see is the woman who loves me. The woman I love. The woman who is mine, who never would have been if not for a Saxon war hammer." He touched his fingers to her lips. "I see you," he whispered.

"The only man who ever has," she replied.

Did you enjoy this book?

How to make a big difference!

Reviews are powerful.

Authors like me, without the financial muscle of a sleek New York publisher backing me, can't take advertisements out in the subways and billboards of the world.

On the other hand, New York publishers would *kill* to get what I have: A committed and loyal group of readers.

Honest reviews of my books help bring them to the attention of other readers. If you enjoyed this book I would be grateful if you could spend just a few minutes leaving a review (it can be as short as you like) on the book's page where you bought it.

Thank you so much!

Tracy

Next in the Once and Future Hearts series.

War Duke of Britain, Book 4.

He is not the enemy she came to fight.

Idris the Slayer is the champion of the northern kings. Undefeated in battle, the dark, lone warrior who rides to war with a black wolf at his side spreads fear before him, even among those counted his allies.

When Rhiannon of Galleva rides to her first battle with Emrys and Cai, she expects to fight the Saxon hoards pouring into Britain. She is not braced to defend herself against Idris' incursion into her heart.

He is a dangerous man to be drawn to, for his allegiance lies with king Lot of Orkney, who holds no love for Uther, the aging High King. Rhiannon's parents, Anwen and Steffan, are loyal to the High King, as is Count Ector, Cai's father. Rhiannon's association with a northern man tears open secrets that have brewed for a generation, forcing Uther and his commanders to fight enemies on two fronts.

Readers have described Tracy Cooper-Posey as "a superb story teller" and her ancient historical romances as "written art". Get your copy of *War Duke of Britain* today!

About the Author

Tracy Cooper-Posey is a #1 Best Selling Author. She writes romantic suspense, historical, paranormal and science fiction romance. She has published over 90 novels since 1999, been nominated for five CAPAs including Favourite Author, and won the Emma Darcy Award.

She turned to indie publishing in 2011. Her indie titles have been nominated four times for Book Of The Year. Tracy won the award in 2012, and a SFR Galaxy Award in 2016 for "Most Intriguing Philosophical/Social Science Questions in Galaxy-building" She has been a national magazine editor and for a decade she taught romance writing at MacEwan University.

She is addicted to Irish Breakfast tea and chocolate, sometimes taken together. In her spare time she enjoys history, Sherlock Holmes, science fiction and ignoring her treadmill. An Australian Canadian, she lives in Edmonton, Canada with her husband, a former professional wrestler, where she moved in 1996 after meeting him on-line.

Other books by
Tracy Cooper-Posey

For reviews, excerpts, and more about each title, visit Tracy's site and click on the cover you are interested in:
http://tracycooperposey.com/books-by-thumbnail/

* = Free!

Vistaria Has Fallen
Vistaria Has Fallen
Prisoner of War
Hostage Crisis
Freedom Fighters
Casualties of War
V-Day

Scandalous Scions
(Historical Romance Series – Spin off)
Rose of Ebony
Soul of Sin
Valor of Love
Marriage of Lies
Scandalous Scions One
Mask of Nobility
Law of Attraction
Veil of Honor

Season of Denial
Scandalous Scions Two
Rules of Engagement
Degree of Solitude

Once and Future Hearts
(Ancient Historical Romance—Arthurian)
Born of No Man
Dragon Kin
Pendragon Rises
War Duke of Britain
High King of Britain
Battle of Mount Badon
Abduction of Guenivere
Downfall of Cornwall
Vengeance of Arthur
Grace of Lancelot
The Grail and Glory
Camlann

Kiss Across Time Series
(Paranormal Time Travel)
Kiss Across Time*
Kiss Across Swords
Time Kissed Moments
Kiss Across Chains
Kiss Acoss Time Box One
Kiss Across Deserts
Kiss Across Kingdoms
Time and Tyra Again
Kiss Across Seas
Kiss Across Time Box Two

Kiss Across Worlds
Time and Remembrance
Kiss Across Tomorrow

Project Kobra
(Romantic Spy Thrillers)
Hunting The Kobra

Romantic Thrillers Series
Fatal Wild Child
Dead Again
Dead Double
Terror Stash
Thrilling Affair (Boxed Set)

Scandalous Sirens
(Historical Romance Series)
Forbidden*
Dangerous Beauty
Perilous Princess

Go-get-'em Women
(Short Romantic Suspense Series)
The Royal Talisman
Delly's Last Night
Vivian's Return
Ningaloo Nights

Blood Knot Series
(Urban Fantasy Paranormal Series)
Blood Knot*
Amor Meus

Blood Stone
Blood Unleashed
Blood Drive
Blood Revealed
Blood Ascendant

The Sherlock Holmes Series
(Romantic Suspense/Mystery)
Chronicles of the Lost Years
The Case of the Reluctant Agent
Sherlock Boxed In

Beloved Bloody Time Series
(Paranormal Futuristic Time Travel)
Bannockburn Binding*
Wait
Byzantine Heartbreak
Viennese Agreement
Romani Armada
Spartan Resistance
Celtic Crossing
Beloved Bloody Time Series Boxed Set

The Kine Prophecies
(Epic Norse Fantasy Romance)
The Branded Rose Prophecy

The Stonebrood Saga
(Gargoyle Paranormal Series)
Carson's Night*
Beauty's Beasts
Harvest of Holidays

Unbearable
Sabrina's Clan
Pay The Ferryman
Hearts of Stone (Boxed Set)

Destiny's Trinities
(Urban Fantasy Romance Series)
Beth's Acceptance*
Mia's Return
Sera's Gift
The First Trinity
Cora's Secret
Zoe's Blockade
Octavia's War
The Second Trinity
Terra's Victory
Destiny's Trinities (Boxed Set)

Interspace Origins
(Science Fiction Romance Series)
Faring Soul
Varkan Rise
Cat and Company
Interspace Origins (Boxed Set)

Short Paranormals
Solstice Surrender
Eva's Last Dance
Three Taps, Then....
The Well of Rnomath

Jewels of Tomorrow
(Historical Romantic Suspense)
Diana By The Moon
Heart of Vengeance

The Endurance
(Science Fiction Romance Series)
5,001
Greyson's Doom
Yesterday's Legacy
Promissory Note
Quiver and Crave
Xenogenesis
Junkyard Heroes
Evangeliya
Skinwalker's Bane

Contemporary Romances
Lucifer's Lover
An Inconvenient Lover
The Contemporary Romance Collection (Boxed Set)

The Indigo Reports
(Space Opera)
Flying Blind
New Star Rising
But Now I See
Suns Eclipsed
Worlds Beyond

Non-Fiction Titles

Reading Order
(Non-Fiction, Reference)
Reading Order 2017